The Mask of Merryvale Manor

PETE SHERLOCK

Fairlight Books

First published by Fairlight Books 2024

Fairlight Books
Summertown Pavilion, 18–24 Middle Way, Oxford, OX2 7LG

A CIP catalogue record for this book is available from the British Library.

1 2 3 4 5 6 7 8 9 10

ISBN 978-1-914148-48-4

www.fairlightbooks.com

Printed and bound in Great Britain

Cover Design © Anna Abola

Dorset, August 1964

The bride and I escaped from the marquee and took the path down the sloped lawn towards the wood. Natasha was tipsy and tactile, unconcerned by the Rubicon she had crossed. I was bitter and bruised. In the morning, she would drive to St Ives to spend her honeymoon in a cottage with a view of the bay. I would sulk at Merryvale Manor, haunted by the image of her husband's fat white fingers fiddling with the buttons of her skirt.

We walked in silence, passing between us a bottle of blanc de noirs we'd snatched from the top table. Bess, the old black Lab, trotted ahead of us, her nose glued to the carpet of pine needles on the path. The air was fresh with the scent of wild mint and pine.

After a while, Natasha said, 'Well, there we go – what's done is done, I suppose.' She had changed out of her wedding dress into a pair of black trousers and a brown cashmere jumper. Her short black hair was sleek and neat, and her face scrubbed free of make-up. 'I wasn't too glum for the photos, was I? I was trying my best to smile.'

'You looked radiant,' I said. It was close to midnight and we held on to each other, shivering a little. 'Listen... can you hear the redwing make its seep-seep sound? Probably came all the way from Norway, poor fellow.' I didn't care much for the redwing, or anything for that matter, but I felt I had to change the subject; the more she spoke about the wedding, the more she seemed to deepen my despair.

Natasha linked her arm in mine. Her lips curled into a half-smile. 'It's poor form to take the bride into the woods on her wedding night, you know.'

'I didn't *take* you. You wanted to go for a walk.'

'Oh, that makes it all right, then,' she said, in a low whisper. 'Just what will people think?' She circled my palm with her thumb.

'Oh, stop it,' I said, pulling my hand free from hers. 'I'm done with being teased. I'm done with all that now.'

Natasha stiffened. The playfulness of her teenage years had hardened into something crueller and more reckless. She said, 'I was getting restless. They're all terrible bores when they're squiffy... and Charles keeps pawing at me.'

'He'll be looking for you.'

She bit her bottom lip and said, without sincerity, 'Your girl seems sweet. I should imagine she's looking for *you*.'

'I should imagine she's gone to bed. She's got blotto on negronis.'

'Oh, she's gone to bed. I wish Charles would.' She placed a cold hand on my chest. 'Are you going to try and kiss me again?'

'No.'

'You can if you like.'

Her flippancy irked me. 'You've just got married.'

'I know, but it doesn't really count.'

I snorted in disapproval.

Natasha's fingers toyed with the top button of my shirt. 'That's why I brought you into the woods. I wondered what you'd do. Do you know, you've become a bit of a prig since you went to Cambridge? I hope you don't mind me saying. It must be all that dreadful poetry you're reading.'

'I don't mind.'

'Mind being a prig, or mind me saying?'

I glanced over my shoulder at the wide old house, set at the top of the hill. Amber light glowed from the grid of rectangular windows. Something about Merryvale Manor's rigid straight lines and imposing facade made me shudder. 'I think we should turn back now. It's too dark to go further,' I said.

Natasha leaned in so close I smelt the elderberry gin on her breath. She slipped her ring finger through the gap in my shirt. 'You can kiss the bride on her wedding night,' she said. 'It's her prerogative.'

I guided her hand away from my chest. 'I'm not going to kiss you,' I said. With a vague sense of defeat and of a chapter ending, I realised I was sober. What was I doing? I should be curled up in bed with Clara, stroking her forehead while she stared at the ceiling and complained of the spins.

Natasha followed the path further into the woods, the moment gone. 'You should have asked me to marry you, you know. I might have said yes.'

'You're my cousin.'

'Well, that never stopped anybody.'

'Upward counterfactual thinking is pointless. Your mother would never have allowed it, for a start.'

'Upward *what* thinking? Are you reading philosophy now?' Nat said, with an impish gleam in her eye.

'Mock me all you like, but don't offer a glimmer of hope in my direction now. It's far too late, and far too cruel.'

'You *have* become serious,' she said. 'Do you have a cigarette?'

'No.'

She stretched her hands high above her head, then reached down to touch her toes. She stayed there a moment, bent over like a folded piece of paper. The old dog sat on its haunches and stared back at us, its eyes lit up by the moon. When Natasha came back up, she said, 'Your mistake was to be too cautious. You could have chanced your arm. But then Charles came along and got there first.'

I came behind her and massaged her shoulders. 'You're too much.'

'I'm glad we didn't marry. You'd drive me mad with all your moral posturing.'

I thought of Charles, the pompous banker almost twice her age. 'Your husband...' I said, but she silenced me with a fierce look.

'I don't want to go back to the house,' she said. 'I want to go to Arcady.'

'Charles will be worried sick.'

'You think he's back there waiting to claim his prize. I don't think so somehow. Let's walk a little further. Don't you want to look Charles in the eye when you see him over breakfast tomorrow? As he pops pieces of marmalade toast into his mouth, you'll have a little secret. Wouldn't you like that?'

I nodded, and something about her mischievous smile persuaded me to go with her, all thoughts of Clara banished.

We followed the path until we emerged from the wood into a clearing. This was Arcady, a grassy meadow surrounded on all sides by acres of thick woodland. In the centre of the clearing was a natural lake, shaped like a wishbone. It had been an oasis of calm in our childhood, but now something was rotten. The air was ripe with the smell of stagnant water and algae. The waters had rescinded, leaving a mulchy layer of leaves and mud on the lake's shores. From deep within the wood, a fox let out a high-pitched bark.

'Remember those summer days we spent here?' Natasha said, and she lifted each foot in turn to remove her canvas shoes as she balanced against me. When she was done, she tossed the shoes to one side and undid the buttons of her trousers. She wiggled out of them and handed them to me, then pulled her sweater over her head, draped it over my arm and stepped forward in her underwear. Her petite feet were engulfed with mud as she walked towards the water's edge.

'Don't go any further,' I said.

She looked over her shoulder and smiled. A full moon lit up her face. 'The water is fine,' she said. 'Quite mild.'

Bess had always loved the lake, swimming in slow circles, her nose cocked to the sky. Now she just dangled a paw at the surface and thought better of it.

Natasha squealed. 'It's pulling at my toes,' she said, and suddenly one foot plunged into deeper water, and she almost toppled over. She righted herself and burst into laughter. 'I always forget how deep it is.'

I slipped off my shoes and socks and left them alongside Natasha's clothes draped over a fallen log. Then I rolled up my trousers to just below the knee and went to her. She was right: the water was warm and murky, somehow sticky. With each step, my toes sank into the mud. I took her arm in mine. 'Come back now. It's time for bed.'

We stood there for a moment. I let myself enjoy the silence, the water, Natasha's touch. I thought of a gnomic piece of advice my mother had given me just before she died. *We are not who we think we are, Benjamin*, she had said, *but we are condemned to be who we think we are.*

Natasha gazed up at the sky with a wistful expression. 'I wish we could live in Arcady,' she said. 'Money doesn't mean anything here. People just fumble around naked, making love and listening to the seep-seep.'

'The redwing.'

'I thought you said—'

Bess let out a low growl and sank down low, her hackles raised.

'What's up, mate?' I called.

The dog spun round, the whites of her eyes showing. She prodded at the surface of the water with her paw.

'What is it, Ben?' Natasha took a few steps back.

I waded towards the dog. When I reached her, she growled and dipped her nose between the reeds.

I knelt down and felt below the surface.

Natasha said, 'Father really did think the Prime Minister was going to come to my wedding, didn't he? I feel rather sorry for him.'

I turned to look at her. She had stepped out of the water and retrieved the bottle of champagne from where I'd left it propped up against the log.

'Stay there,' I warned, and then I was back to the task, inching forward through the gloomy water.

Bess had snatched something from the lake.

'What have you got?' I said, prising the slimy object from the dog's jaws and examining it.

I was looking at a high-heeled shoe covered in thick black mud. It took a further moment to realise skeletal remains were encased within the shoe. A wedge of ankle joint, the irregular form of the metatarsal bridge.

Natasha said, 'I suppose the Home Secretary was a decent enough replacement for him to salvage some pride.'

Bess whimpered and licked my hand with a hot tongue.

'He got terribly excited by the chap from Special Branch with a pistol in his blazer pocket,' Natasha said.

'I think we should go back to the house.'

'What are you holding?'

'Just shut up a moment, will you, and let me think.'

'There's no need to be sharp.' Natasha had slipped on her jumper and folded her arms across her chest. She yawned, impatient to return to the house. She'd had her fun, concluded her transgression.

Much later, when all this had played out, I considered what might have been if I had placed the shoe back in its resting place among the mud and reeds of Arcady. What if I had returned to Merryvale and never told a soul? The next day Natasha would have headed for St Ives, for a cottage with a view of the bay. Life would have gone on. I would have returned to Cambridge with Clara, free at last from my childish infatuation. It was, of course, the most pointless of counterfactuals.

'Darling, I've found something rather alarming,' I said.

Act I

Chapter 1

Dorset, 1959

My mother was an unhappy woman whose husband had died in the last year of the war, attempting to take a German bridgehead in Kapelsche Veer in the Netherlands. Where I came from a few years later, nobody in the extended family seemed to know, though I presume my mother must have had an idea. She had no other children, and lacked a maternal instinct, something my Aunt Eva referred to as her 'chilly heart'.

There had been a man. He had greasy, side-parted hair and a brown corduroy suit, and when he came into our house the scent of cheap cologne would linger for hours. They went to the pictures together on Sunday afternoons, and when she came back my mother bore a quiet air of satisfaction. I came to call this man Uncle Billy, and he sometimes brought me a small brown bag of liquorice sticks or a piece of fruit.

One morning, at Ealing Tube station, the day after my fourteenth birthday, my mother stepped out from the crowd of commuters on to the tracks. She was a woman who had survived the Nazi bombardment of her home city during the blitz, who liked to dance and go to the pictures, who drank the occasional sherry and sang along to Andy Williams records on the gramophone. I suppose she must have felt that didn't add up to very much.

*

It was Aunt Eva who picked me up from the school gates and whisked me into a waiting black cab. She was silent at first, but later, as I munched on cucumber sandwiches in a first-class carriage from Paddington, she dabbed a handkerchief to her eyes and gazed out of the window at the limestone hills and rolling vales of Dorset.

'You must put this behind you,' she said, stubbing the butt of a thin cherry-scented cigarette into an ashtray on the arm of her chair. 'Nothing good ever came from looking back.' She took off her dark glasses. 'Do you understand?'

I nodded, but said nothing. Whole moods danced and flickered in Aunt Eva's eyes, and then, just as quickly, disappeared.

'I asked if you understand.'

'Yes,' I replied.

My aunt had only ever been a fitful presence in my life, making the occasional visit to my mother's house when she was in London. She would bring a comic and a bar of chocolate, which I would take upstairs with a glass of milk. The two sisters would sit at the kitchen table and drink gin from teacups. It always started off amicable, but within an hour or two – whether it was the alcohol, or my mother's depression, or just the sheer incompatibility of the two women – I would hear raised voices, whereupon I'd sneak onto the landing and eavesdrop. One time, as my aunt marched towards the front door, I overheard her say, 'The boy will grow up dull-witted living here. Be that on your head, Margot.'

Now she gave me a curious look, then lit another cigarette and turned her gaze towards the window. She had the habit of pinching the curls of her jet-black hair and pinning them behind her ears. After a while, she said, 'You'll be coming to stay with me at Merryvale Manor. I didn't have time to pack a suitcase, but everything you need will be at your disposal.'

At Dorchester railway station, a gruff man with a wide chest and a full red beard waited in a silver car with leather seats. Aunt Eva introduced him as 'Mr Cresswell, the oil in our engine.'

'All set, then, lad,' Cresswell said. He caught my eye in the driver's mirror and lifted his palm to his forehead in salute.

Eva wound down the passenger window and ran her fingers through her hair. 'The poor woman left a note,' she said quietly to Cresswell.

Cresswell shook his head. 'Rest her soul.'

Eva closed her eyes as the breeze rushed in through the open window. '*Be it on your head now.* That was all she wrote.'

Cresswell pulled out of the car park. 'She wasn't of sound mind.'

Eva rolled her eyes. 'Oh, she was of *per*fectly sound mind,' she said, and she fumbled for the packet of cigarettes in her handbag.

We drove for several miles along twisting country lanes, either side of which loomed high hedge banks. Sometimes, the view opened up to wide moorland, which was dotted with isolated farmhouses. We drove through villages with strange names such as Melplash and Grimstone. Dozens of bulky, long-woolled sheep grazed on the surrounding green hills.

After about half an hour, Eva looked over her shoulder and said, with a smile of anticipation, 'Welcome to your new home.'

On the brow of a hill, looking down over a vast lawn towards a patch of woodland, stood Merryvale Manor. It was a large red-brick country house with a white porch and a peaked roof of purple slate. A set of four Doric columns rose from the base of the porch to a wide triangular gable.

'A little piece of London for you,' my aunt said. 'Georgian architecture at its finest.'

I gave her a blank look. My mother's house was a cramped terrace, set on a grey and ugly street. In contrast, everything about Merryvale was in perfect proportion, straight and proper and clean.

'Have you ever visited Buckingham Palace? It's the same style, if a tenth of the size.'

I shook my head.

'She really *did* make you spend your childhood in that grimy terrace, didn't she?'

Cresswell stopped the car in front of the house's wrought-iron gates. He got out to unlock the padlock and push them open. From a cottage to the right of the house, a black Labrador dashed across the gravelled forecourt. Cresswell knelt to greet it. The dog wiggled on its back legs and licked his face. 'Have you missed me, Bess, my girl?' he said.

Eva said, 'I do apologise, Benjamin. I'll try to stop being resentful of your mother. We're all doing our best, or something like that. It's just I always told her she could come here, bring you, start a new life.'

Cresswell got back in the driver's seat and drove the car onto the gravelled forecourt. In a flowerbed that surrounded the perimeter of a pond, vibrant orange dahlias competed with pink snapdragons. Half-submerged in the green water was a statue of a young boy holding a flask to his lips.

I got out of the car. The scale and sense of Merryvale Manor was overwhelming. I stood for a moment, shielding my eyes from the sun as I took it all in. Bess sniffed at my legs, her tail wagging.

At the top of the front steps, under a marble porchway, a boy and a girl appeared, both a few years older than me. They waved, and skipped down the steps towards us. They were Tom and Natasha, my aunt explained, the twins.

Tom was tall and rangy, with a mop of thick blonde hair and the languid movements of a cat. He gave a polite handshake and said, 'Our cousin from the capital. What a delight.'

Natasha, with her pixie crop and slight frame, was as light as a woodland creature. She had elfin ears and a thin nose with narrow nostrils. When she spoke, her words came out in a tumble. 'We're very sorry for your loss, and there's not a proper way to behave, if that's what you're thinking. Last year, when Willy died, I felt nothing for a week... didn't shed a tear, or even think of him much. It was only when I was taking French class with Miss Horley and instinctively reached to my lap to stroke him that I realised he was gone.'

Tom observed her with a faint smile. 'What my sister is trying to express is that she has a tendency towards narcissism, which she is constantly trying to keep in check.'

Natasha gave her brother a light cuff on the ear. 'What Tom has just revealed is a tendency towards sadism,' she said. 'You will find he likes nothing more than to tease.'

'My dear sister,' explained Tom, 'claims the cat was eaten by a fox, but I think she just got fed up of it mewing and ditched it in the woods.'

Natasha rolled her eyes. 'You'll get used to Tom spouting lies; he's addicted to them.'

The twins led me up the stone steps and into Merryvale Manor. We passed through a small vestibule, where a knight in a suit of armour brandished a shield emblazoned with a coiled python.

'That's Alphonse,' Tom said, touching the knight's helmet as we passed. 'Keeping out the heathens since 1342.'

'That's another lie,' Natasha said.

'You cry foul, but—' Tom protested.

'But *what*, you idiot? The house is only a hundred and fifty years old.'

Tom smiled. 'Good Alphonse, nonetheless. He's on the right side.'

We came into an oval-shaped hallway, which was dominated by a sweeping twin staircase that curved its way to the upper floors. A series of four bronze chandeliers hung from the high ceiling. The hall, Natasha explained as she pointed to various doors, led to the dining room, the salon and the study. There was a third set of stairs that led to the snooker room in the basement.

'Do you play snooker?' she said, tugging at my arm. 'You really must learn. What card games do you know? We're rather obsessed with gin rummy at the moment.'

Eva had followed us inside. 'Oh, children, please. Give the boy some space.'

'*Chil*dren,' Natasha said, screwing up her face. 'We're sixteen.'

'Welcome to Merryvale Manor,' Tom said, and, with his back to me, he unhooked an object from the wall and held it to his face. When he turned to face me, he was wearing a macabre mask. Its face was part human, part beast or devil, and its bulging eyes, one placed slightly lower than the other, looked as though they had witnessed something terrible. It had large bullock horns that jutted out from its temples, and flowing locks of hair made from matted rope. Under its chin was a thick white beard that looked like it had been woven from sheep's wool. There was a repulsive bulge on its forehead.

'That's enough,' Natasha said, snatching the mask from her brother. 'You've scared him.'

Tom chortled to himself. 'Sorry, I couldn't resist. Poor old Alphonse is guarding the front door, but little does he know the devil itself has already got in.'

Natasha hooked the mask back on the wall. 'Learn to be kind,' she said. Turning to me, she said, 'That horrible thing is called the Ooser. An old relic that for some reason my father won't throw away.'

Tom scoffed. 'He won't throw it away because he thinks he can sell it for a lot of money.'

'This family thinks money is worth more than kindness,' Natasha said.

'Oh, do fuck off,' said Tom. 'You make a terrible moralist.'

Eva said, 'Your *lan*guage. Wherever did you hellish children come from?'

'From you, obviously,' Natasha said.

Eva enveloped her daughter in her arms and rubbed the top of her head. 'I do wish you'd grow your hair out, however *du jour* you insist this boyish look is.'

Over the next few days, I came to realise these first exchanges were typical of the twins. Often, Tom would gently tease until Natasha's cheeks glowed pink and she searched for the most hurtful retort. It often spilled over into physical violence: a wrestling match or a cuff round the ear. And yet, within the next hour, they would be crossing the lawn to the tennis courts arm in arm, as if nothing had happened at all.

When they had exhausted teasing each other, they turned their attention to me. Did my mother resemble Aunt Eva? Where was my father? Why couldn't I keep eye contact when talking to people? The questions kept coming.

Tom was constantly amazed at my ignorance when it came to politics and literature, his favourite topics. 'My father,' he said, one time, as the three of us lay on the back lawn in the sunshine. 'You don't seem to know who he is.'

'Who wants to know about a politician?' Natasha said with a sigh.

'It's not that he should know, it's that he *doesn't* know, which is just frightfully strange, don't you think? It's as if he descended from the moon to live among us, but doesn't show the least bit of curiosity about who we actually are.'

Natasha rolled her eyes. 'Ignore him, Benji. We are a boring family from a boring part of the world.'

'Well, that's not strictly true,' Tom countered. 'Our father is a Member of Parliament. He could be on the phone to Khrushchev in the study and Benji here would be none the wiser.'

Natasha stretched out her bare foot and poked Tom in the ribs with her toes. 'They wouldn't trust him with anything important, and you know that. He can't even outmanoeuvre Mother.'

'Do you know who Khrushchev is?' Tom persisted. 'He's First Secretary of the Communist Party of the Soviet Union.'

I blushed and looked away.

'Have you heard of Harold Macmillan? He's my father's boss.'

'Stop it,' Natasha said.

'Which of the following have you read? *The Tenant of Wildfell Hall*, *Great Expectations*, *Ulysses*—'

'*You* haven't read *Ulysses*,' Natasha pointed out.

'That's not the point... I'm asking Benjamin here how he's gone through life knowing next to nothing about—'

'Oh, go away,' she said, landing a sharp kick below his ribs.

Tom grabbed his sister's ankle and yanked it round until she screamed. 'You spiteful cow,' he said.

Natasha pulled her leg back and went for another kick, but Tom sprang to his feet and walked away, muttering something to himself.

When he had gone, Natasha said, 'We will not let you be defined by tragedy, do you know that? Your mother must have been very sad to have done such a thing.'

'I suppose she must have,' I said, and the first swell of anger bubbled up from the knots of my stomach.

The morning she died, she had licked her finger and rubbed a piece of jam from the corner of my mouth. Then she'd stepped back to inspect my school uniform, undone the top button of my shirt and said, 'Make the right choices in life, darling.'

Natasha must have seen my pained expression. 'I mean, it's not her fault she was sad. Women are told all sorts of things about what they should be and how they should behave. It becomes oppressive.'

I looked down at my grass-stained knees.

Natasha touched my arm. 'What they don't tell us – as if it's some bloody male secret – is how we can be *happy*.'

I sought her out, in those first few weeks, as my initial crush soon turned into infatuation. 'Have you seen my cousin?' I would ask, as I searched the salon where she had flute lessons with a stern woman with blue-rinse hair. If that failed, I would go to her bedroom, where she would often be sitting cross-legged on the bed, a Robert Traver or Daphne du Maurier novel on her lap. I loved her easy physicality, the way she rubbed the back of my neck with those long fingers.

The Drummonds, Tom in particular, treated my infatuation with curious teasing. They called me Willy Mark Two after the old cat that used to pad around the house seeking Natasha's affection.

'They seem unlikely sisters, don't you think?' she said to me one morning as we strolled through the wood with Bess at heel. Rays of light filtered through the branches in the elm trees. 'What was your mother like? Was she a sad woman?'

'I don't know.'

'You never wondered?'

I thought of the occasional visitors we had to the house – lachrymose war widows and do-gooder pensioners who squeezed their stout frames into the armchair while my mother served tea and made pleasantries about the rotary club, the weather and the plight of so-and-so, who had never been the same since her other half passed away. I thought of Uncle Billy taking her to the pictures on a Sunday afternoon. 'She had some friends,' I said.

'That's good – that makes me feel better. Isn't it horrid to think of living your life and dying and nobody really caring when it's all over?' She put her hand over her mouth. 'I'm not saying no one cared about Aunt Margot, and it must be terrible for you to be left all alone like that. You don't mind me talking like this, do you?'

I shook my head.

'I'm thinking a lot about what I'm going to do with my life, you see, and I think it's important that we talk about these things, otherwise you just go through life in a daze and before you know it...' She paused. Bess had spurted ahead in pursuit of a rabbit or a bird that had shot off in the thicket. We watched her crash through the bushes. 'I mean, before you know it, it's all over, isn't it?' she went on. 'There's really not much time to get it right.'

I nodded.

'I'm troubling you, aren't I? Silly cousin getting all pseudo-intellectual on you. Drop that horrid leaf and take my hand – it's a bit sweaty, I'm afraid.'

We walked in silence for a while.

Bess came ambling back with an oversized stick dangling from the side of her mouth. Natasha wrestled it from her jaw and feigned throwing it. The dog shot off, then stopped and looked back, confused.

Natasha said, 'I wasn't being mean about Aunt Margot, you know. I just never got to know her, and so I'm probably making horrible assumptions, but it's important to think about these things. I want to be happy in my life, and I don't want to do things just because other people say you should do them, because that seems like such a horrible waste, but I don't know what it is I want to do, and nothing seems important anyway. Do you know what I mean?'

We had emerged into the clearing at the heart of the wood, where the sunlight shimmered across the surface of the lake.

Natasha took a deep breath. 'All *this*,' she said, and she sank to the grass and sat with eyes closed and legs crossed.

The truth was I hadn't much thought about my mother. I certainly hadn't understood the finality of her death. It was as if I was on holiday at Merryvale and, on some level, I imagined she was still pottering around the grease-stained kitchen, boiling carrots to a watery pulp in the pan. Only later, after years of therapy, would I come to realise the five stages of grief are long and tedious.

When I found the words, I said, 'I love the way you talk.'

She opened her eyes and looked at me with a grateful smile. 'That's a kind thing to say. What do you love about the way I talk?'

'I don't know.'

'You're not very expressive, are you? You're a watcher, I can tell. That's OK, you'll come out of your shell. We are a loquacious bunch; we very much like the sound of our own voices.'

I watched Bess plunge belly-first into the lake. She lifted her snout out of the water and paddled around in small circles.

'Come and sit down and enjoy it with me,' Natasha said, patting the grass beside her. 'An ancient paradise. We're very lucky. You'll come to realise that living at Merryvale can be rather exhausting. One needs one's privacy – one needs a place to be at peace. Tom and I call this clearing Arcady.'

I gave her a blank stare as I sat down. A sparrowhawk circled overhead. From deep within the wood, a bird let out an angry screech. I had the uneasy impression someone was watching us from the trees.

'I presume you didn't do Greek at school. Arcady was a special place, unspoiled and innocent. There's a god of the wild called Pan. He's most peculiar. He has the body of a man, but the legs of a goat. He lived there.'

'In Arcady?'

'Tom will tell you all about him. Creatures that are half-man, half-beast – mermaids, satyrs, centaurs – when he was younger, Tom used to obsess about them. He read every book in the salon he could find. Do you know, he's convinced that silly mask in the house is somehow related to the myth of Pan? Personally, I think he just has a wild imagination.'

Bess emerged from the lake and shook the water from her fur. She lay down on her front paws with a satisfied grumble.

Natasha tilted her head towards me. 'This is rather awkward, but Tom and I had a chat this morning, and we really want to help you.'

'Help me?'

Natasha gritted her teeth. 'Mother says she plans to send you to St Francis's next term. And it's just, well, Tom and I have been there since we were eleven, so we know all about it, and it's rather a cut-throat place at times, very competitive. It really shouldn't be like this, but if, you know, you're sort of... not up to scratch, then the other pupils can be very mean.'

It took a moment to realise she was looking at me with pity. My cheeks burned with shame.

'I told Mother you would really benefit from a preparatory year, but she's not having any of it, so Tom and I thought, well, we get bored in the summer holidays anyway, so we thought we would teach you some things, give you some books to read.' She looked away. 'We don't think you're stupid or anything.'

And that was how my education at the hands of the twins began. After breakfast, Tom and I would go to the tennis courts to work on my backhand. He was a patient coach, who gave out words of wisdom while sweeping the ball around the court with effortless grace. At least twice a week, after our match, we performed a routine of push-ups, jumping jacks and sit-ups until our muscles burned. If it was raining, we stayed indoors and he taught me to play rummy, the card game of choice among kids at St Francis's.

After lunch, Natasha and I would set off for Arcady with Bess and a satchel of books. We'd spread a rug out on the grass and pour cups of tea from a Thermos flask. Every few days, Natasha introduced me to a new book from the salon – *Wuthering Heights, Jude the Obscure, Great Expectations*. She would lie on her front, propped up by her elbows, her chin cupped with an upturned palm. They were precious hours.

'You're the cleverest person I know,' I said, one morning. She was wearing a blue and red striped shirt she had tucked into a baggy pair of denim shorts. She had taken off her shoes and was kicking her bare feet up into the air. She had a purple bruise the size of a grape on her calf. Her eyes danced and flickered over the pages. From time to time, she rolled the tip of her tongue over her teeth.

She said, 'That's a kind thing to say, but really I'm just rehashing everything I've read. This is a terrific short story by Camus – it's called "The Adulterous Woman". There's a couple called Marcel and Janine and they're travelling through Algeria on a business trip. They've been married a long time and she's middle-aged and a bit porky, and he's getting on a bit and has lost all his spark. At one point they're on a coach and there's a young soldier giving her the eye, and she's very flattered because it's delicious to be desired again. Later on, they visit a fort, but Marcel couldn't care less about it, so they go back to their hotel. Later, in the middle of the night, she sneaks back to the fort, and you wonder whether she's going to get it on with the soldier from the bus, but he's not there, so she just runs around full of passion for life, for the fort, for everything, and she ends up on her back staring at the stars.' Natasha's eyes glowed. 'She had finally stopped running from fear,' she said. 'I want to be like Janine. I don't want to be fleeing from anything.'

Later, in the sanctity of my attic bedroom, and as the house slept, I wrote in my diary: *Love is everywhere at Merryvale Manor.*

Chapter 2

The day she arrived was a day like any other that summer. We had a breakfast of croissants and coffee on the verandah. Flat, white clouds drifted across blue skies. The air was rich with the sweet scent of white hydrangea. On the lawn, Cresswell wrestled with the cord of the lawnmower, cursing when he failed to ignite the petrol engine. From the wireless within the house, a newsreader read the morning headlines. The Queen had arrived in Newfoundland to begin a forty-five-day tour of Canada. Billie Holiday had been rushed to hospital following an overdose at New York's Metropolitan Hotel. At the table, Eva, Rupert and his brother, Uncle Channing, plotted their approach to the constituency meeting in Dorchester later that morning. I had no such responsibilities, of course. The day would unfold in now familiar segments. Some study by the lake, a lunch of salmon sandwiches, an afternoon of card games, maybe some tennis if the weather held, then perhaps a book in the salon with a hot chocolate before bed.

After breakfast, I followed Natasha to Tom's room, where he was trying on a new pinstripe suit. He had slipped out of his pyjamas and was standing in front of the large wardrobe mirror in his underpants. He had a pale, lean, hairless body.

'They'll be no tennis today,' he said. 'Father wants to take me into the village on constituency business.'

'He's trusted *you*,' Natasha said. She was peering over his shoulder at her reflection in the mirror and applying some eyeliner.

'I hope Ruth from the Anchor is going to be there,' Tom said. 'She's been putting out, did I tell you? That's the rumour, anyway.' He rifled through the bundle of clothes in a heap at the foot of the wardrobe and pulled out a white shirt. 'What do you think? Do you think she'll put out for me?' He ran his hand over his chest, then tugged at the waistband of his pants and peered down. 'I need muscles, don't I? I look like a girl.'

'A pale Adonis,' Natasha said. 'Put some clothes on, brother. Mrs Kinney's new girl is dusting in the next room.'

'She might be pleasantly surprised.'

'Get dressed, Tom,' she repeated, more firmly.

Tom mumbled something as he slipped on the shirt and fiddled with the collar.

Natasha came over to the bed and ran a hand through my hair. 'What are you reading?' she said.

'Sherlock Holmes.'

'Oh, *dreary*.'

Tom slipped on a corduroy jacket and then got in a tangle with a navy-blue tie. He smoothed his hair back into a quiff with a squirt of Brylcreem. 'Father is master of ceremonies, sis, did you know?'

Natasha shook her head. She traced her finger over the spine of my book. Her scarlet nail polish was chipped and her fingertips were stained with black ink.

Tom pouted at his reflection. 'Come if you like – it'll be fun.'

Natasha looked at her watch. 'It won't be anything of the sort, and anyway, *she's* coming today, don't you remember?'

Tom turned from the mirror. 'Who?'

'My French friend. Mother says I must tidy my room. She'll be here in time for lunch.'

We both looked at her blankly.

Natasha sighed. 'You know this, Tom, you just never listen. Father thinks my French is appalling and has arranged for a tutor to spend the summer here. She's staying with the vicar in Upwey. Her name's Meryam and she's from Paris. *Que j'ai hâte!*'

Tom pulled a face. 'Dear God, she wants to swap Paris for that old bastard in the vicarage? She'll be gone by the end of the week.'

'She needs the money, I suppose. She's more interesting than you two anyway. I bet she doesn't read Sherlock Holmes, and she sent me a marvellous letter. She's lived in Paris and London and she's only twenty-five. She makes her own dresses and her favourite poet is Gertrude Stein. She's quite *magnifique*, I just know it already.'

'I'm sure we'll all get on famously,' Tom said. 'Is she a looker?'

'That's completely besides the point. Mother says I must be as near as fluent by Christmas.'

'Why? Are we all moving to Paris?' Tom said.

'*Pas de chance*,' his sister replied, and she leaned back with a sigh. 'Just boring, boring Merryvale.' She tapped my shoulder. 'Come on, Benji, let's take Bess for a walk before she gets here.'

During the walk to the lake, Natasha told me everything she knew about Meryam from the handful of letters they had exchanged. Not only did she make her own dresses, but she was halfway through knitting Natasha a red beret. 'She also paints watercolours,' she said. 'Can you imagine someone so gifted wanting to come and spend the summer with *me*? I'm so lucky. I had begun to think I might die of boredom these holidays.'

I couldn't focus on my book when we arrived at the lake. Instead, I stood by the water's edge and skimmed stones across the surface. A pair of swans glided by.

'Careful of those two beauties,' Natasha said. She was sitting on the rug on the grass, reciting her French vocabulary.

I carried on regardless.

'Don't frighten the swans,' she said, this time raising her voice.

I dropped the handful of stones.

'Are you *sulk*ing?'

I turned to face her, my bottom lip quivering. 'I didn't realise I was so boring.'

Natasha smiled. 'Oh, sweetheart, I'm sorry. I was being careless with my language. Now come over here and test me on my verbs, and leave those bloody swans alone.'

We must have lost track of time. When we returned to Merryvale, the family was already seated in the dining room.

Eva's eyes followed us as we crossed the room and took our seats at one end of the grand oak table. The smell of smoked fish and cigarettes hung in the air.

Next to her, Rupert, fresh from his constituency event in a splendid grey suit, gave his wife a nervous glance. Uncle Channing filled the bowl of his pipe with strands of tobacco.

Seated to my aunt's other side was the vicar. He cupped his hands together and gave a thin smile in our direction.

On the other side of the table, Tom was seated next to a woman with a tangle of curly red hair. She was laughing at something Tom had said, and the sound of her delightful cackle seemed to suck the centre of gravity in the room towards her. So this was Meryam, I realised, with a sinking feeling.

'You're both very late,' Eva said, placing her knife and fork down. 'I seem to remember asking you both to be at table for one.'

Addressing his daughter, Rupert said jovially, 'This marvellous young lady has been waiting to meet you.' He gestured towards Meryam, who lifted her glass and said, '*Enchantée*.'

As Natasha took a seat, she said, 'So you've been tasked with teaching me the subjunctive. I don't envy you.'

Meryam licked her lips and smiled. She had a round, open face with an arched nose and a smattering of freckles. 'I don't think anybody has envied a teacher of the subjunctive,' she said.

Eva had not taken her eyes off her daughter. She said, 'I'd have thought you might have wanted to make a more endearing first impression. Firstly, your bedroom remains a pigsty, and secondly, a young lady should not be neglectful of her timekeeping.'

Tom said, with a sigh, 'Mother, it's only ten past.'

Rupert said to the room, 'We abhor lateness in this household,' and laughed, as if to suggest he thought nothing of the sort.

I took a seat next to Natasha. 'Please accept my apology,' I said to my aunt. 'It was my fault. I wanted to take Bess for a walk.'

Natasha whispered, 'How very sweet of you.'

Eva's nostrils flared. She said, 'That's salmon on your plate, and a potato dauphinoise. It's most probably cold.'

Uncle Channing peered out from under a cloud of pipe smoke, one hand playing with the extremities of his wiry black moustache. He had returned to Merryvale from a trip to London several days ago. He said, 'Not only do we have a guest, but it happens to be a special occasion.'

Rupert rolled his eyes. 'My birthday is not something to celebrate, dear brother. Fifty-bloody-one is perhaps the least special occasion I can remember, but thank you, every day is a blessing.' He fixed his eyes on the vicar. 'That's how it should be – am I right, Reverend Hardcastle?'

The vicar was a small man with a greying beard, a flushed face and several strands of greasy hair he had combed over his balding scalp. He gave a thin smile and said, in a light Dorset accent, 'Every day is a new opportunity to take the right path, yes indeed.'

Eva chewed a mouthful of fish slowly. When she had finished, she said to Meryam, 'My husband's timekeeping is absolutely ghastly. So he naturally aligns himself with the children's tardiness. In fact, they most probably have picked up the habit from him.' She looked up and surveyed the room. 'I don't know where he is half the time, and that's obviously quite all right, isn't it, darling?' She gave a light, hysterical laugh.

Rupert said, 'I don't like to be wedded to my timepiece, no.'

Meryam picked up her wine glass and fixed her eyes on Rupert. Flecks of hazel seemed to radiate out from her green irises. She said, 'I hear in the English countryside, everybody wants to know where you are and who you are with.'

Rupert's face turned crimson. He said, 'It's true I'm a city soul in a country house, but...'

The vicar did not let him finish his sentence: 'You're all such bohemians,' he said, with a false chuckle that signalled he was uncomfortable with the conversation.

'Not all of us,' Eva said, and she picked up her wine and finished it one gulp.

Channing said, in full voice, 'I heard this morning that William Rudgely wants to stand for election again in Torrington, Rupe. What the hell do you make of that?'

'He bloody won't. You don't gift the Liberals their first by-election victory in thirty years and get a second chance.'

'It's always Devon,' Channing said, filling his glass with red, before offering the bottle to Meryam on his right. 'Something about the Liberals and Devon. They're all piss and wind down there.'

Rupert smiled. 'I'm sure, brother, you will find some such information to disseminate about Mr Rudgely. The dark arts indeed.'

Channing nodded. 'There happens to be a rumour that Mr Rudgely's dear wife is getting roasted by the handsome young man who serves behind the bar in the Silver Oak.'

Eva licked her lips and smiled. 'You're a revolting man.'

The vicar dropped his eyes and said, with a degree of irritation, 'There are impressionable young women around the table.'

'A revolting man who uses revolting language,' Eva said.

Channing held his hand up. 'My apologies, ladies, for using an ugly term.'

Natasha popped a slice of potato into her mouth, and when she had finished chewing, she said, 'What are you still looking at me for, Mother? I'm mildly late for lunch.' She glanced at the vicar. 'A forgivable sin, don't you think?'

Meryam snorted through her nose and was forced to spit out a small mouthful of wine into her napkin.

Channing said, 'She's sixteen going on twenty-one, eh?'

Eva gave Meryam a withering look and said, 'Are you quite all right, Miss Martin?'

Meryam scrunched the napkin into a ball and held it out of view under the table. She said, 'Forgive me, a piece of food...' and she pointed to her throat.

'Went down the wrong way, of course it did,' Eva said. 'We should all eat purposefully for that very reason.'

Tom licked his knife clean of cheese sauce and said, 'Mother, you're coming on very thick, I must say.' He gave Natasha a look of support across the table.

'You *must* say?' Eva said. 'I think we'd all rather prefer it if you didn't.'

'We're all just doing our best,' Tom mumbled, his commitment to standing up to his mother clearly wavering.

Rupert nudged the vicar at his side and, with a smile, said, 'We're all doing our best, isn't that right, Mr Hardcastle?'

'That napkin was hand-embroidered by Francois Meganne,' my aunt said, not shifting her gaze from Meryam.

Tom let out a loud sigh and dropped his knife onto his plate.

At that point, Meryam caught my eye across the table. Her nose was peppered with red freckles and, when she smiled, she revealed a missing tooth.

Natasha said, 'Excuse me, everyone, but I was asking the Reverend if he thought being late was such a sin.'

The vicar poured some more wine. 'I don't think He would take great offence, Natasha, not at someone as thick-spirited as you. I quote you Colossians: *And whatever you do, do it heartily, as to the Lord and not to men.*'

Natasha scooped up a piece of fish with her fork and held it a moment in thought. 'I like that one, sir. That one's really not bad at all.'

'Do it heartily,' Meryam repeated. 'What means this word?'

'With gusto,' Natasha said.

'Gusto?'

'Like you really mean it.' Natasha squeezed her hand into a fist. 'Like you love it with every fibre of your being.'

'Heartily,' Meryam said, rolling the word over her tongue.

Channing resumed the conversation about the Conservative candidate's by-election loss the previous year, which seemed to take the sting out of Eva's ire. She lit a long, thin cigarette and sucked at it eagerly.

Tom looked at his sister's empty plate and said, 'You've the manners of a pig, dearest Nat. You've finished and you've only just walked in the door.'

Natasha took a gulp of water. 'Whatever you do, do it heartily. That's right, Mr Hardcastle, isn't it? We can all take a lesson from that. Corinthians.'

'Colossians,' the Reverend corrected her.

'Colossians,' Natasha repeated back. 'I've never heard of that one. Genesis, Exodus, Leviticus, that's as far as I can get. We will do extra penance and read that one before we go to bed, won't we, Benji?' She grinned at me.

'I know that one off by heart, actually,' I said.

'Of course you do, darling,' Eva said, 'of course you do.' And the faces around the table broke into laughter. When the laughter subsided, she said, 'We've some good news for you, Benjamin dear. We plan to enrol you at the twins' school next month, but we fear that perhaps you are not up to speed in several subjects. It will be essential to do some preparatory learning, and Mr Hardcastle here has kindly offered his services.'

'Natasha—' I began to say, but my aunt silenced me with a look.

'My daughter is not here to tutor you,' she said. 'Besides, she is going to be very busy for the rest of the summer. The vicar here is an excellent teacher of Shakespeare.'

The vicar placed his knife and fork side by side on his plate. He gave a slight nod and said sombrely, 'Tomorrow morning at nine is when we'll commence.'

Natasha winced in my direction and mouthed an apology.

Chapter 3

The Reverend Jonathan Hardcastle stood in front of his wall-to-ceiling bookcase in an ill-fitting brown suit and thick grey socks pulled up over his ankles. The living room was dull and confined, with mustard curtains and a two-seater sofa peppered with brown stains. There was a strong smell of cat piss and tobacco smoke. With a little yelp of pleasure, the vicar retrieved a dusty volume from the shelf. He sat down alongside me on the sofa and placed the book on his lap.

'Which character in these inimical verses of Shakespeare confounds you the most?' he said.

'Confounds, sir?'

'Perplexes, puzzles,' he explained, and, when I continued to look at him blankly, he added, 'it's not a test, just a question between two enquiring minds.'

'We didn't read much Shakespeare, sir,' I muttered, staring down at the beige carpet, which was stained with cigarette ash.

'Does that surprise me? Let me consider.' He sucked his bottom lip and shook his head. 'Then I see I must begin at a base level. There was a man called William Shakespeare, who was born in 1564 in Stratford-upon-Avon in the West Midlands. Do you know who reigned over England at that time?'

'No, sir.'

'It was Elizabeth I.'

'Of course, sir.'

'Shakespeare went on to become this country's greatest ever poet and playwright, and no young man can expect to go forth in life and prosper without knowledge of his work, as well as the Holy Bible, of course. You have read the Bible?'

Outside, a blackbird sang a mellow song. The milkman greeted the villagers on his morning rounds.

'I asked you a question, boy.'

'I've read the Bible, sir.'

'Of course you have – you're a good boy, just rather unpolished. We can work on that.'

He opened the book and thumbed through the pages. A curious smile played on his lips as his fingers traced the words. 'Let's dive right in, shall we? This is a story about a noble general called Othello and his beloved wife, Desdemona. At the very beginning, we meet Roderigo, a dissolute Venetian who is in love with Desdemona, and is appalled to learn of her secret elopement with Othello, who, as well as being a proud and well-respected soldier, happens to be a black man.'

The vicar read slowly from the book, savouring the cadences of the verse. I listened, but the words washed over me. The twins were free to roam the grounds of Merryvale while I suffocated in the drab vicarage.

Hardcastle paused and turned his face to mine. 'Well?'

'It's very good, sir.'

'Very good?'

'Excellent, in fact, though there are some words that are new to me.'

The vicar rubbed his greying beard with nicotine-stained fingers. 'Which words exactly?'

As I pondered the question, Meryam came into the room carrying a tray with a jug of lemonade and two glasses. She was wearing a lemon-coloured sundress with loose straps over her shoulders, and a red bandana as a headscarf. On her upper arm was a large black and white tattoo of a man with an elephant's head.

The vicar said, 'Benjamin is discovering Shakespeare for the first time.'

Meryam poured the jug of lemonade into two glasses. 'You're lucky it's not the Bible,' she said, with a faint smile.

'My lovely new house guest,' the vicar explained, 'sometimes likes to goad. We are rubbing along very nicely, though, aren't we, dear?'

'*Oui, bien sûr.*'

'Although I don't approve of that ghastly heathen tattoo.'

Meryam shrugged. 'He's Ganesh. He brings me luck.'

'He won't bring you a husband. It's unladylike, ugly.'

Meryam glanced at the figure on her arm. 'I don't think it's ugly.'

The vicar watched her leave the room with an uneasy smile, then got to his feet and closed the curtains. 'I hope you don't mind, but my mind works best in the gloom,' he said. 'I have what's called photophobia – I'm positively vampiric,' and he forced a chuckle and sat back down. 'Now, tell me what you've learned so far,' he said. 'What do we know of Othello? This great man, this Moor, this general. Elopement with a nobleman's daughter would be an imprisonable offence. A crime, don't you think? We haven't met Othello, but we have learned one thing, haven't we? He can't keep it in his pants.' The vicar's fingers drummed on the coffee table and his knee bobbed up and down. He studied me for a reaction, but I remained silent. 'I'm talking about Othello's penis, Benjamin. He can't keep it in his pants.'

I stared at the gap between my feet.

The vicar's knee brushed against mine.

'And Cassius, what about him?' he went on. 'Alleged to have been bedding his boss's wife. Do you know what they would have done with such a man?'

I shook my head.

'They would have carried out a shaming ritual. Wait, you're looking at me as though I'm speaking Dutch.'

'A ritual, sir?'

He touched my leg. 'Listen, we're a strange bunch down here, Benjamin, with customs quite peculiar to this part of England. We have tended to do things a little differently. If it had happened around here, the ritual would have looked something like this. There's poor Cassius, sleeping in his bed, and he's woken all of a sudden by a tremendous clamour outside his window. He gets up, looks out the window, and he sees something quite terrifying. Men in masks with gongs and cow-horns, whistles and rattles, maybe some tin cans. These men would be rhythmically crashing and hooting and slamming. And they would be chanting and singing too.'

The vicar clapped his hands and stamped his foot. When he paused, his cheeks had turned a deep pink and beads of sweat peppered his forehead. 'They called it "charivari". It's an old hobby of mine, you know, researching the old ways of this land.' The vicar placed his hand on my thigh for a second time and strummed his fingers. 'It was for people who transgressed,' he said. 'Adulterers, thieves, wife-beaters. The vengeful villagers would turn up in the middle of the night, rip them from their beds, and beat them or strip them and parade them. Sometimes, they would go further.' He paused, as if considering a question, then said, 'Do you know, you have quite muscly thighs for a young boy. Do you play sports?'

'No, sir. Well, a little tennis.'

'Excellent – a fine game. Your uncle used to play for the village team. Then he claimed he got too old. It happens to the best of us.' He chuckled to himself. 'You know that despicable-looking mask hanging in the entrance hall of Merryvale?'

I nodded. It made my skin crawl every time I hurried past.

The vicar shot me a lopsided grin. He had two lower front teeth missing. 'That mask was most likely used for charivari back in the old days. It was probably an instrument for inflicting fear and pain. They called it the Ooser, back in the day.'

The telephone rang in the hallway. A moment later, Meryam reappeared. 'It's for you,' she said. 'Don't ask me who, I didn't ask.'

The vicar took a few attempts to raise himself off the sofa. He muttered something to himself as he left the room.

Meryam stood in the doorway, one hand gripping the door. She looked over her shoulder, then came into the room and shut the door behind her. She picked up the Shakespeare and flicked through the pages. 'He thinks it's all in books,' she said, without explaining further. Then she went to the piano and played a sequence of minor chords. 'I always wanted to play the piano, when I was a girl,' she said. 'I don't know why I bothered. You'll probably think the same way about *Othello* in twenty years' time, or maybe not.' She stopped playing, went to the window and opened the curtains. I winced at the sunlight.

'It must be hard for you, being here with these people all of a sudden,' she said, her back to me. 'Natasha told me your mother died.'

'Yes,' I said, and, though I wanted to say more, I found myself mute. Meryam made me feel funny in my stomach, like it was all knotted up.

'That's a shame. At least you have a new family. They're quite something, aren't they? In France, we say *ravissant*.'

She turned from the window to face me. 'You don't say much, do you? You're what, fourteen?'

'Yes.'

'When I was a little girl, I was a proper chatterbox – my papa got so angry, but I couldn't stop. Everything needed a label. That's a flower, that's a bee, that's a milk cart.' She sighed. 'Tell me, do you hate coming to this stuffy cottage when you could be in the outdoors, breathing fresh summer air?'

'I don't mind,' I replied.

'You're very polite,' she said, and sat down with a flounce on the armchair opposite. 'You're also a terrible liar. Shall I tell you a secret? Just between you and me, I get restless when I've been indoors all day, and I hate Shakespeare.'

I risked a smile. She crossed a leg over her knee. She had broad feet with toenails painted red. After a while, she said, 'Tell me, your uncle is an interesting man, isn't he? Is he very powerful?'

'He's a Member of Parliament.'

'I know that. And Natasha? What about her? You like her, don't you? Your eyes follow her. It's very sweet.'

My cheeks burned. 'She's my best friend.'

Meryam smiled. 'She told me to look out for you here.'

'Why?'

She looked at the closed door. 'Why do you think?'

The collar of my shirt felt damp with sweat.

Meryam fingered the strap of her dress. She shifted forward and said, in a lowered tone, 'There is something you could do for me, actually. If I were to give you something very important for Uncle Rupert, would you make sure he receives it?'

I nodded.

She rummaged through a leather handbag at her feet and pulled out an envelope. 'Wait till he's in his office and give it to him there. It's a reference from a family in London. He's been asking for it.'

She passed me the envelope. Her fingertips briefly rested on my forearm. 'But say nothing to anyone else, OK?' she said, and she fixed her eyes upon mine until I felt compelled to look away.

I slipped the note into my satchel.

'Good boy,' she said, and she glanced at the door. 'If you're ever frightened here, speak to your aunt, OK?'

'It's all perfectly fine,' I said, but the truth was I was frightened, and I desperately needed to pee.

Meryam pressed her cold fingers on my wrist. 'Look at me,' she said.

I did as she asked.

'Our secret, OK?'

'Our secret.'

The vicar opened the door and came back into the room. 'We keep all doors open in this house, young lady,' he said.

Meryam gave him a hard stare. 'We were having a conversation.'

The vicar turned away. 'Well, the boy and I have plenty of work to do, I'm afraid, and so do you. The Drummonds are expecting you shortly for your first lesson with Natasha.'

'I can manage my timetable perfectly well,' she said, and then she pressed her fingers onto the back of my hand and said, 'I'll be upstairs if you need me.'

The vicar sat back down on the sofa. When we were alone, he said, 'The charivari would come for her, that's for sure. Introduce the concept of shame.'

I said, 'My aunt's expecting me home for lunch shortly.'

Hardcastle screwed up his nose. It was red and bulbous with nostrils that sprouted black hairs. 'Well, we haven't finished yet. We've at least half an hour left.' He got up, went to the bookshelf, and pulled out another book. 'I was telling you all about the ancient customs of Dorset, wasn't I? You see, charivari is very interesting as a social development. It tells us a little bit about ourselves.'

'I don't understand.'

He opened the book and returned to the sofa. 'Charivari emerged in the absence of God,' he said. 'You see, these villagers saw there was not really any rhyme or reason to who succeeded and who failed in life, who got punished for their sins and who got away with it. They said prayers, and the prayers went unanswered. Their lives remained shit and miserable. So rather than reject God outright, they invented charivari. They thought, "We might as well do this morality thing ourselves." They decided to become God's punishment squad, seeing as He didn't seem to care less what happened to any of them.'

'But what did God do?'

The vicar sank back into the sofa with a sigh. 'He did nothing at all, of course.'

I didn't understand. 'You don't believe in God, sir?'

The vicar threw his hands up in the air. 'I didn't say that, did I? What I said was that man's attempt to play God results in some pretty grim consequences.'

'But you said He didn't seem to care less.'

The vicar scratched his greying beard and rolled his tongue over his teeth. 'Does God exist?' he said. 'What big questions you ask. Well, yes, it doesn't seem likely, does it? People like your uncle get elected to Parliament. And his insolent daughter mocks the Bible at the dinner table and faces no consequences. That says it all, really, doesn't it?'

Later that evening, Tom entered my bedroom without knocking. I had been writing a letter to Uncle Billy, who had been kind enough to send me a small note saying how sorry he was about my mother, that he missed going to the pictures with her on Sunday afternoons, and how he hoped my new family was treating me well.

Tom picked up the large volume of Sherlock Holmes from my desk and studied the back cover. 'I rather like these strange stories,' he said. 'Don't mind if I borrow it off you, do you?'

'No, please do.'

'Ta very much.' Tom trailed a finger over the bed frame. 'I haven't been up here in a very long time. I don't think Mrs Kinney's girls have either.' He inspected his filthy finger. 'I'll ask her to rectify that immediately.'

'It's not a problem.'

Tom waggled a finger. 'That's not how we do it here. If someone has fallen short of their duties, they shall be reminded. The Drummonds don't prize modesty. In fact, I don't think it should be considered a virtue at all. Jesus wasn't modest, was he? No, he was a complete showman. Swanning into Jerusalem on a donkey is false modesty. He was making a bloody scene, and he knew it.'

I smiled. When one was alone with Tom, he was warm and pleasant. It was only when the twins were together that sparks flew.

'Drop all modesty,' he said, peering over my shoulder. 'Who's Uncle Billy?'

I tried to shield the letter. 'Just a friend of my mother's.'

'Oh, I see. A friendly friend.'

'Watch it,' I said.

Tom read from the letter. '"Everybody is very kind to me, particularly my cousin Natasha." What about me? Don't I get a mention at all?'

I grabbed the letter and stashed it in the desk drawer. 'I haven't finished yet,' I said defensively.

'Don't worry, I'm only teasing. Of course dearest Nat gets all the acclaim. She, by the way, is someone who eschewed modesty a long time ago.' He perched on the edge of the bed. 'Hey, listen, I wanted to ask you something.'

I swivelled my chair round to face him. 'Sure.'

'How was your lesson with Reverend Hardcastle?'

'It was fine.'

Tom plucked a piece of hardened skin from his big toe and flicked it across the room towards the dustbin. 'I used to have private tuition round there, that's all. Does he still stink of his pipe and pickled onions?'

'And cat food. The whole place stinks of cat food.'

'Does he do that annoying thing of sitting too close on that little sofa?'

'Yep.'

'I bet he still pulls the curtains shut too.'

'He says he's sensitive to light.'

'Wanker,' Tom said, breaking into a wide smile. He leaned forward, elbows on knees, and in a softer voice said, 'You can talk to me, you know that, if there's anything you feel the need to talk about. You're right to think Nat magnificent, but Cousin Tom can rise to the occasion too.'

'Thank you.'

Tom winked as he stood to go. 'You're a good egg.'

When he had gone, I took Uncle Billy's letter from the drawer. My pencil remained poised over the page for a long time before I wrote, ...*and Tom too. Both the twins are very kind to me.*

Chapter 4

In his study, Rupert swivelled in his chair like an overgrown child trying out a fairground ride. He coupled his hands together behind his head and stretched with an ostentatious yawn. Sheafs of paper, empty mugs of tea and cigar ash littered his desk. There was a small transistor radio relaying the cricket commentary. He gestured to me to approach.

He said, 'How was the old rascal at the vicarage? I hope you're getting some benefits, as he's not cheap, you know. A man of God is more often than not a man who knows how to keep his wallet fat. It's the Church of England's doing, you see – their salary is pitiful. When I was a boy, I told my father I was to become a churchman, a Member of Parliament or a swashbuckling all-rounder for Somerset and England. I said he could choose. Do you know what he said? Banking. Get yourself into the City, make your fortune, and then you can do what you ruddy well like. There's some wisdom in that, for sure, but I do sometimes question whether I would have been happier turning out at Lord's.' He mimed a batting motion with his hands. 'I suppose I didn't have the natural talent,' he said, and he gave a wistful smile and motioned for me to sit.

I took a seat, removed the envelope from my satchel and slid it across the desk towards him.

Rupert eyed the envelope as if I had deposited a dead cat under his nose. 'What is it?'

'A reference.'

He waved his hand. 'Oh, I don't deal with references, dear boy – that's Eva's domain. Or rather, Mrs Kinney usually takes a reference for the girls in the kitchen, and the girls who come in once a month to spring-clean. We don't want them to be light-fingered, do we?'

'It's from Meryam.'

Rupert pounced on the envelope. 'Yes, she did say she would be sending something over. She's also a young woman who knows how to keep her wallet fat. It's the French, you know. Crafty buggers, the lot of them.' He ripped open the envelope, pulled out a piece of paper and read with a half-smile. Then he wetted his lips with his tongue and slipped the note into the breast pocket of his smoking jacket. 'I do hope you three children will appreciate the education I'm giving you. The costs make my accountant weep.'

'Most grateful, sir.'

My uncle appeared to sense my discomfort. 'That's my grandfather,' he said, following my gaze to the portrait of a white-haired man in a tightly tailored coat and high collar. 'His name was Sir Edward Drummond.'

I nodded.

'He was born in 1851, the year of the Great Exhibition, the highpoint of Victoriana. I never knew him, but by all accounts he was a terrible bastard. He never came to terms with the fact that with privilege comes scrutiny. A minister in the great Liberal government of Lord Russell, a man of great privilege and wealth, but he was spiteful and unaccommodating to others. There's a story about him, which is by no means apocryphal. I'd like to tell it to you now.

'Back then, there was a Jewish lawyer called Henry Gilbert, who was elected to the House of Commons in a by-election in Woolwich. Some people thought this Gilbert fellow should not be allowed to take his seat because he refused to take the Christian oath, but he was a persistent bugger: he took his seat on the benches regardless and, in reasonable fashion, argued it was his right to be there, as he commanded a huge majority.

'Sir Edward, my grandfather, refused to accept this, and launched a vociferous campaign against poor Gilbert, until the poor fellow was asked to withdraw by the Sergeant of Arms. I think of that story sometimes when I regard this painting. Look at his face. Proud, isn't he? Proud of all that hatred and bigotry. You can sort of see it in his smirk. I'm afraid that's no way to live, no way to live a life at all.' He chuckled sadly to himself and then fell silent. After a moment, he gripped the edge of the desk and said, in a lowered tone, 'What did the French girl say to you?'

Something in his look startled me. 'Nothing, sir, just to deliver the note,' I said.

'You didn't open it?'

'No.'

Rupert breathed in through his nostrils. 'It's an invoice, you see, for her tuition work, and because she charges top dollar, I've decided to keep the whole thing away from the eyes of your ever-worrying aunt.' Then he took a pen and began scribbling on a piece of paper. When he had finished, he folded it in two, slipped it into an envelope and sealed it with a lick of the tongue.

I stared at the floor.

Rupert rested his gaze on me and said, 'Your aunt thinks I'm rather frivolous with money, and I'm trying to counteract that false accusation. It never bloody works, but hey ho, one must try.'

'Yes, sir.'

My uncle opened a drawer and pulled out a bottle of dark amber liquid. He reached for a glass tumbler and poured himself a generous dash. Then he lifted the glass to his nostrils, took a sniff and knocked it back in one. He said, 'Try to be open to everything in life, Benjamin. There's no black and white, only lots of grey.'

I glanced up at the painting. 'What happened to…?'

'To Henry Gilbert? Not a lot. Think he's buried in the Jewish cemetery in West Ham.'

The housekeeper, Shelagh Kinney, came into the room and waved her hand in protest at the clouds of smoke. She muttered under her breath as she picked up the mugs from the desk and put them on a tray.

Rupert said, 'Come on, woman, it's the only room in the house in which smoking is permitted…'

'And the conservatory, and the salon, and wherever else you light up those foul things,' Mrs Kinney said, but with a reluctant smile.

Rupert said, 'Take the rest of the afternoon off. You look tired, my dear woman.'

'You do know how to flatter a woman, Mr Drummond. I would say you are an angel, but you're not, you're a politician.'

Rupert snorted a little laugh.

When Mrs Kinney had left the room, he said, 'And you run off too. You're a fine addition to the family. Shy, yes, but you'll grow into being a Drummond. You're like a blank slate: unspoiled and yet to blossom. This is the perfect place to flourish.'

I nodded.

'Are you enjoying your lessons over at the vicarage? I know he's a strange old fruit, but he's a fount of wisdom. What are you studying?'

'Shakespeare, sir.'

'Ah, the bard – what a place to start. Your mind will be opened. Listen, I'm not very comfortable with "sir". I don't like to make hierarchies. Call me Rupert.'

'Thank you.'

'Run along, then, I have work to do. Go and say goodnight to Natasha, she's in the salon, and remember, we don't talk of invoices or anything like that. Money is very much off-limits with your aunt.'

I went to go but, before I had reached the door, Rupert called my name.

I turned to face him.

'There's so much grey in every story,' he said. 'Never judge a person in black and white. That's what my grandfather always did. He used to exercise judgement on every Tom, Dick and Harry. He would have been quite comfortable donning that hideous mask in the hallway and indulging in judgement, shame, retribution. It's enough to make you weep. Whereas I'm a romantic at heart, very different to that old bastard. Do you understand?'

'Yes, sir.'

Rupert beckoned me back towards his desk. 'Please make sure the French girl receives this,' he said. 'Be discreet. I may be paying over the odds, but the truth is, one's daughter's education is worth the price of the moon. You'll know that one day when you have a child of your own.'

In the salon, Natasha was sitting on the Persian rug in front of the fire. She hugged her knees to her chest as she stared into the flames. Behind her, Meryam was sitting cross-legged on the chaise longue with a book on her lap. She had thick yellow woollen socks pulled up over the hem of her jeans. Her hair was tied back with a black bandana.

'He just *walked in* while you were dressing?' Natasha was saying. 'That's beyond the pale.'

Meryam gave a dismissive wave of her hand. 'I don't think it was like that. A mistake, perhaps, an accident.'

'It doesn't sound like a mistake,' Natasha said, sounding flustered. 'He should have knocked; he should have waited until you gave permission for him to enter. I'm going to speak to my parents and get you moved into Merryvale. I don't know why you're staying all the way over in Upwey anyway. It's intolerably rude of them to board you over there.'

Meryam untied the bandana and let her mass of red curls fall over her shoulders. 'I can help myself, you know,' she said.

'You can look after yourself, you mean?'

'I can look after myself, yes, I can.'

'I don't doubt it,' Natasha said. She took off her slippers and tilted the soles of her feet towards the warmth of the flames. The room smelt of spiced cocoa. 'But Upwey is a strange village, full of backward people who believe people like the vicar deserve respect because he wears a dog collar, rather than anything the grubby man has said or done. You'd be better off over here with me.'

'With *you*?'

'Yes, with me.'

Meryam spotted me in the doorway and gave a wave.

Natasha looked round. 'What have you been up to, mister?'

I told her I'd been studying at the vicarage.

'Oh goodness, yes, of course. That must be trying.'

I came forward with the copy of Othello the vicar had lent me. 'I wanted to ask you something about Desdemona's speech in Act 4.'

'Her soliloquy?' Natasha sprang to her feet. 'Sorry, darling, but we're just about to start French class. Do you want to come by the fire, M, or shall I come to you?'

'Over here,' Meryam said, patting the space next to her on the chaise longue. 'We start with Céline, *d'accord*?'

Natasha sat next to her and opened a leather-bound red book. She studied it for a moment and then said, 'Don't assume the vicar is a nice person. He's acting like a Peeping Tom.'

Meryam traced her finger over the page. She looked older than twenty-five, I thought. There were fine lines round her eyes whenever she smiled. She said, 'I like to presume at first that everybody is nice. The vicar, your mother, even the drunk guy from the pub who followed me into the woods. I'm naive, huh?'

Natasha snorted her disapproval. 'You are rather. Well, I'm sure we'll do something to shatter the illusion because we're actually all rather terrible. Except for Benji over there, he's quite benign. Sooner or later, Mother will say something horrible to you, or the vicar will burst into your room again when you're completely naked, and— wait a minute, who on earth followed you into the woods?'

'Oh, it was nothing,' Meryam said. 'There was a man with a black dog. He had had too much to drink. He followed me from the village into the woods for a little while, but it was nothing. I walk fast.'

'Have you seen this man?' Natasha said, looking at me with a cross expression as if I was somehow to blame.

I shook my head. She surely hadn't seen Mr Cresswell and Bess?

Meryam touched Natasha's bare toes. 'I don't believe you're terrible. Are you telling lies?'

'No, I *am* terrible. Awful, actually.' Natasha gave an uneasy laugh. 'Are you *chatouilleuse*?'

Natasha bit her lip. 'Ticklish? Is that what you mean? Not very.'

'Ticklish, what a funny word.' Meryam traced an index finger down the sole of Natasha's right foot. 'Let me see whether this is true.'

'Stop it,' Natasha shrieked, pulling her foot away and then performing a perfect backward roll off the chaise longue and onto the rug. She spun round to face Meryam. 'Bet you didn't know I could do that, did you?'

'You're a little *folle*, aren't you?'

'Oh, don't say that, that's what they all say.'

Meryam patted the cushion next to her. 'Come back – we have work to do.'

Natasha said, 'Pull me up, Benji.'

I reached for her hand and helped her to her feet. 'What do you think, cousin? Do you think she'll tickle me again? She's absolutely not to be trusted.' Her breath smelt of peppermint and garlic.

My hand lingered.

Natasha said, 'Look, I know we normally have a little moment at this time of night, don't we? A hot drink and some quiet time with a book, and here I am all giddy and breathless and not ready for bed at all. But tonight is my French lesson and, as you can see, we're having tremendous fun.'

Meryam patted the cushion again. '*La leçon commence maintenant*,' she said.

Natasha waggled her finger and said, 'You must promise not to tickle.'

Meryam's tongue darted out over her bottom lip. 'I will not.'

Natasha cautiously took a seat. 'You will not *promise*, or you will not tickle?'

'I will not tickle,' Meryam said, as she sidled up closer. 'See, I'm keeping my hands to myself.'

'You are the devil and you are not to be trusted,' Natasha said, and she ran her fingers through her cropped hair.

Meryam placed a hand on Natasha's midriff. 'See, no tickling,' she said.

Natasha took a deep breath. 'OK, I might just trust you. But only the teensiest bit,' and then, without looking at me, she waved a dismissive hand in my direction. 'Run along now, Benji, and give us some privacy.'

I realised I still had the note from my uncle in my satchel. I hesitated.

'Don't stand there like a fool,' Natasha said. 'Leave us alone.'

I hurried out of the salon and climbed the three flights of stairs to my attic bedroom, one of the smallest and least decorated rooms in Merryvale. There were two mahogany cupboards either side of a single bed, an armchair and a writing desk. On the wall facing the bed was a faded pastel painting of a woman sitting alone on a beach with a violin. Everything in the room was painted a lacklustre brown or green. There were mouse droppings in the iron grate by a bricked-over fireplace. The only way to breathe light and air into the place was to stand on the armchair and push open the gable window. On the desk was a King James Bible and a dictionary. I opened the latter and looked up the definition of the word benign.

Mild, or unharmful.

Until that moment, I had never really felt the burden of being judged by others. In my old life, before coming to Merryvale, I went to school, did my household chores and, at the end of the day, cleaned my teeth and said the Lord's Prayer. I supposed I was obedient; I trusted my mother loved me well enough, but I lacked the imagination to see myself through another person's eyes.

Now I knew.

They didn't really see me at all.

Chapter 5

Over the next week, Natasha spent all her free time with Meryam. There were no more morning walks to Arcady with Bess and a satchel full of books; no more evenings in the salon drinking hot chocolate and playing games of chess. Instead, I trudged to the vicarage every morning and spent hours in the company of Reverend Hardcastle. Since Meryam's arrival, his behaviour had become increasingly erratic. He gave off an odour of liquor and cat food that was nauseating to endure for hours on end. He underwent wild mood swings, and on his worst days would rant about the excesses of the Drummonds and the vacuous political ideas of my uncle. One time, when he returned from the bathroom, he was clutching a pair of Meryam's stockings. 'Look at the slut,' he said. 'These were left on the stairs. She treats this house like her own personal whorehouse.'

I longed for some innocent intimacy with Natasha, a touch of her hand on the walk to the lake, the feel of her fingers in my hair. In her absence, I had taken to exploring her bedroom when the opportunity arose. The pink bedspread, always casually tossed to one side; the silk nightdress that smelt of lavender and vanilla, stained with something oily she had consumed in bed, the crumbs of which peppered her bedsheets; the floppy rabbit she had borne an affection for to the cusp of adulthood, its ears gnawed and torn. Then there were her books stacked in a neat pile on the bedside cabinet – the Brontës, Agatha Christie, Eliot, as well as the secret novels she kept in a box under the bed – Céline, D. H. Lawrence, Henry Miller.

It was *Tropic of Cancer* I was thumbing through one afternoon when I heard footsteps in the corridor.

I froze. Natasha and Meryam were meant to be in Dorchester on a shopping trip.

The doorknob rattled.

As the girls entered the room, I rolled under the bed and lay still, unsure whether I'd been spotted.

'Look at this mess, Natasha – if your mother sees this, she gets mad, huh?' It was Meryam's voice: sing-song, throaty and exuberant. She sat on the bed, plunging the mattress towards my face.

I remained motionless.

Natasha said, 'Mother knows better than to come in here. She'd probably find something that makes her very uncomfortable, and then she would struggle whether to confront me or not, and would have to defer to Daddy, and, well, it would be oh so much for fragile nerves.'

'You like to fight with your mother?'

'Oh, I don't really. It's all a pretence.'

'That's sweet, just playing at being a fighter,' Meryam said. 'Your mother makes me scared, you know? She watches me.'

'Well, she likes to do that. Doesn't miss a trick.'

'A trick?'

'Oh, she likes to be in control. Poor Daddy doesn't have a chance. She probably suspects he likes you. He has been known to stray.'

Meryam tapped her foot. 'She wants me to leave, you know.'

'She said this?'

'She tells me with her eyes.'

'People can read whatever they like into other people's eyes.'

'It's not a problem if I have to go,' Meryam said. 'It's very quiet here.'

Natasha scoffed. 'Don't tell Mother that – she likes to think she's quite the progressive. She wouldn't like to think she lives in some backwater.' In a sulky tone, she added, 'So, there's a boy back in London, is there?'

'Not exactly.'

'What's his name, then?'

'David. He's from Scotland.'

'And what does *David* do?'

'He's a film critic, for *The Times*.'

'Ooh, very nice.' I heard the sound of a record being slipped out of its sleeve. There was a crackle of needle on vinyl, then the jingle of a tambourine. 'Do you know the Crystals?'

The bassline kicked in, then the vocal harmonies. 'This is nice,' Meryam said.

Natasha lay back on the rug with her hands clasped behind her head. If she turned her head to the side, she would see me, and no doubt think me a ridiculous sneak. I would be caught. She said, 'Look, see out the summer for me – there's only three weeks to go. I'm sorry we've been such dreadful bores. Mother normally throws more parties, and they're quite fun. Sometimes people come from London.'

'All the way from London?' Meryam said, with a tease in her voice.

Natasha crossed her legs and jiggled her foot in time to the music. 'Don't laugh at me,' she said. 'Go back to London with your film critic boyfriend if that's what you want. I'll just die of boredom here, slowly, day by day.'

'You are very funny, Miss Drummond. I will write you letters.'

'Oh, don't, *please*. I don't want to hear all about your exciting life while I'm sat here staring out the window. So, when are you leaving? How long before I sink back into a lonely torpor?'

'Do you ever speak without irony, sweet girl?'

'No – why should I?'

'Stubborn, sad, sweet girl.'

Natasha got up; I heard her cross the room and lift the sash window. 'Listen, who are you, anyway? You're a lousy teacher.'

'I'm not suited to teaching, this is true.'

I heard the flick of a lighter. Natasha's yellow pumps were just visible as she stood on tiptoes to lean out of the window.

'Your mother knows you smoke?'

'No, absolutely not.'

'Why not tell her? You're a woman now.'

'Oh please. I'm sixteen.'

Meryam was wearing a floral skirt and sandals. She had a birthmark the size of a grape on her left calf. She said, 'You have much to learn about freedom. We should read Camus next.'

'Piss off with your French philosophers – they didn't have to negotiate my parents, for starters.'

'You need freedom from this house, from your parents. Do you understand?'

'Oh, I bloody do all right. I've read Camus – he says I'm free to do what I want. That's what's so fucking terrifying.'

'Bad, bad mouth.'

'Potty mouth – we say potty mouth.'

The bed slats bulged towards my face as Meryam shuffled backward. 'Potty mouth... where does this phrase come from?'

I heard Natasha shut the window with a thud. 'You should at least stay until my birthday. It's going to be a fabulous party.'

'I don't have any clothes for parties.'

'You've got some nice dresses.'

'I have plimsolls and sandals.'

'Oh, don't worry about that. I've loads of things you could borrow.' Natasha padded across the room and I heard her open her wardrobe. I could picture her sifting through the pile of clothes discarded at the bottom. 'What size feet are you?'

'Six.'

'Snap. Here you go, then, how about these?'

I fought the urge to cough.

Natasha came back to the bed with a pair of shoes. 'Try these – they're ever so pretty. That starfish on the toe-tip is crystal. You must be very careful.'

Meryam lifted one foot and slipped off her sandals. Then she took a shoe from Natasha and tried it on. She bent down to tie the strap at the back of the heel, then stood up and walked towards the standing mirror.

'Beautiful, aren't they?' Natasha said.

'They pinch my toes.'

'You get used to it.'

There was a rap of knuckles at the bedroom door. 'Are you coming for afternoon tea, darling?' Eva said.

After a pause, Natasha replied, 'We had lunch in town.'

'Is Benjamin with you? He's not in his room.'

'I haven't seen him.'

Eva's footsteps sounded down the corridor.

Meryam said, with just a hint of derision, 'You're treated like the Queen.'

'Oh, please.'

'It's not normal, how you're treated.'

Natasha lifted the needle from the record's surface. 'Do you know, I've got a frightful headache. And I can't think of anything worse than having tea and cake while all the time I'll be thinking of how lonely I'm going to be when you go back to London. Come to my party, please.'

'*Oui, oui, oui, pauvre petite.*'

'You're not very sympathetic, are you?'

'This is not true,' Meryam said, patting the mattress.

Natasha sat down next to her and dangled her bare feet over the bed. There was a red insect bite on her heel.

'You've gone all pink from the sun,' Meryam said. 'Your nose, even your neck is pink. What do you call this part?'

'The nape. It's called the nape of your neck.'

'The *nape*. You have little white hairs on the nape, did you know? Like a duck.'

'Like a *duck*?'

'It's pretty.'

'I've never been compared to a duck before.'

Meryam spoke softly. 'Your heart is here in this *maison*. C'est *normale* – you're very young.'

'How tremendously patronising,' Natasha said. And with sudden animation, she went on, 'Hey, why don't you let me come to London with you for a weekend? We would have such fun.'

'Are you serious?'

'There's a Cézanne exhibition at the National Gallery. We can drink martinis at a bar by the river.'

'You *are* serious. Your mother would never let you.'

'We don't need to tell her.'

'I don't think that's a good idea.'

The room fell silent. A tickle crept into my throat. Natasha said, 'What do you say, Meryam? Will you take me to London?'

Meryam whistled through her teeth. 'You are going to end up getting me into a lot of trouble,' she said.

'What kind of trouble?'

'Don't look at me like that. It's quite disconcerting.'

'Like what?'

'You know like what – you're not naive.'

'Every possibility exists at every moment,' Natasha said, in a whisper. 'Isn't that right?'

Another silence. It was broken by the frantic cawing of a crow on the windowsill.

'Oh, you're too much,' Meryam said, with a groan. 'Enough. I'm leaving you to study.'

That night, I dreamt I was standing among the villagers of Upwey near the front door of the vicarage. There was the vicar, stooped and greasy-haired, rhythmically tapping a cane on the ground. Besides him, a hooded man with a black dog by his side started a slow handclap as a procession of masked men came down the High Street. As they came nearer, I saw they were dragging Meryam along by a rope. She had been stripped naked and smeared from head to toe in black mud. The vicar pushed me hard in the small of the back, causing me to stumble into her path. She lifted her gaze towards me, her green eyes alert with rage. 'Please,' she said. I shook my head. Meryam put her hand to her mouth and whimpered. That's when I realised I was wearing the Ooser.

Chapter 6

A week later, over the dining table, Aunt Eva was laying the ground rules for the twins' seventeenth birthday party, dictating that the girls were allowed one glass of champagne on arrival and one when food was served. She was scanning the guest list. There was an untouched bowl of fruit in front of her.

'That's rather mean,' Rupert mused, and he appeared to consider challenging her further, before opting for a little sigh and a shake of the head. 'I suppose we don't want a bunch of giddy teenagers, do we now?'

Mrs Kinney, her grey hair scraped back into a ponytail, nursed a cup of steaming tea between her hands. 'The girl is turning seventeen, would you believe it? She still behaves like a child.'

'This is true,' Eva said vaguely, as she trailed the pencil down the guest list. 'Tom has invited Vaughan Fletcher. Do you remember he broke my bust of Queen Victoria in the entrance hall?'

'Was that in 1952, or 1953?' Rupert mused.

'Don't jest. He was a clumsy little boy, and no doubt he's turned into an apology of a young man.' She looked up from the table. 'The food is all in check, then, Mrs Kinney? The band will play from nine. What time is it now? Goodness, the morning has evaporated – it's almost midday. Rupert, make sure Cresswell knows to open the gate for the arrival of our guests from three. Benjamin, you seem to be idling. Make yourself useful. There are balloons you could blow up in the entrance hall.' She frowned. 'You look pensive, my dear. What is it?'

Tom looked up from a copy of the *Telegraph*. 'There'll be no drinks restrictions on the boys, surely, Father? We're expecting to get stuck in.'

Eva said, 'You're expected to behave, that's what.'

Meryam came into the dining room wearing a peach ballgown. She was holding up yards of fabric, which fell in folds onto the floor. A waft of hairspray, citrus perfume and tobacco followed her into the room. With one hand, she held in place her red hair, which had been piled into a bouffant and decorated with a purple bow. As she approached the table, she said, 'Natasha says someone might be able to help take up this dress.'

Rupert's gaze swallowed her up. 'Ravishing, my dear,' he said.

Eva gave him a quick glance, her lips curving into a slight smile. 'Not quite the language we should be using, darling.'

'Resplendent,' Rupert corrected himself. 'You look resplendent.'

Addressing Meryam, Eva said, 'Let's hope the birthday girl doesn't feel too upstaged. How is she doing up there?'

'We have a little problem with the back of the dress, you know. I came down for some safety pins.'

Tom said, 'Well, I say...'

Eva lightly cuffed the back of his head. 'You must get changed soon, darling. I don't want you showing up your sister.'

Tom made a noise of disapproval. 'I happen to have been born a minute before her, but I'll always come second place.'

'Nonsense,' Eva said.

Rupert said, in his most mellifluous tone, 'How is the vicar treating you, my dear? I appreciate he may not be the most welcoming of guests. He's lived alone for many years, bar the odd lodger.'

Meryam circled the top of her mouth with her tongue. 'Well, the vicar thinks I make too much mess, but really he hasn't dusted in a long time.'

'He's got no personal hygiene, that man,' Tom said.

Eva's expression was blank. 'I should think he's being very generous in putting you up at all,' she said.

Meryam gave her a hateful glare.

Rupert said, 'Well, we probably could find some space in the staff quarters, couldn't we, darling? They are tiny rooms, but it would make life a whole lot easier. You and Natasha are obviously getting on splendidly. Mrs Kinney, what's the situation?'

Eva said, 'I'm not sure that's going to be possible for a while, I'm afraid. Mrs Kinney needs a little spare capacity.'

Shelagh Kinney shrugged. 'Not until the start of Christmas, to be honest, when the new girls are getting trained up.'

Eva stood up and moved to the open sash window. She lifted the window a little higher and poked her head out. 'It's a fine day,' she said. Then she turned back towards the table and said, 'No, I think it wise if Meryam stays where she is for now. Natasha tends to obsess over her close friendships, and I firmly believe a tutor should keep some distance.'

Meryam's eyes burned with indignation, but she said nothing.

Tom stood up. 'If everybody is going to dress so dreamy, then I suppose I must make an effort. You've shamed me, Meryam. You look a million dollars.'

Meryam tried to hide a smile. 'You should hold your compliments closer to your chest. They'll all wear off by midnight.'

'Yes, Tom, bugger off,' Rupert said grumpily. 'Young Meryam is a guest, not—' But he failed to finish his sentence. There was a clatter of footsteps, and a moment later Natasha burst into the room. She had on a black dress with a flared skirt and a fitted waist. In one hand she held a pair of black heels. 'There you are, darling,' she said, grabbing Meryam's arm. 'Quick, quick, guests are arriving in three hours and I'm nowhere near ready. Did you get the safety pins? I can't have my boobs falling out.'

Eva came across the room to inspect her. 'This neckline is a little plunging. It's lucky you have no chest, sweetheart. Is there a necklace you could wear? Something chunky. Your thing is showing.'

'My what, Mother?'

'Please, darling.'

'My what? Oh, my scars, you mean? Yes, of course, I'll cover them up to make you feel at ease.'

Eva spoke softly. 'It's not me that needs to feel at ease.'

Natasha's eyes widened. 'Is that right?' she said. 'Because I can assure you I am feeling absolutely tickety-boo.'

Eva stepped forward and planted her hands on Natasha's shoulders. 'Darling, deep breaths – your nerves are getting the better of you. Come and sit down, we need to talk to you about a few things. Firstly, there will be one glass of champagne on arrival, and one when food is served.'

'Oh gosh, that's rather tight,' Natasha said with a frown. 'I am seventeen, Mother, not seven. We're not going to be playing pass the parcel, you know. Please stop being such an old woman. You're not even fifty.'

Eva said, 'I'll think about it, darling, but I don't want to get into trouble with the girls' mothers. Lord knows I'm not a prude when it comes to alcohol.'

'Now there's a truism,' Rupert said.

The girls hurried out of the room.

Eva turned to her husband. 'I'm sorry to say this, Rupert, but the French girl is irritating me. She's not getting the best behaviour out of Natasha, quite frankly. She's trying to act above her age.'

'Oh, she's rather charming I think,' Rupert said, affecting an air of nonchalance.

'Charming to look at, that's for sure,' Tom said. 'She's not like the drab girls in Dorchester.'

'Your contribution is not needed,' Eva said. 'Please go and get changed into something smart.'

Tom shrugged. 'She's thrown you, hasn't she, Mother? She's a bit too modern for dusty old Merryvale. Personally, I think she's a marvel.'

'Just go,' Eva said, in a shrill tone she seemed to instantly regret. 'Just go and get changed,' she added, regaining her composure.

Tom ambled out of the room, sporting a bemused smile.

Eva came behind my chair and massaged my shoulders. 'What do you think of her, Benjamin? What's she like at the vicarage? Am I the only one not understanding why she's supposed to be so fabulous?'

'She talks about the vicar badly when he's not around,' I said, but the remark made me feel snide and I regretted it.

'Oh, everyone does that, Benjamin.' Rupert snorted. 'It's practically a parlour game.'

Eva said, 'You look terribly out of sorts, darling. I'm going to take you out for cake while the girls get ready and we're going to have a proper chat. I've been neglecting you these last few weeks. Let's spend some time together.'

'Marvellous idea,' Rupert said. 'I'll fetch the car.'

Eva glanced at her husband. 'No, darling, I'd like to talk to Benjamin alone.'

Half an hour later, we were sitting at a round table near the window of the village tearoom in Upwey. Dull paintings of rural scenes decorated the dark green walls. Candles and glassware lined the shelves of a mahogany sideboard. Union Jack bunting hung from the ceiling. From the kitchen wafted the scent of cinnamon and freshly cooked bread.

Eva took out a small mirror from her handbag and examined herself. 'Have you heard the expression "crow's feet"?' she said with a sigh, not expecting an answer.

A middle-aged woman with a pinched expression and a ruddy complexion placed a teapot on the table, along with two scones and a pot of cream. 'All well at Merryvale, Mrs Drummond?' she said.

'Oh, quite all right I suppose, Mrs Chilvers.'

'Miss Drummond was in here the other day with her new friend,' Mrs Chilvers said.

Eva forced a smile. 'Well, she's technically her tutor.'

'Perky thing, isn't she?'

'She's a bit too *du jour*, if you understand my meaning, but Natasha seems quite smitten. She's a very impressionable young girl at times.'

Mrs Chilvers nodded. 'I thought at first the French girl was in drink, but then some girls just like to make a bit of noise, don't they?'

Eva took off her silk gloves, took some change from her purse and handed some coins to Mrs Chilvers. 'I hope Natasha wasn't contributing to any unseemliness.'

Mrs Chilvers pocketed the change. 'Your girl's a good 'un, Mrs Drummond. Don't you worry about her,' she said.

When she had gone, Eva poured for us both; then she brought her cup to her nose and breathed in the aroma. 'How calming, the scent of a good cup of tea,' she said.

We sat in silence for a while as I ate my freshly baked scone. It was sugary, with plump raisins and a thick crust. Eva stared out of the window, seemingly lost in thought. After a while, she said, 'I think you're rather upset at all the attention Natasha is giving our guest, but you have to remember, she's just a teenager, and can be thoroughly self-involved. I suppose we all were at that age; I certainly was.' She brought the cup to her lips and closed her eyes for what seemed like a long time. When she opened them again, she said, 'Tomorrow, and tomorrow, and tomorrow, creeps in this petty pace from day to day.'

I was aware of the sound of my chewing, and of the clank and rattle from the kitchen.

Eva said, 'Your friendship with Natasha is very charming to witness. Please don't let this affect it... The family has its flaws, but I'm sure you'd agree, we manage a certain level of success. None of it comes easily, though some people seem to think we have it served up on a plate. We've had to...' She paused as if reflecting on what exactly it was she had had to do.

'Everyone is very kind,' I said.

Eva reached across the table and clasped my hand. She said, 'Creeps in this petty pace from day to day, to the last syllable of recorded time. What wonderful verse.'

'I've not heard that one.'

Eva shook her head. 'No, no, I didn't think you would. It's about this sodding life of ours.'

She picked up a knife and cut her scone into four small squares. Then she picked one up and popped it into her mouth very quickly, as if afraid someone might see. When she had swallowed, she said, 'So your lessons at the vicarage are progressing well, I trust. What are you studying?'

'We've just finished *Othello*, and started *Julius Caesar*. We've done some algebra. Miss Martin is going to teach me some French.'

'What can you tell me about Miss Martin?'

'Nothing much.'

'Nothing at all?'

'I don't know.'

Eva loosened her grip of my arm. 'In what way don't you know? You're going to have to learn to communicate with more precision. Do you mean she's different? A little strange?'

'I suppose so.'

'In what way? In a kind of modish way, perhaps a way you're not used to? Women wearing clothes that show off their flesh.'

I nodded.

'She's what we call a woman of the world. Or perhaps she'd like to be a woman of the world. Unfortunately, she's just a tart.'

I stopped chewing and stared at my plate.

'Forgive me,' Eva said. 'We shouldn't speak ill of people we barely know. It's just an impression I get, that's all. Your uncle has a more favourable impression, I think. He wants to extend her stay up to Christmas, but I'm really not sure. Natasha has been acting up since she's been here. Would you agree?'

'She is…'

'Let's try again. What do you really think of Meryam?'

'I think she's nice.'

'Nice is a very dull adjective, Benjamin. It doesn't really convey any information at all. Is she flamboyant? Does she have a sensitive soul?'

'Not really.'

'Not really? What is she, then, for God's sake?'

'She's just nice.'

'Just nice,' Eva repeated. 'Just bloody nice.' She pushed her plate towards me. 'Have mine – I'm not hungry.'

I looked at the half-eaten scone, but dared not touch it.

Eva said, 'I am going to ask you a direct question now. Have you seen Miss Martin doing anything inappropriate? Anything you think I should know about?'

I shook my head.

'You'd tell me if you had, wouldn't you?'

'I promise.'

'Good.' Eva picked up her fork and tapped it on the china teapot. 'My mother, your grandmother, used to have this habit. She used to tap things with her knife and fork. Tap, tap, tap on her plate. Tap, tap, tap on the table. It used to drive us all mad.'

The bell rang and an elderly man with white hair and a pot belly walked in. When he saw us, he held his right hand to his temple in salute. 'Mrs Drummond, fine day,' he said.

'Delightful to see you, William, as always. We heard you whis-tling from halfway down the street.'

Eva leaned across the table towards me and, in a calm half-whisper, she said, 'Let me tell you something about your new family. We have a sense of fidelity to each other that overcomes our flaws as individuals and makes us a strong and successful unit. Your mother never knew it, but external appearance is everything. Once it slips, you become vulnerable.'

She sat back in her chair and wiped her mouth with a napkin. A V-shaped red mark had spread across her throat.

She said, 'You see, I am going to tell you something, because I am feeling rather alone on this issue and need your help. You must promise not to tell.'

I nodded.

Eva put her napkin down. She said, 'I don't think Meryam is quite who she says she is. She claims to have been an au pair for a family called the De Blooters, in Fitzrovia. Rupert, you see, would never chase references – not for him the meagre task of due diligence. I, however, made some calls and... well, there was such a family, and by all accounts they were a very nice one. Trouble is, a bomb landed on their lovely home in 1942 and killed the bloody lot of them. Well, all but one. A daughter survived. She is a woman now with children of her own. They live in a far more modest home in the suburb of Norbury. I wrote to her, and she told me the De Blooters' family home is now a coffee shop. So you understand what I'm saying? Miss Martin is a liar. She also happens to be brash and modern, and she laughs like a tramp, and she really should wash her hair and scrub her face.' Eva paused, then laughed at herself. 'I'm sorry, darling, I'm getting carried away. I shouldn't be telling you all this. I am trying to articulate the most oppressive of thoughts that have been plaguing me since her arrival. And she stinks of cigarettes, doesn't she? I've noticed a whiff of smoke on Natasha's clothes, too. That's a new development.' Eva clasped my hand in hers and placed it on her chest. Her heart was pounding.

She said, 'That's what she does to me, that girl: she causes me terrible anxiety. Will you keep your eye on her for me? Will you be my second pair of eyes?'

I felt a constriction in my throat and my shoulders tensed. Ever since Meryam's arrival, I had sunk to the bottom of Natasha's priorities. I had been of novel interest for a week or two, but Meryam was the new spectacle, and I was on the fringes.

'There is something,' I said.

'You're such a good boy, a rare ray of light in this household. You've come to me from my sister as a gift, and I want to make the very best of you. What is it you want to tell me?' A warm glow of camaraderie spread through my chest as my aunt squeezed my hand.

That night, an intoxicating atmosphere took hold at Merryvale Manor. On a makeshift stage in the entrance hall, a four-piece band played a high-tempo skiffle. Waiters came and went from the kitchen with canapés of salty fish and flutes of ice-cold champagne. On a table by the fireplace, neatly wrapped presents had been stacked into a precarious pile. I had latched on to Tom's band of close friends from St Francis's, who had formed a semicircle near the foot of the staircase. Dressed in crisp white shirts and blazers, they observed a group of girls standing nearby.

A stout boy called Fletcher said, 'Laura Gleeson's got fat.'

'She was ever thus,' another shot back.

'Victoria Bland is blossoming,' Fletcher said.

'But who on earth is the redhead holding court?' said Brendan Causwick, a granite-jawed hockey player from Edinburgh. Their attention switched to Meryam, who was wearing the peach ballgown, which fell off one shoulder.

'She's supposed to be teaching my sister French,' Tom said, then he added, with an air of wistful resignation, 'I think we've all fallen a little bit in love with her this summer.'

At the top of the grand staircase, Sir Rupert appeared with Natasha's petite frame at his side.

The head waiter struck a gong and the hall fell silent. 'Ladies and gentlemen, Miss Natasha Drummond,' he announced.

Tom handed me a flute of champagne as the band segued into a rendition of 'Happy Birthday'.

'Have some of this cuvée – it's delicious,' he said. 'Quick, before anyone sees.'

I took a sip, then another, and before I knew it I had emptied the glass.

'Was that wise?' Tom said, giving me a wary look, but, before I could answer, another of his friends had bowled over – a Charles or a Lawrence – and they were bear-hugging and slapping each other's backs, and, once again, Ben Butler from Ealing fell back into the shadows.

'My twins,' Rupert said, lifting his glass into the air. 'May they be healthy, may they be happy.'

'May they be healthy,' I said, raising my empty glass. 'May they be happy.'

Chapter 7

Meryam and Natasha emerged from the woods at the end of the lawn and walked slowly towards us. They stopped about fifty yards away and sat on the freshly cut grass with their backs to us. It was the day after the party, and I sat in silence alongside my aunt and uncle in the heat of the verandah, awaiting the girls' arrival with a sense of dread.

Rupert tapped the sole of his shoe against the stone floor with the regularity of a metronome, until Eva silenced him with a glance. She brought a cocktail glass to her lips. It rested there a moment as she formulated a thought. Then she said, 'I did not want to ruin the birthday celebrations, but if what Ben says is true, we will have to ask the girl to leave immediately.'

Rupert snorted and took a puff of his cigar. He said, 'Our daughter might consider that her father is a Member of Parliament.'

Eva closed her eyes and sipped the pale green liquid. A moment later, she said, 'It is useful, I suppose, that every problem shines through your prism. It would be worse if you sat here uninterested.'

'Oh, how I admire your higher moral purpose.'

'Let's not go there, Rupert. Things would get rather messy quite soon, don't you think?'

'Not in front of the boy.'

'Agreed.' Eva turned away from her husband and rested her gaze on the girls.

'Morality, morality,' Rupert muttered. He rested his cigar in the ashtray and sighed. Looking at me, he said, 'Your aunt seems to believe she has a monopoly on it.'

Eva's eyes flared with indignation. 'And your uncle...' she began, then it passed, and she took another sip of her drink and closed her eyes. When she resumed talking, she was back on the subject at hand. 'I will preserve morality among my children, that's for certain. That's where my influence still holds sway.'

At that point, Tom appeared behind us in just a pair of tennis shorts and flip-flops. Tucked under one arm was a pair of racquets. His cheerful demeanour contrasted with the sobriety of the room. 'Who's up for a game, then? Benji? Father?'

Eva said, 'Your father and I need to speak to Natasha about something very important. Would you go and fetch the girls? They're on the lawn.'

Tom screwed up his face. 'Benji?' he said, waving a racquet in my direction. Streaks of white sunscreen glistened on his bare chest.

Eva said, 'Benjamin needs to be here too. Go and fetch the girls, will you? We can't wait any longer.'

Tom sought my gaze, but I stared dumbly ahead. Natasha had taken off her shoes and was performing wonky handstands. Her long legs, bronzed from a summer estivating at Merryvale, struggled for balance, and she flopped to the ground.

Tom nudged my leg with a racquet. 'This is all very peculiar. You look white as a sheet.'

'Go and get the bloody girls,' Rupert bellowed.

Tom went through the patio door with a shrug. He approached the girls and said a few words. They exchanged a worried glance, then stood up and brushed themselves free of grass.

'May I be dismissed?' I said.

Eva gave me a fierce look. 'Out of the question. What we set in train, we must finish – however painful.'

Moments later, the girls were standing before us.

'What is it, Mother?' Natasha said. She was standing on the verandah, one knee stained with grass.

'Benjamin...' Eva began, and she struggled to find the words, but eventually landed on, 'Benjamin has told us you two girls had something planned.'

Natasha gave me a confused look. 'What are you talking about?'

Rupert said, with a wave of his hand, 'I mean, it may be entirely misinterpreted, or in any case it's hardly the end of the world as we know it, but we think maybe we need to nip things in the bud.'

Eva said, 'While your father is mincing his words, I'm going to be straight. Meryam, my nephew tells me you were planning to take my daughter to London without my permission. I'm afraid that constitutes gross misconduct and you are therefore dismissed.'

Natasha put her hand to her mouth. 'This is intolerable.'

'Your cousin overheard things he has quite correctly passed on,' Eva said. 'Natasha has only just turned seventeen.'

'But this is a lie,' Natasha said, with a slight whimper. 'Oh my gosh, the little cunt.'

Eva winced in disgust. She said, 'Composure, darling. Don't demean yourself any further,' and she looked steadfastly ahead, her lips pursed and her face white with anger.

I went to move away, but Eva grabbed my arm and held me in place.

Rupert addressed Meryam in the way he might an awkward member of the household staff who had been caught with his hand in a private drawer. 'There'll obviously be no reference forthcoming, but it wouldn't do to make a song and dance of all this with the agency,' he said. 'If you pack your bags tonight, we'll get Cresswell to take you to the railway station first thing in the morning. I believe the train to Paddington arrives just before ten.'

Eva said, without turning her head, 'It's Sunday tomorrow, Rupert. There will be no trains.'

'So it is.'

'She'll go this afternoon.'

'Yes, she will.'

Meryam sported an ironic smile. She stared at Rupert, head cocked slightly to the side, like a dog straining to understand its owner. She said, 'Mr Drummond, is this *really* what you want?'

Eva tutted and flicked back her head. 'I don't particularly like the way you talk,' she said. And she turned to Rupert. 'What agency did you say you used? We'll never use them again.'

Meryam stood, arms folded across her breast.

Rupert stood up and said loudly, 'Come on, let's not end on a sour note. Some situations work out very well, some not to plan. There's no need to lay on the melodrama with a big trowel.'

Eva said, 'I rather object to being called melodramatic.'

Rupert said, 'We don't want to leave anybody out of pocket. Come to my study and we'll write you out a cheque for the month.'

Eva's mouth opened. 'Oh, you are too much.'

'I'm just saying that there's probably more to this unfortunate situation than meets the eye. Our darling daughter can be a funny sort, we all know that.'

'What agency was it, Rupert? I want to make a note.'

Rupert said, 'It wasn't a fucking agency. It was a friend from the office who recommended her.'

'A friend from the office?' Eva repeated quietly.

We all waited a while, listening to Natasha sob. After what seemed like an age, Eva said, 'Go to your room, darling, if you're going to carry on like this. This really won't do, you know. Your deportment is...'

Natasha fixed her eyes on her mother. 'My deportment? Is that what you just said?'

'Yes, darling, a French word – thought you'd be rather good at that.'

Natasha stepped forward, her finger wagging accusingly. 'You make me shudder at times, do you know that? My own mother.'

'Come, come,' Rupert said, without much conviction.

Eva spoke in a staccato rhythm, rising in pitch and tempo. 'Wipe your nose, go to your room and draw a line, young lady. Don't step any further over it. Do you understand me?'

'Did I not even rattle you with that?' Natasha said. 'I said you make me shudder. Like a ghost has passed through my body.'

Rupert got to his feet. 'You're forgetting yourself now, darling. Now come, come.'

Eva turned to Meryam. 'You've been here, what, two months, and you've managed to turn our daughter into some sort of hysteric.'

Meryam, fully composed, said, 'And I was having so much fun.'

Rupert said, without a hint of irony, 'This is all getting rather heated.'

Eva said, 'Nothing is getting heated, darling. I want my daughter in her room and this woman out of my house, and that will be the end of it. Ask Cresswell to take her to the station immediately.'

Meryam said, 'I'll be ready in half an hour by the front door.' She touched Natasha's forearm lightly and whispered something inaudible in her ear.

At that moment, Tom came back in with a quizzical expression on his face. 'Are you sure everything is all right? You're all making an awful racket.'

'Get out, Tom,' Rupert said. 'It's a matter for your sister and your mother.'

Tom pointed at me. 'What's he doing, then?'

Eva said, 'Ask Cresswell to have the car ready outside the front door in half an hour.'

Tom looked from face to face. 'He's in the village, Mother, it's his day off.'

'I'll go,' Rupert said.

Eva said, 'You damn well won't.'

'I can do it,' Tom said quickly. 'Where are we going?'

Rupert said, 'Meryam has to terminate her contract early. She needs to be in Dorchester for the last train to London.'

Meryam said, with a raised eyebrow, 'It seems I'm no longer wanted.'

Tom smiled. 'That's nothing but a bloody shame of the highest order. If you get ready quick, we can have a swift half in the tavern.'

'You'll do no such thing,' Eva said. 'You'll go straight to the vicarage to pick up her things, and then you will go straight to the station and then you'll drive straight back.' She looked skywards and took a deep breath.

Tom appeared to belatedly accept the severity of the situation; his eyes appealed to mine for help.

Meryam took two steps towards the table where my aunt was sitting.

Eva sat placidly, as if refusing to engage further. She picked up her glass and took an audible sip.

Meryam said, 'Your daughter is halfway through that door, you know. I just showed her it was open.' And she turned and with a trembling lip walked across the room.

Natasha sank to the floor as all defiance slipped out of her body. She remained there, cross-legged, staring at her knees.

My aunt for a brief moment looked at Rupert, who had gone over to Natasha's crumpled form and was attempting to haul her gently to her feet.

Rupert's face twisted into a grimace. He held Natasha into his large frame and stroked her head.

Tom said, 'I assume the tank doesn't need filling. Cresswell always handles that side of things.'

Eva breathed in and said, 'Just get her out of my house, Tom, before I do something I regret.'

Later that evening, I was reading in bed when Natasha came into my room. She stood in the doorway in her white nightgown.

'I'm so sorry,' I said, putting the book down.

'You're *sorry* – that's all you can say? With your stupid adventure book in your lap. I have been so kind to you.'

'Yes, you have.'

'Do you know why that was?'

I stared at her blankly.

'Because I felt sorry for you. For your situation, for who you are. I thought I'd be kind. I preferred the company of Meryam because she was brilliant and funny and open and clever, and those people are a light to me, and I will flicker around them like a moth, and I will never compromise on that.' She paused a moment, then said, 'Your whole silly little running-to-mother act prevented nothing of any consequence happening. Though it has achieved something. It's hardened my heart a little. If that's something you can be proud of as you put down your stupid Walter Scott novel, then so be it. I presume, however, it will have the opposite effect, and it should. I hope you feel bloody awful.'

I lay in the darkness after she left, struggling with dark thoughts. My mother used to say I was a delicate flower, not quite ready for the world, and she would hold an imaginary stalk between thumb and forefinger and gently blow. *You're a dandelion*, she would say. What would she say of me now?

At some point I fell asleep. When I woke, Tom was standing in the doorway. He had turned on the light. There were flecks of what appeared to be mud on his face.

'Do you know where Mother and Father went?' he said, in between deep breaths. 'The car's not here. Did they say what time they'd be back?'

I sat up. 'I've no idea. Are you OK?'

'Perfectly fine,' he said.

'What time is it?'

'I don't know exactly. The sun's almost up.' He took several deep breaths. 'Listen, I think I've got myself into trouble.' His hair was mashed to one side and the top buttons of his shirt were undone. There was a look in his eyes that was at once wild and somehow pleading. I had the sense he wanted me to say or do something to comfort him, but if that was the case he had come to the wrong room. I was frightened and confused.

'What trouble?' I said.

Tom silenced me with an upturned palm, stood in the doorway for a moment, then left without saying another word.

Act II

Chapter 8

Merryvale Manor, 1964

Clara put her novel down and peered through the windscreen, which had become smeared with dust on the drive down from Cambridge. As the wonder of the place took hold, she said, in a tone of rising hysteria, 'Oh my gosh. Ben, how dare you tell me you're upper-middle class? Your family live *here*?'

'Welcome to Merryvale Manor,' I said, rolling the car onto the gravelled forecourt next to my uncle's shiny blue Triumph. It felt good to be back; returning to the old place was like sinking into a hot bath.

Clara leaned out of the window to glance at her reflection in the wing mirror. Ruffling her hair, she said, 'Two questions, do I look a state? No, don't answer that, it's quite obvious. I need a hairbrush before I speak to anybody. Second question, is the Prime Minister *really* coming?'

I shrugged. 'He's been invited. Whether he comes...'

The lanterns above the porticoed entrance flicked on, and a moment later Rupert and Eva emerged at the top of the stairs. They were dressed in evening wear and clutching glasses of champagne.

Clara whispered, 'Oh fuck, are they *really* posh?'

'They like to think they're down to earth.'

'On a scale of one to ten?'

I gave a reassuring squeeze of her knee. 'They wear tweed and ask people, "Where did you school?"'

She took a deep breath. 'An eleven, then.'

The first time I met Clara she was standing precariously on the seat of her rickety old bicycle, which had been propped up against the wall of a terraced house. I was walking home with my house-mate George, a broad-shouldered rugby player from Surrey with a buzz-cut and Labrador eyes.

Clara, wearing leather boots over her blue dungarees, was leaning against the brickwork with one hand, and with her free hand she was wielding a tree branch above her head in the direction of a second-floor window. 'This isn't going to plan,' she said, when we stopped to ask what she was doing.

George stabilised the wobbling bicycle with a firm hand.

'Up there, above my head,' Clara said, 'Georgina is having wild sex with a French waiter, which I really don't hold against her, but the trouble is she's walked off with my wallet and I can't buy a drink at the pub quiz.'

She reached up on tiptoes, but the bike wobbled and she slipped, falling backward into my arms with a shriek. When we had disentangled ourselves, she had said, 'Maybe you two want to buy me a drink? I promise I look better without pieces of tree in my hair.'

Now she had retrieved a hairbrush from the rucksack at her feet and, with tilted head, she grimaced as she untangled a stubborn knot.

I said, 'Steel yourself – they might be squiffy. And don't ask too much about the groom. They've been a bit secretive about it.'

'You don't know?'

'I suspect he's someone tremendously unsuitable.'

'This is going to be wild,' Clara said, shaking her head.

We exited the car, to be greeted by warm embraces from Rupert and Eva.

'Good to have you home,' Rupert said, patting my back firmly. He gave off a strong whiff of musk and tobacco. 'I hope you stay the full fortnight, and don't shy off back to Cambridge when the family drama gets a bit much.' He released me from his grip. Wisps of grey hair from his quiff blew about in the evening breeze. 'It's going to be terrific next Sunday. The cricket club is playing a match on the sandbar in the Solent for charity. They say you get three hours' play when the tide is out.'

Before I could answer, Eva threw her arms around me. 'Oh, Rupert, this young man has far more interesting pastimes than watching you and your old codgers play silly games in the sea.' She kissed me firmly on the lips, then stepped back for an examination. 'You're looking pale, Benjamin. Are you getting enough fresh air? Or are you spending all your daylight hours locked up in your bedroom with...' She turned to Clara. 'This fine young lady. Who has redder hair than Clara Bow. What a delight.'

Clara gave an amused smile.

'Welcome to our home,' Eva said, flinging up her arms, and just managing to avoid spilling champagne from her glass.

Rupert moved to her side with the speed of a cat and took the glass from her hand. 'Not the cuvée, sweetie, it's more expensive than gold.' He ushered Clara towards the house. 'Come, come, we have nibbles and things, some marvellous liquor.'

Eva said, 'Come and meet Merryvale.'

'The house is not a person, darling,' Rupert said.

'The house has personality,' Eva insisted.

Bess appeared with a tennis ball in her mouth, followed by Cresswell in his flat cap and green dungarees. When the dog spotted me, she ran across the forecourt, tail wagging.

'Ladies and gents,' the gardener said, doffing his cap. He went to retrieve our suitcases from the boot of the car.

Rupert said, 'Take it to the attic room, will you, old chap? Apologies if it's not on the light side – he's got company.'

'Mr Cresswell, it's been too long,' I said, with a smile.

He grunted something I didn't catch.

I tried again. 'You're still feeding Bess the most foul-smelling meat. Her breath could skin a cat.'

Cresswell opened the boot and pulled out our suitcase. 'It's fish, lad, she'll eat pilchards or nort.'

Rupert placed an arm round my shoulder as we mounted the front steps. He appeared larger than I had seen him last, broader and more padded, and he bore the comfortable ease of a man at the peak of his powers. It was as if five more years in Parliament, two as permanent undersecretary of state at the Home Office, had lent his life a sense of purpose. He said, 'Tom's been back since Wednesday. He's been waiting for his old mucker to return. And Natasha, well, you know how she misses you...' He paused, and changed the subject. 'I'm hoping you can have a look over one of my speeches, actually. You have a mastery of the written word.'

We saluted the knight Alphonse in the vestibule, as had become customary, and passed into the entrance hall, where Tom was waiting with a warm smile.

'Welcome to the madhouse,' he said, and he gave that sheepish smile that made girls weak at the knees.

Eva said, 'We're nowhere near ready for tomorrow, so Rupert and I are sitting in the salon drinking this fabulous cuvée instead. Nat's sulking in her bedroom for some reason. Mr Cresswell has the weight of the world upon him, as if the wedding prep is all too much of an imposition. Channing is pissed as a newt. I must say,' she ruffled her hand through Clara's hair, 'this colour red is just *su*per.'

'We are overjoyed at your courtship,' Rupert said. 'Just no weddings for a while, because my bank account is cleared out. My children will be the ruin of me.'

Tom said, 'Father, just how much cuvée?'

'Not enough by a long shot,' Rupert shot back. 'Come and have a glass.' He led Tom away, leaving the three of us in the entrance hall.

Clara took it all in: the black and white chequered marble floor, the high ceiling, the twin staircase.

'Please, go and discover,' my aunt said, following her gaze to the sixteenth-century tapestry that dominated the far wall.

We crossed the room. The tapestry showed a robed man on the ground in front of a baying mob.

Eva tugged my sleeve. 'Help me out with this, clever clogs – I always make the story up.'

'It's the Death of Ananias and Sapphira,' I said. 'They were a married couple who refused to hand over their money to the apostles, so God struck them down dead. That's Ananias there – he was first to go. His wife is counting her cash in the corner. Presumably, she'll be next.'

Eva let out a throaty laugh. 'It's one of the most appalling episodes of the New Testament, but I love it.'

'And the Latin?' Clara asked.

I reread the inscription. 'It's something like, "I will repay each of you according to your deeds".'

Clara moved on to a framed black and white photograph adjacent to the painting. The photograph of the Ooser had been framed in the entrance hall since the original mask went missing, but even its image gave me a shiver: the wild eyes that seemed always to be looking somewhere else, somewhere dark and unforgiving.

Eva said, 'We like to contrast the Bible with a little devilry.'

Clara nodded. 'Oh, I know all about this particular devil, Mrs Drummond,' she said.

Eva gave a quizzical look.

With a smile, I said, 'Clara has been looking into aspects of our strange old mask as part of her studies.'

'Her studies?' Eva replied.

'Have a guess what she's writing her dissertation on,' I said.

'Thomas Hardy? Surely he's the only thing of note to come out of this backwater.'

I shook my head.

'It's always Thomas Hardy. There's nothing else,' Eva said.

I gestured towards Clara. 'She is writing a history of the ethnology and folklore of south-west England.'

Eva's eyes twinkled. 'Oh, aren't you delightful! So brilliantly niche.'

Clara explained, 'I'm looking specifically at charivari.'

'You've lost me there,' Eva said.

Clara was in her element. 'Oh, well, you see, it was a folk custom in some villages down here. Used as a form of social coercion. The Ooser was almost certainly made for that purpose.'

I said, 'Clara wants to trace the Ooser's history, its origins.'

Eva sipped her champagne.

Clara said, 'It's mentioned in a lot of texts, you see, but the Merryvale mask is the only one known to have survived. Until—'

'Yes... until it disappeared from under our noses,' Eva said. 'I'm afraid we have no hope of ever seeing it again. It's just a thing that Rupert's grandfather picked up from somewhere.' She gripped Clara's arm and said, 'Your work sounds rather splendid – but now come and let me fix you a drink.'

The salon was one of the cosiest rooms at Merryvale, but it didn't have much competition. A matching pair of tobacco-brown chesterfield sofas had been placed either side of a rug that had grown so worn you could barely make out its floral patterns. Floor-to-ceiling oak bookcases lined every wall. It was reassuring to be home, where life unfolded in comfortable little vignettes – the port and lemon on the verandah, a game of evening cricket, reading a whodunnit in the salon before bed.

Tom said, 'It's marvellous that you've finally arrived. These oldies have no stamina.' He pointed at Uncle Channing, who was asleep in the armchair by the cast-iron fireplace, the frame and canopy of which was decorated with a dragon and thistle design. Turning to face Clara, he said, 'Ben tells me you're going to be a brilliant historian.'

Clara gave me a sideways glance. 'Well, I'd rather be a playwright.'

'You'd be great at that too,' I said, kissing her on the cheek. 'You understand people.'

Rupert leaned towards his wife's ear and said, 'Oh dear, I fear our insufferable pretensions will be laid bare, my love.'

'You'd best not be boring, then, darling. No long-winded stories,' Eva replied. She gestured towards the bookcases and said to Clara, 'There are hundreds of history books in this room if you want some inspiration.'

'I think Clara will be inspiring us, Mother, not the other way round,' Tom said, with the light flattery he wielded so effortlessly.

Rupert handed me a glass of Scotch. 'How's Cambridge, son?'

'Jolly hard work,' I said.

Tom said, 'English literature jolly hard work, my arse.'

Rupert smiled and ushered me to the couch. 'These years will probably be the most memorable of your life. My own life has certainly never quite hit those dizzy heights again. You are in an exquisite city, in the seat of learning, embarking on a love affair.' He put his hand on his heart. 'Gosh, who would not trade places?'

Clara said, 'I think you'll find Ben is a home-boy at heart. He talks of you all with great affection.'

Eva murmured approvingly, 'That makes me happy.'

Tom sank into one of the sofas and surveyed the room. 'Where's sis, then?'

Eva glanced at Rupert, then went to the champagne bucket and refilled her glass. 'She's in her room, darling. She won't be down,' she said.

'I can't bear the suspense any more,' I said. 'Is anyone going to enlighten me on the man who has finally swept dear Nat off her feet? It seems she's only known him five minutes.'

Rupert coughed into his hand. 'She's known him a little longer than that.'

'She's told me his name is Charles, that's all,' I said. 'It's not like her to keep her cards so close to her chest.'

There was a moment's silence, then Eva sat down and said hurriedly, 'You know him, actually, darling. It's Charles Hogan – a very nice man indeed.'

I glanced at Tom, but he averted his gaze.

'Charles Hogan the banker? Please tell me it's not the same chap.'

'He makes her very happy,' Eva said.

Rupert raised his eyebrows. 'And that, my dear boy, is no easy task, as you very well know. Your aunt and I have come to the conclusion it's probably quite all right.'

'Did you know about this?' I said to Tom. Natasha had written to me a series of short letters, each one alluding to the relationship she had embarked upon with a man twice her age. There were mentions of a 'sweet Charles, who puts up with much', but she had not elaborated.

I said, 'I have to say I find this incredibly troubling.'

Eva waved a dismissive hand. 'She's been perfectly all right, hasn't she, Rupert? Charles brings solidity in her life. He's good for her.' She looked at her husband for reassurance, but he said nothing.

Channing began to snore, his large moustache quivering.

Eva went on, 'I will freely admit that I was quite taken aback when she told me she was... that she was... in a *relationship* with this man, but I've thought an awful lot about it, and he's... well, he's strong, and she needs some guidance.'

Rupert said, matter-of-factly, 'We have a hundred and fifty guests arriving tomorrow, including the Home Secretary, and we'll all have a jolly good time.'

I said, 'So the Prime Minister declined?'

Rupert nodded. There was no escaping that his political career had so far been defined by mediocrity. There had been a minor scandal involving undeclared donations to his campaign when he was elected to the Commons in 1955 and, ever since, Rupert had battled the impression he had bought his seat. Tom once pointed out a piece in the *Telegraph* that quoted Tory sources describing his father as 'boorish and out of touch', which seemed a harsh but not unfair assessment. Nevertheless, he had become a minor minister in the Douglas-Home government, and the promotion had brought him a degree of personal satisfaction and professional pride. He folded his arms and said, 'The PM is in Italy this weekend,' leaving it hanging as a choice piece of insider knowledge nobody sought to unpick.

Tom said, 'Charles Hogan is not fit to lace her shoes.'

Eva took a sip of wine and held the glass between her hands as if in prayer. 'Perhaps we should celebrate the fact that, since being engaged to Charles, Natasha has been rather less uptight.'

Rupert got to his feet and rubbed his hands together. 'Come now, everybody. It's a celebration, and we have a guest, who is very politely ignoring our family nonsense and pretending to read' – he peered over Clara's shoulder at the bookcase – '*The Life and Times of Saint Benedict.*'

There was a murmur of laughter.

Clara said, 'Oh, don't mind me,' but Rupert had already taken the book from her hand and was guiding her towards the sofa where Eva had taken a seat. 'Do sit down and let me fix you another drink. Saint Benedict is the patron saint of Europe – that's all I can remember about that man. God knows why we surround ourselves with such piety.'

Eva said, 'Bring us both a glass of Scotch, darling,' and she forced a smile and said to Clara, 'My daughter has had a challenging few years.'

Tom said, 'She got kicked out of school for setting fire to her room-mate's pillow.'

'For God's sake, Tom,' Eva said.

'Well, she did, Mother.'

'Nobody came to any harm. The girl had bullied her.'

Rupert came back with glasses for the two women.

Clara swirled her glass and said, 'Summer weddings are the best. My best friend Charlotte is getting married next month in—'

Eva spoke over her. 'Rupert and I married in summer, in Sicily, a most wonderful place called Giardini something. We couldn't take a gamble on the weather – we're both extreme heliophiles.'

Rupert said to Tom, with a boyish grin, 'There are two Special Branch officers currently inspecting the grounds. They showed me their Smith and Wessons.'

'Marvellous.' Tom grinned. 'Who'd have thought the Home Secretary had any enemies? He's as inoffensive as an old lamb.'

Clara said, 'I hear he has a streak of steel, actually.'

'Naxos,' Eva said, to nobody in particular. 'It was called Giardini Naxos.'

'One last question, then I'll let it rest,' I said. 'How old is he? Does anyone know?'

Eva said, 'You'll let it rest now.'

There was a loud cough and splutter from Channing, then a terrific wheeze as his lungs filled with air. His eyes opened and he looked around the room, licking some saliva from his lips. 'He's forty-four – almost my age,' he said, reaching for the bottle on the coffee table next to him and refilling his glass. He drank, then noticed our surprised faces and said, 'What? You're talking about that old bastard Charles. He's forty-four, believe me. I asked him the other day.'

I said, 'Forty-four, and she's twenty-two.'

Channing yawned, shut his eyes and nestled back in the armchair. He said, 'She was down here earlier, Eva darling, when you were eating. I have to be perfectly honest and tell you that she was very agitated about tomorrow. I think you do need to have a conversation with her. What's done is done.'

Rupert said nervously to his brother, 'You old doomsayer. Just have another whisky – it will see you off for the night.'

Channing let out a low rumbling belch. 'Do excuse me. That Scotch keeps repeating on me.' He held his hand to his mouth and swallowed, then said, 'She was asking me whether I thought Charles was a bore.'

'And what did you say?' Eva said.

'Well, he's no Jack Benny,' Channing said. 'He bores the pants off me.'

Eva closed her eyes and said softly, 'Go to her, Ben, would you? We promise to entertain your guest.' She placed her hand on my chest. 'This wedding is *very* important. Charles is a good thing – you'll see that in time.' She stroked my cheek with a cold finger, then moved in for a hug. 'I'm glad you're home, darling. We're all so bloody glad you're home.'

Chapter 9

Natasha was sitting upright in bed with her hands on her lap and her eyes closed. She was still beautiful, but she had grown thinner, her collarbone more visible underneath the silk nightgown that hung loosely over her petite frame. She opened her eyes, sniffed and wiped her nose with the back of her arm. 'I know I look awful,' she said. 'You'd think I was getting married tomorrow. What a fucking drama.'

I slipped off my shoes and took up a position on the bed alongside her. The room had hardly changed since she was a teenager. The poster of a red-faced alien in front of a skyscraper holding a ray-gun, the sewing machine she never used, quotes from books she had written on felt paper and stuck to the walls with Sellotape. There were dying plants in little pots on the windowsill and dozens of record sleeves scattered across the floor.

She reached for my hand; the cluster of diamonds on her white gold engagement ring pressed into my palm.

'I've missed you,' I said, which was a half-truth. The more time I spent away from Natasha, the more I felt freed from the intoxicating spell she seemed to cast upon me. After Meryam's departure, she had refused to speak to me for three months. And then, at Christmas, when we had returned from St Francis's for the school holidays, she presented me with the book *Fishing for Trout* by Robert Traver. 'I suppose I should get over it now,' she had said, planting a kiss on my cheek. 'Just don't be such a shit again, OK?'

Natasha gave the flesh of my palm a playful pinch. 'Strawberry, vanilla or chocolate?'

'Strawberry.'

She squeezed harder. 'Strawberry was the wrong choice. That was the worst one.'

'You would have said that whatever I said.'

'Maybe,' she said, her tongue darting over her bottom lip.

I pulled my hand free and shifted position to face her.

'Hmmm,' she said, running her hand through her tomboy crop and averting her eyes. 'I sense a lecture coming on.'

I held her pale wrist. 'Why didn't you tell me it was him?'

She looked down at her hands. 'Because you'd disapprove, and you know I don't like disapproval. Mother does it all the time – please don't do it too.'

'I'm the only one you might listen to.'

'I only listen to you because you don't give advice.'

'This is your life.'

'It's an aspect of it,' she said, cradling her hands. 'There are lots of things that happen in one's life.'

'There's still time,' I said, not sure if I should say what was unsayable.

There was a flicker of hope in her eyes. 'The Home Secretary is coming,' she said.

'I know.'

'I can't call it off. How *bad* would that look?'

I sighed. 'This family is obsessed with how things look. It really is rather tragic.'

She jutted out her chin. 'Didn't somebody say the world is a tragedy to those who feel?' she said.

'The doomed heroine.'

Natasha cast a look of disapproval. 'You're being all unkind. I haven't seen you in yonks. Tell me something about you. You've brought a girlfriend. Has Mother scared her witless yet?'

'She's coping admirably.'

She turned to face me. 'Is she prettier than me?'

'That's enough.'

'Cleverer than me?'

'Probably.'

'Bitch,' she said, breaking into a half-smile. She shuffled closer and rested her head on my shoulder.

I put my arm round her waist. 'You've got so skinny, like a little sparrow.'

'I honestly don't know why. I'm eating like a horse.'

'Listen, tell me one thing about this man.'

She pulled away from me. 'Please stop calling my fiancé *this man*. His name is Charles, and you don't know him.

'I do,' I insisted. 'He's a dull bank manager from Dorchester who is old enough to be your father.'

'He can't help falling in love,' Natasha said vaguely.

'You deserve more.'

'When you meet him, you'll regret going on this moral crusade.' There was a small leather book by her side; she took it and flicked through the pages. 'This is what I wrote when he asked me to marry him, and I promise you it's what came from my heart.' She steadied herself, then began to read, 'No more secret Natasha, no more hiding in plain sight. You will have a husband who knows you, and you will not be able to hide. You will not be allowed to hide.'

Her words pinched my heart. '*I* know who you are.'

She rolled her eyes. 'You know the tip of the iceberg.'

I gazed at the opposing wall. It was bare but for a single oil painting, which depicted Oberon, Titania and Puck dancing in the woods. She was probably right, I thought. Since I had moved to Cambridge, our friendship had lost its intimacy. I wrote at first, at least twice a week, but then the gaps between letters became months, and whole passages of time would go by in which we weren't participants in each other's lives. I had weaned myself off Natasha until I was able to live my own life, so why did the thought of her marrying Charles Hogan fill me with dread?

In a low whisper, Natasha said, 'Hand in hand, with fairy grace, we shall sing, and bless this place.'

I tried again. 'If you have any doubts about going ahead with the wedding, then we can call it off – that's what we'll do.'

'That's what *we'll* do?'

'Everybody will understand. That's not to say they won't be very upset at first, but it's your life. You want to...' But I couldn't think of anything she wanted to do. We had grown apart.

We sat in silence for a moment. The only sounds in the room were the ticking of the clock and Natasha's sniffles.

There had been a time, nothing more than a fleeting moment, when we were closer than cousins. Rupert had thrown a summer party for his boorish and rapacious Westminster chums. Natasha and I sneaked upstairs to her bedroom with a bottle of champagne. We leaned out of her window and smoked cigarettes. When she had finished hers, she flicked the butt towards the crowd of men in grey suits gathered on the lawn below. One man threw his hands up into the air and swore. We ducked out of view and sat on the floor with our backs to the wall. The commotion outside died down. After a while, she told me she was not going to take up her place at Bristol. I accused her of being reckless. She gave me a defiant look, and then she cupped my cheek with a cool palm, closed her eyes and kissed me on the lips. Our awkward half-open mouths pressed together without finesse. It was the single most erotic moment of my life.

'What I want to do is sit and stare at that painting and smoke cigarettes,' Natasha said. 'If someone wants to marry such a person, then so be it.'

I said, 'When you told me you were not going to university, you said not to worry, because – do you remember this? – you said, "Don't worry, because whatever I do, I'll do it gloriously."'

Natasha gave a flash of recognition. 'Is that when we had that drunken snog? That wasn't glorious.' She forced a cruel laugh. 'I think I was just trying to shut you up.'

'Now *you're* being unkind. The point is, you said you'd live your life gloriously.'

She threw her hands above her head in exasperation. 'Well, I fucked it all up when I set fire to that girl's bed,' she said. 'I'd really only meant to teach her a lesson because she said I looked like a sparrow. I thought I'd singe the pillowcase. I didn't realise she'd been spraying hairspray everywhere.'

'You are a little birdlike.'

'What are you talking about?'

'Light and fragile, though you claim to be tough.'

There was a knock at the door.

Natasha jerked forward with a start. 'Who is it?'

'It's Mother, darling, just checking in.'

'I'm perfectly OK.'

'Is Benji with you?'

'Yes, he's here.'

There was a pause, then Eva said, 'Are you coming downstairs? You haven't met Clara yet. She's anxious to get acquainted.'

I said, 'We'll be down in ten, Evie.'

There was a moment's silence, then my aunt said, 'Ten minutes maximum. Any more would be discourteous.'

Natasha snatched my hand and pressed it to her chest. 'So, is she incredibly clever? Is she a square?'

'She's very bright.'

She slipped down into the bedsheets until her head was on the pillow. 'I don't want to feel like a thicko around her.'

'You're not a thicko,' I said.

'I hate feeling like one. Just because I turned down Bristol doesn't mean I wouldn't have been a success there.'

'Look, I just want to say, and then I won't say another word… I don't think marrying a man you don't love is all that glorious.'

Natasha spoke with her mouth obstructed by her thumb. 'Perhaps I've given up on glorious.'

'We can go downstairs now and say you're not getting married. That would be glorious – that would be like you.'

She took her thumb out of her mouth and said, 'Stop saying "glorious". I didn't even mean it back then. I was drunk. I certainly don't think it now.'

I reached for the comb on the bedside table and ran it gently through her hair. 'Hand in hand, with fairy grace, we will sing, and bless this place,' I said.

'That's nice,' she said, turning on to her side and closing her eyes.

After a few minutes, her breathing softened. I touched the hair that curled over her earlobe and stroked the soft down at the back of her neck. She whimpered, already halfway to sleep.

I had to be vigilant with my feelings, I told myself. It was true I had weaned myself off Natasha, but that was easy enough in Cambridge when I would not see her for months on end.

She mumbled something.

'I can't hear you, darling,' I said.

'I said I missed you.' She opened her eyes and turned to face me. 'I'm really glad you're home.'

Chapter 10

The following morning, Clara and I descended the staircase into a hive of activity. A man in a white tuxedo played Doris Day's 'When I Fall in Love' on the grand piano, his voice tender and melodic. Rupert's older sister Marion was speaking to Bob, the elderly Conservative party chairman from Dorchester, who nodded his head and tried not to look ridiculous in a suit a size too big for his spindly frame. At the bottom of the stairs, Mrs Kinney had lined up a dozen waiters for inspection. She made her way down the row, bemoaning the lopsided bow ties on show.

Clara tugged at my sleeve and whispered, 'This girl from Swindon feels really out of place.'

'You're the most authentic person here,' I replied, taking her arm. Hundreds of fresh lilies potted in green vases permeated the room with a spicy scent.

'My dad gets the bloody *Morning Star* delivered every day,' she said.

'Perhaps don't mention that in small talk,' I said, guiding her across the room and through the vestibule, where I saluted Alphonse.

We went outside, where my aunt had asked us to join the welcoming party for the Home Secretary. At the top of the stairs, under the portico, Rupert and Eva surveyed the mayhem below with fixed grins. Dozens of cars snaked down the winding path from the gate towards the house, where a stressed Cresswell faced an uphill task directing them into ordered slots on the forecourt.

Eva glided over and kissed Clara on both cheeks. 'This outfit, my dear, is rather bohemian,' she said, as she stepped back and admired the paisley print dress Clara had borrowed for the occasion. She dabbed at Clara's lips with a handkerchief. 'The rouge is a little too severe, though, if you don't mind me interfering.'

Clara had squeezed into a pair of tan high heels, which threatened to topple her with every step she took. 'One hell of a knees-up, Mrs Drummond,' she said.

Eva leaned closer and said quietly, 'We're terribly sorry our daughter did not come down to see you last night. She is nothing if not a melodramatist, and I'm afraid it's all part of the Drummond disease. We struggle with simplicity.'

Clara said, 'Oh, we all need drama. Nobody wants to go out with a whimper.'

Eva gave a half-smile, as if she was trying to guess whether Clara was taking the piss.

'Come, darling, you must imbibe,' she said, and she hooked an arm over her shoulder and ushered her away.

Rupert spotted a break between greeting guests and sidled up to me. He said, in a hushed tone, 'She's all right, then, is she? Our little girl.'

'She's fine,' I said, tersely.

'Ah, goodness me, the trials life throws at us,' he said, and he turned to greet a man whose greying hair was slicked back over his tanned, wrinkled face.

'The Right Honourable Mr Cathcart – what a delight.' He shook the older man's hand with vigour. 'I promise you will positively drool over a cigar I have set aside for you after dinner. A J. C. Newman all the way from Cleveland.'

The old man's eyes twinkled as he shuffled into the house.

Rupert said to me, 'That man used to be the secretary of state for health.' He waited a beat. 'Now he's the secretary of state for poor health.' And he forced a little chuckle and said, 'God knows, we need a little levity today. The forecast says it's going to piss down like billy-o later.'

'It'll be fine. She'll be fine,' I said.

Rupert examined his wristwatch. 'That girl changes her mind more times in an hour than...' But he left the comparison unsaid. 'The election, dear boy, is on a knife-edge. I could do without my daughter creating a public drama.'

Clara appeared in front of us clutching two flutes of champagne. She handed me one. 'I'm so sorry, Mr Drummond, I should have got three.'

Rupert said, 'Oh no, you go ahead – my wife has already chided me for drinking too much champagne this morning. I think she fears I'll be sloshed for the speech. What she doesn't know is that I am made of strong stuff.' Then he spotted another arrival and bounded down the steps with open arms.

Clara sipped champagne. 'Shit, this is good stuff. Have you tried it?' Then, leaning in closer, she said, 'Your Uncle Channing's squeeze is a hoot. She's a cover girl for *Fiesta* magazine.'

'Porn?'

'Fashion, you dolt. She's got all these old toffs eating out of her hand. Squeaky-voiced little thing from south London.'

The sound of chattering voices died down as a black motorcar with shaded windows pulled up in front of the house. The driver stepped out of the vehicle and came round to the passenger side. There was a tremor of excitement as a small, puckish man with round glasses and a perfectly bald head emerged. Rupert was on him like a rash, shaking his hand and sweeping him into Eva's waiting embrace. The guests gathered on the portico broke into applause.

Rupert turned to face the crowd with a wolfish grin. 'Ladies and gentlemen,' he said. 'It is my very special pleasure to introduce one of the most formidable talents of the decade.'

Clara whispered, 'He's over-pitched this somewhat.'

'He is a man who needs no introductions,' Rupert went on. 'The Home Secretary of Her Majesty's government, Sir William Randolph Malling.'

The crowd gave a few whoops of approval.

Sir William raised his hand and gave a thin smile. Eva placed a gloved hand on his elbow and guided him towards the steps. Rupert grimaced as if his guest was standing at Everest base camp.

Sir William took slow, steady steps. Halfway up, he paused, and for a moment I thought he was going to keel over, but he just stood a moment, arm on his waist, taking deep, wheezy breaths.

Rupert said, 'Perhaps, Sir William, you'd like to take the back entrance. There are no stairs.'

The old man turned to face him with a pinched face. 'Do you take me for a cripple, Mr Drummond?'

Rupert gave an awkward grin. 'Indeed, sir, that is not what I meant at all. I just...'

Sir William breathed in through his nostrils and resumed his slow ascent.

Clara said in my ear, 'This is going to be more fun than I thought, Ben,' and with that she quaffed back her remaining champagne and followed them inside.

Chapter 11

The Gothic chapel was a compact building made for private worship, with eight rows of timber pews. Plaster peeled free from the brickwork, cracks ran through some of the stained glass and the slate roof was blanketed in green moss. It had been built, Rupert had told me, as an afterthought, and did not feature in the original plans for Merryvale. There was a theory that his great-grandfather had built the chapel following a series of calamities that befell the family at the turn of the nineteenth century. 'He thought he'd fob God off with this,' Rupert said, 'but the sins of my forefathers were too great to get Him off their back.'

I found myself in the second row, with Tom to my left and Rupert's sister, Lady Marion, to my right. She stared straight ahead with a rigid smile she occasionally forgot to maintain. From time to time, she opened the order of service, appeared to read, then raised it to her face and used it as a fan.

In the front row, Eva clasped the Home Secretary's arm with both hands and roared with laughter. A small blush appeared on the side of his spindly neck, then faded as fast as it had come.

At the front, the Reverend Hardcastle stood before the pulpit, scanning his notes. Whether it was the noted guests or the unfamiliar surroundings, he appeared uneasy, shifting his feet and toying with his beard. Next to him, Charles played with his top button and straightened his bow tie. A best man, a younger brother perhaps, bit his bottom lip and fiddled with the ring box.

I leaned closer to Tom and whispered, 'Can't believe we're having the wedding in here. It's worse than a crypt.'

'A fucking morgue,' Tom agreed.

Eva turned her head and said to us both, 'The Home Secretary was just telling me he's sure the landscape painting in the vestibule is a Richard Wilson. Isn't that exciting?'

Tom and I nodded in ignorance.

The elderly politician turned his domed head and said, 'It's virtually a crime it's been hanging there all this time. It should be *seen*.' He spoke with an accusatory flourish that gave me a tremor of unwarranted guilt.

The remaining benches filled with aunts and uncles, second and third cousins and friends in high places. I thought of Clara back at the house with the free champagne, the side split in her bohemian dress, and the men no doubt gravitating towards her.

Tom said, 'What are the odds? I say ten per cent chance she bails.'

'She won't bail.'

'Let's put a bet on it.'

'She won't bail.'

'I suppose she knows what side the butter is spread,' he said.

'What does that mean?'

'She doesn't want to risk getting cut off.'

There was a chatter and hum from the back of the chapel. We all turned at once in expectation, but it was Channing and his girlfriend Caitlin slipping into a space on the back row.

At the front of the chapel, the vicar shuffled his papers on the podium, coughed and said, 'Ladies and gentlemen, please.' The low bellow of the organ pipes filled the room.

'Well, well,' Tom said, craning his neck. At the start of the aisle, Rupert and Natasha had appeared.

Eva turned to the pair of us and said, 'Isn't it marvellous? Our little girl is becoming a woman.'

Natasha glided up the central aisle on the arm of her florid, beaming father. When they reached the pulpit, the vicar removed her veil and she turned to face us, as pale as a ghost.

'She's scrubbed up since this morning,' Tom whispered.

'She's making a mistake,' I said.

Tom said, with a sly nudge to my ribs, 'We all know you had an adolescent crush on her. You can officially put that to bed.'

Eva silenced us with a stare.

I endured the ceremony with head bowed, unwilling to make eye contact with the bride. Tom was right; whatever it had been – a crush, an infatuation – it was over, and I was free to give my heart to somebody who would reciprocate.

As the couple exchanged rings, Lady Marion turned to me and said dryly, 'The groom's playing out of his league, is he not? That never ends well.'

When the wedding party emerged from the chapel and rejoined the other guests on the lawn, the smattering of white clouds had cleared, and Merryvale was bathed in sunshine. A jazz band tuned their instruments under a red marquee, which had been erected on the lawn. From the house appeared a phalanx of waiters with trays of canapés.

I found Clara alone on the verandah, her finger curled round a champagne glass. 'That was mercifully quick,' she said.

'If it were done when 'tis done, then 'twere well it were done quickly,' I said.

'That old codger over there,' she said, pointing to a stooped man with a pencil moustache, 'just asked me if I wanted to holiday with him in Biarritz.'

'I hear it's pleasant in September.'

'The sense of entitlement,' Clara said, knocking back her champagne. 'It's enough to make you gag.'

The old man glanced in our direction, raised his glass and winked.

Natasha sashayed up to us with her husband on her arm. She kissed me on each cheek. 'I'm terribly sorry we couldn't fit you in the chapel,' she said to Clara. 'There simply wasn't space for everyone.' The two women had been introduced over breakfast earlier that morning. Clara had asked cheerful questions about her wedding dress, but Natasha had been fidgety and unwilling to engage.

Now she held out her hand to show us her ring, a ruby nestled on a thick gold band.

'Beautiful,' Clara said, with the same enthusiasm as if she had just been shown a dead wasp.

Charles gave my hand a vigorous shake. 'You are standing before a very proud man,' he said.

'Welcome to the family,' I said.

With my hand still in his grip, he said, 'I never could have imagined the Home Secretary would attend my wedding.'

Natasha said, 'He was almost nodding off during the vows. Did you see, Charles?'

'I was simply looking at you, darling,' he replied, with an obsequious smile. He finally released my hand, gestured towards the marquee with a dramatic flourish, and said, 'Now onwards, we must eat and be merry.'

The Home Secretary droned on with the unmistakable air of someone who would rather be anywhere else. He stopped every now and then, gazed at the guests assembled round the four long tables in the marquee, and played with the ends of his moustache. Natasha was, he explained, a young woman embarking on a new life with her husband, who, as if misplacing his name, he referred to throughout as 'the esteemed banker'. He praised Merryvale Manor as a secluded paradise where the Drummonds had dwelled for more than a century; then he nodded towards Rupert and made comforting assertions of friendship and political partnership.

My uncle fondled his wine glass and smiled ruefully; his large face had turned a healthy rose colour and his eyes a watery green. There would be no late-career flourish that led to holding one of the great offices of state, he seemed to realise at that moment. No, he was simply a Home Office minister, and a Home Office minister he would remain; but at least he had this, a Tory grandee heaping praise on his family in front of two hundred guests.

The Home Secretary cleared his throat, then resumed his peroration. 'What a fine occasion for a family that has only one aim, and has performed that aim dutifully throughout the ages – service to its country,' he said, and he appeared to contemplate whether it was too early to take a seat, before he looked at a scrap of paper in his hand, and went on, 'I would like to raise a toast to Sir Rupert, to his lovely wife, and to the twins.'

Rupert clapped loudly, until everyone caught on. The applause died down and he stood up, and continued clapping like a demented seal. There was a weariness about my uncle, I noticed. Whether it was the stress of the day or something more fundamental, I couldn't tell. His grey quiff had morphed into an awkward position, so it appeared he had just emerged reluctantly from his bed.

He pulled out his spectacles, placed them on the rim of his nose and said, 'Firstly, I would like to thank the Home Secretary for such a fine address, and for his attendance here today. I know my dear daughter is honoured to have such a fine array of guests witness these sombre vows to her new love, a man who has come into our family with grace and strength.' He paused, then said, 'No doubt the latter he will require in spades.' There was a smattering of laughter; Charles smiled and cast his eyes down. Rupert continued, 'It is at times like this that we come together, as old friends, as another summer passes, as a general election looms, as uncertainty rears its ugly head, and perhaps unsettles us in the night hours. It is at times like this that we realise there's nothing too much to worry about – two youngsters fall in love and marry, the world keeps turning. We raise a toast, we laugh, and dance, and drink ourselves silly.'

I whispered to Tom, '*Youngsters*. Channing said he was forty-four.'

'Quite,' Tom said, and refilled my glass.

Rupert continued, 'My two children – Tom and Natasha – and my dear wife, Eva, are my inspiration and my joy. They all are, in their own peculiar ways, magnificent people, and I am lucky to share my life with them.' He stopped and looked at Eva, who was discreetly tugging at the sleeve of his jacket. 'And of course my nephew Benjamin,' Rupert added quickly, 'who has come into the family and become one of us – a Drummond.'

'Ouch,' Clara said, glancing at me and gritting her teeth.

'He's just pissed,' Tom said, by way of an apology.

Rupert raised his voice. 'I would like to raise a toast to the Drummonds. We have been blessed with this wonderful place we share today, but take the people away and I would have nothing.'

Then he turned to Natasha, whose crumpled face appeared on the verge of tears, and said, 'Dearest daughter, you befuddle and bewitch me; you are as infuriating as you are sensational. You are, in the most literal sense, a puzzle, the pieces of which I will continue to put together for the rest of my life, but putting together that puzzle has been and will always be my greatest challenge and my greatest joy.' He made a few steps towards her, lifted her to her feet and planted a kiss on the top of her head. Then he took her hand in his and raised them both in some sort of awkward salute. They were both in tears. 'To Natasha Drummond, to my family, to happiness, to the whole bloody brilliant lot of you. Now let's go and get blotto.'

With a sudden surge of freedom, Clara and I spilled out of the marquee and onto the lawn. The day had entered a new phase where the conversation was looser, the gossip a little fruitier. It was a time for guests to act upon the subtle flirtations exchanged earlier in the day. A new shift of waiters emerged from the house with trays of brightly coloured cocktails. The air was thick with the scent of sandalwood, cigarette smoke and roast beef from the kitchen. A fat yellow moon hung low in the night sky.

We passed minutes in huddles with second and third cousins I had not seen for years, swapping brief summaries of our lives.

'*Fuck*ing hell,' Clara said, sipping at her negroni, when we were finally alone. '*Bijou*? Her parents thought it was a good idea to call her that?'

'Isn't it French for jewel?'

'It's ridiculous, that's what it is.'

'You know,' I said, losing my patience with her cynicism. 'You're very quick to say these people are shallow and self-absorbed, but you seem to forget these people are my people. I grew up here.'

Clara bit her bottom lip. 'Understood,' she said, and she knocked back what remained of her drink. 'Bijou told me she supports the slum clearances in Johannesburg. She belongs to your world, not mine.'

Tom appeared with gritted teeth, mouthing an apology. It took me a moment to understand. Alongside him was the vicar, who offered a feeble smile. He had once seemed a tall man, but his frame was now diminished, his beard had thinned and the strands of hair stretched over his balding head had become fewer. There was an angry patch of red skin on his neck that he scratched from time to time.

'Boys,' he said, with open arms. 'Your teacher has grown old while you have both bloomed. How in God's name are you?'

Tom said, 'Well, we're fine and dandy, Mr Hardcastle. But this is who you were really after – the delightful Clara Baxter.'

The vicar took Clara's hand and brought it to his lips. 'Eva tells me you are a budding Cambridge scholar,' he said.

Clara pulled her hand away with as much tact as she could muster. 'I'm on a scholarship, yes.'

Mr Hardcastle said, 'She told me about your project, which I must confess gave me a shiver of excitement. You see, it really is rather rare to have somebody cast an enquiring eye into the funny old ways of us Dorset folk. I'm an amateur historian myself. Written a few pamphlets over the years. You may still be able to pick up one or two in Dorchester library.'

'I'm specifically looking into the Ooser,' Clara said.

'Ah yes – as a man of God, I've long found the old devil a source of fascination. I've done a little bit of research myself.'

'Well, I'd love to have a longer chat while I'm here,' Clara said, suddenly interested. She looked at her empty tumbler. 'Preferably when I haven't had three negronis.'

'I don't think we'll have time for that,' I said.

'We've got two weeks, haven't we?' Clara said, screwing up her nose.

'I recently came across what I believe is the first use of the word "Ooser",' the vicar said. 'I believe it may have its origins in the word *ooset*, meaning a horse's skull on a wooden pole. "Ooset" appears in some verse penned in Wiltshire in the seventeenth century. Perhaps that was the first stirrings of charivari before it swept south.'

Clara touched the vicar's wrist and held her fingers there. 'Reverend, we really *must* talk further.'

The vicar scratched at the sore patch of skin on his neck. 'I thought you would be interested. I may not be a Cambridge scholar, but there are a few things I know about this county. Come and see me. You can't miss the vicarage in the village. Just fifty yards past the tea shop.'

Clara put her hand to her heart. 'Is tomorrow too keen?'

'Not at all. I consider it a date,' he said, and then he turned towards me. 'Always a pleasure to see you, Benjamin.'

When he had gone, I said, 'He's not really somebody you want to be spending your time with. It wasn't very pleasant when I had lessons there.'

Clara was trying to read my concerned expression. 'Did he touch you?'

I shook my head. 'Not as such. He was just deeply inappropriate.'

Tom said, 'He was touchy-feely.'

'He made us feel uncomfortable, that's all,' I said.

'Oh Ben, what's an old repressed homosexual going to make of me?' Clara said. 'Not a lot, I should imagine.'

Tom said, 'Sorry about bringing him over. I was stuck with Aunt La-di-Da from Diddly Dee, and she wouldn't stop going on about the azalea festival she's hosting next year, and then the vicar came along asking for you, and I considered it an opportune moment to get away. Did you know, azaleas are so toxic that to receive a bouquet in a black vase was once considered a death threat?'

'The vicar makes me nervous,' I said.

Clara put her hand on my chest and said, with the slightest slur in her speech, 'I can't handle being around Bijou, but I can absolutely assure you I can handle a touchy-feely vicar. Now let's go and dance.'

Back in the marquee, Rupert gamely attempted the twist, rocking his large frame on the balls of his feet and jutting out his arse.

Natasha hurried towards us. She was now wearing a pair of black trousers and a brown cashmere jumper. Her eyes were wide and insistent, and there were beads of sweat on her brow. 'Where've you been? I managed to get everyone dancing. Look at Daddy. He's like a bear taking a shit.'

Tom took Clara's hand and asked if she wouldn't begrudge him a dance. She looked back with a fake-pained expression as he led her towards the dance floor.

Eva spotted me standing alone. She came over and gave me a hug. Her jet-black hair, so neatly tied in a bun earlier that morning, had come loose and fallen over her bare shoulders. She said, 'Even the Home Secretary has lost his gravitas. Every good party should loosen one's morals.'

On the dance floor, Tom held Clara close to his chest, then swung her out in a breakaway spin.

Eva followed my gaze. 'Too much of that and you'll see what I mean.'

Natasha had returned to the top table, where she attempted to wrench Charles to his feet. When that failed, she took the Home Secretary's hand, and to raucous cheers shimmied onto the dance floor, holding his hand aloft. The old man did his best, one foot in front of the other, a little shimmy, then he twirled the bride.

Eva planted a kiss on my cheek. She said, 'When I brought you into my home, I knew it was for a reason. I thought it was because it was the right thing to do, and of course it was, but the real reason was something far more fundamental than that. What I didn't realise was that you would help steer Natasha through her rocky adolescence.'

'Well, I think I'm the only one who should be showing gratitude,' I said, and once again the sense of my mother, of the past life we had shared, hovered at the edges of my contentment. The smell of her skin after she washed with soap made from lavender water; the criss-cross of cuts on her fingertips from the clumsy chopping of vegetables, as she gazed out of the kitchen window at a narrow strip of untended turf.

'You look lost in thought,' Eva said.

'Just that I'm grateful, I hope you know that.'

'We're family, and that's what matters,' Eva said, with a closed smile.

The two of us stood in quiet reflection as the band played the final few bars, and the dancing came to a halt. There was applause for the Home Secretary, who took a polite bow, and even risked a smile.

Rupert, his hair slicked back over his head, clapped his hands once, twice, then called for a moment's silence. When it finally came, he boomed, 'Ladies and gentlemen, please join us outside for a spectacular fireworks display.'

We all headed outside.

I found myself alone with Tom on the lawn as the guests headed for the best vantage position on the terrace.

He fumbled for a cigarette and said, 'Charles is a miserable so-and-so. Not wanting to dance at his own wedding.'

'Well, we all knew that.'

Tom offered me a cigarette. 'What's up? You're not off with me because I danced with Clara, are you?'

'No, no,' I said, shaking my head. 'I think she thinks we're all quite ridiculous.'

Tom gave my shoulder a light punch. 'And she'd be *wrong*?'

'She doesn't need to make it so explicit,' I said.

A rocket soared upwards with a loud screech; there was a second's pause as it hung in the air, then, with a bang, it exploded into thousands of blue and yellow stars. Another one went off, and another, and soon the night sky above Merryvale Manor was lit up with colour. Guests roared their approval.

'Where did she get to, anyway?' Tom asked.

I pointed to the verandah, where Clara was in animated conversation with Brendan Causwick, Tom's hockey-playing friend from St Francis's.

'Oh,' Tom said. 'Wicky's having a go, is he?'

Natasha appeared alongside us, clutching a bottle of champagne she had snatched from the top table. She put her free hand on my shoulder and said, 'Would you come for a walk with me, darling? Just like old times, when you followed me about this place like a faithful old tomcat. I thought perhaps we could go down to the lake. I need to clear my head.'

On the verandah, Clara threw back her head and roared with laughter.

Tom followed my gaze. 'Don't make trouble,' he said.

Natasha hooked her slender arm in mine. 'Bugger off, Tom, we'll only be twenty minutes.'

Several fireworks shot up at once and exploded, filling the sky with red and blue and yellow. I was drunk by then, nostalgic for a past I would never get back, the summer at Merryvale when I fell in love. *Twenty minutes*, I said to myself.

Act III

Chapter 12

The morning after a party, a mournful and dull atmosphere always descended upon Merryvale Manor. The marquee was hauled down, the bunting had come free from the walls, and the house, stripped of guests and glamour, betrayed its age. I had managed a few fretful hours of sleep after stealing one of Eva's pills from the bathroom cabinet. Now, as tired faces gathered round the dining room table for breakfast and the stench of fried mackerel hung in the air, a deep sense of unease spread from the pit of my stomach.

Clara nudged me in the ribs and said, under her breath, 'What the hell happened last night?'

'It's complicated,' I said, unable to look her in the eye. I had sneaked into the bedroom in the early hours of the morning and found her sprawled out on top of the bedclothes, still in her dress from the night before. I had sat on the end of the bed and stared at her small pale feet, her painted toenails.

'Is that all you can say? Tom said you went for a *walk*.'

'I was feeling unwell,' I said, contemplating the vodka and tomato juice in front of me with a queasy stomach.

'Well, that's a bloody weird thing to do,' she whispered. 'I was stuck with that bore Brendan.'

Eva hovered over Clara's shoulder with a large jug. 'Have some Bloody Mary, darling, it's a family tradition after an indulgent night,' she said. 'They have a terrific kick, so go easy.'

Clara put her hand to her temple. 'I think I went overboard with the negronis.'

My aunt said, 'No fish left, I'm afraid, but plenty of eggs, some bacon in the hotpot. Mrs Kinney is fetching some more olive bread from the kitchen.'

Rupert, with his paunch squashed up against the edge of the table, lifted his hands above his head and yawned. 'Are you paying the price as much as we are?' he said to me. 'We've decided just to get stuck in again. Food, booze, the lot.'

I held my hand to my throat as the feeling of nausea swelled. An hour before breakfast, I had briefed Rupert in his office on the discovery I had made the night before. He had nodded sombrely and shaken his head. Now here he was shoving a forkful of scrambled eggs into his mouth.

'Last night—' I said, attempting to command the attention of the table.

Rupert spoke over me. 'Just to shake it all out, we'll be going for a wee ramble this afternoon before lunch. Clara's game for some fresh air, aren't you? I'm sure Natasha has some boots you can borrow if you've not brought anything suitable.' He picked up a piece of sausage from his plate and popped it in his mouth.

Clara said, 'I'm afraid I really must do some work on my dissertation.'

Natasha, whose eyes were smudged with black mascara, said, 'Daddy, don't eat like a pig.'

Eva said, 'Goodness me, I feel fragile.'

'And so you should the day after your only daughter gets married,' Rupert said, and he raised his glass towards Natasha and Charles.

Channing, who had been smoking by the window, slammed it shut and said, 'The guests staying at Hotel Grange are going to meet us halfway if all goes to plan. We suggested the old track that runs through the wetlands and over Simone's Mount. Strenuous, but you get the most striking views and the sea air blowing in.'

Charles lifted his mug and blew on the hot coffee with pursed lips. 'We'll be heading off to Cornwall before lunch, I'm afraid. There's a grand old fish restaurant by the harbour that we're booked into for seven. Lobster and champagne – can't be bad, can it, Rupert?'

My uncle replied with a sly smile, 'Bloody marvellous.'

Tom said, 'You should get going straight away. The roads to Cornwall are tediously slow.'

Natasha lifted her head and said, 'I want to swim in the sea tomorrow. I do hope it's warm.'

'It's going to be *quite* warm, I believe,' Charles said. 'For the rest of the week at least.'

'I'll bring my new bathing suit,' Natasha said. 'It's from Annie's in Dorchester, black with white polka dots. It's quite scrummy, isn't it, Mother?'

I tried to catch Natasha's eye across the table, but she looked away. Why was she bleating on about swimming?

Eva was playing with an unlit cigarette between thumb and forefinger. 'It's certainly *du jour*,' she said. 'I hope fellow bathers don't take offence. Where's the delightful Caitlin this morning?'

'She's not an early riser,' Channing said.

Eva said, feigning surprise, 'Oh, is she not?'

Rupert surveyed the room and, to nobody in particular, said, 'London ways.'

'You are Dorset through and through, though you pretend to be a modern when you're in London,' Natasha said.

'The capital is for prigs and braggarts,' Rupert replied.

Natasha said, 'Caitlin was dancing on the snooker table last night. She's a complete hoot.'

'Oh dear, the baize is not cheap,' Rupert said, scratching his forehead.

'With bare feet,' Clara quickly clarified.

Eva dipped her eyes towards mine. 'Benjamin, I assume you will be joining us on our walk,' she said. 'It will be no fun at all if it is just us oldies. I forbid you to leave my side; you're going to tell me all about your studies. No, not your studies – who cares about that? I want to know about your *life*, darling.' She spoke with an ironic chuckle, and it crossed my mind that she was already tipsy.

'There's something I need to say,' I said.

Tom had his head in his hands. 'I couldn't walk more than two hundred paces, I'm afraid, Mother. I'm going to have to go back to bed. Do excuse me, everyone.'

'Fresh air is the perfect antidote to all this fuzzy-headedness,' Rupert said, clapping his hands as if to raise us from lethargy. 'Let's finish up here and retire to our rooms for half an hour. We'll meet back in the hallway in our walking gear.'

'I must insist,' I said, raising my voice.

Rupert waved his hand in a dismissive gesture. 'Not now, Benjamin. You'll disturb the even tenor of the day.'

Channing appeared alongside Rupert. He put his hand on his shoulder and said, 'Better say *some*thing, old boy.'

Rupert's expression soured and he rubbed his brow. 'If I must,' he muttered. 'Frightful business, frightful.' Then he put on his spectacles, stood up and clasped his hands together. 'Right, everyone, this is a briefing of sorts. I am afraid I am going to have to deliver some news. Benjamin has informed me this morning that he and Natasha made a grisly discovery down by the lake yesterday evening. It seems, and we will have to leave it to the police to investigate, but there are parts of...' Rupert paused, as if unable to speak the words, then he shook his head and said hurriedly, 'There's no way other way to say it: they think they found human remains down there.'

Tom fixed his eyes upon me. 'Are you serious?'

Rupert nodded gravely. 'It was part of a woman's foot.'

Under the table, Clara gripped my wrist. 'Why didn't you say anything?' she hissed into my ear.

Eva said, 'I do hope one of the wedding guests didn't wander off drunk and choose to go for a swim.'

Channing shook his head. 'Oh, fuck no, this appears to have been there a very good while.'

'A high-heeled shoe, some bones,' I said.

Rupert said, 'The police have been made aware and will be carrying out a search up there. No doubt the press will get wind at some stage, so I will be issuing a statement.'

Eva said, 'Well, it's absolutely nothing to worry about. It's a huge lake used by many people. Sometimes sad things happen.'

Rupert cleared his throat. 'It's deeply unpleasant, but should not colour the celebrations. It seems that some poor unfortunate has undergone an accident, or an act of self-inflicted desperation, and it so happens to be on a piece of land that is technically part of the estate. I had been meaning to ensure the gate was closed, but the villagers do enjoy a bathe during the summer months, and it seemed rather cruel to kybosh that little joy. We will have to close it in future.'

'Thoroughly sensible,' Charles agreed, then turned to Natasha. 'But tell me, darling, what possessed you to head for the lake at such an hour?'

'Not now, Charles,' Natasha said.

'Pray tell,' he insisted.

'I wasn't feeling very well,' she muttered. 'I wanted to clear my head.'

Clara tilted her head towards me and said, under her breath, 'The plot thickens. I thought you were the unwell one.'

Eva sipped her Bloody Mary and wiped her bottom lip with her napkin. 'I very much doubt we will shed any light on the matter whatsoever, but we will do everything we can to help.'

Rupert said, 'Channing, please draft something I can say to the press. I'm happy to stand out the front and read it if the blighters want pictures.'

'Of course,' Channing said.

Eva stood up and said, 'I think the main business of the day is to enjoy a fine walk. This is perhaps the last good weekend we'll see this summer. Leave this unfortunate business to Channing – that's what he's paid for.'

Rupert drained his mug. 'My goals for the day are to rid myself of this bloody hangover, and to send my daughter off on her honeymoon. No more mention of the thing in the lake.'

Eva touched her husband's arm and said, 'This will all just be a distraction, nothing more.'

'An unwanted distraction with a month to go,' Rupert said, shaking his head.

'I find it all quite alarming,' I said.

'Always the worrier,' Rupert said.

'For this to happen on our doorstep,' I persisted.

'Hardly our doorstep,' Eva scoffed, and she rose to indicate an end to the conversation. 'Walking boots? Size nine, no?' she said as she passed.

And then everyone was standing, breakfast was over, the subject dismissed. Moreover, we were going on a hike.

Later that afternoon, I found Clara sitting cross-legged on the bed with a newspaper on her lap. She was wearing one of my woollen sweaters over the top of her lime green pyjamas. It reminded me of when we first started dating, when she was ever present at the house I shared with George. Every morning, she would sit at the breakfast table in those pyjamas with a pot of tea, screwing up her nose at more difficult clues of the *Guardian* crossword. Now, completing the look with her thick-rimmed reading glasses and a beanie hat, she looked like an eccentric old aunt who might stop by on Boxing Day for a glass of sherry. When she heard me come in, she looked up and said, in a brittle voice, 'That was a long walk – it's almost dinner.'

'We stopped at the Black Pig.'

'Of course you did. Was it fun?'

'Oh, it was all right. Channing was dropping some delicious gossip about Westminster. Did you know the sitting MP for Chatham South is suspected of being a Russian spy?'

'I don't believe a word he's said to me since I got here,' she said.

'He told me there's a paper trail that runs all the way to the Kremlin.'

'You're too easily impressed, do you know that?'

I slumped onto the chair in front of the writing desk and surveyed the room. The attic was very much like it had been five years ago: small, dark and dank. Mrs Kinney had perhaps run a duster over some of the surfaces and had filled a bouquet vase with white and pink peonies, but seeing Clara perched on my childhood bed, with its yellowing bedspread and only the gable window for light, I felt a stab of resentment that the Drummonds had not accommodated the pair of us somewhere more comfortable. Rubbing the back of my neck, I said, 'Look, I'm really sorry about last night. It was just meant to be a short walk.'

'It was disrespectful to leave me like that.'

I nodded. 'I had too much to drink and made a bad decision. I thought you were flirting with that Brendan fellow.'

Clara squinted at me as if I was talking French. 'We had a brief conversation because my boyfriend had gone off with his former flame.'

'*Sorry?*'

Clara said, 'It's quite obvious you have an unhealthy attraction to your cousin. Your *cousin*, may I stress.'

'I don't know what you're talking about.'

'I mean, she's beautiful, but she's also very rude, and she can't stand me.'

'You've really got the wrong end of the stick.'

Clara rolled her eyes. 'Anyhow, I don't know why I'm even talking about that – it hardly seems important now, does it?'

'You're important to me. I'm terribly sorry I left you feeling disrespected.'

Clara gave a withering look. 'Ben, you found body parts.'

I closed my eyes. The nausea that had affected me all day had not gone away. I pictured the long, grey metatarsal bones, the knobby ends covered in pondweed.

'*Body* parts, Ben, and yet you've all been taking a yomp through the countryside, and then you sat in a pub for several hours getting drunk, and your aunt appears to think it's just a minor distraction. It's all quite incomprehensible.'

'I think she's in shock,' I said, but that wasn't the term for it; it was more a lack of curiosity. During the walk, I had tried to broach the subject with Eva, but she had shown more interest in dissecting the personalities of some of the more eccentric wedding guests. 'Did you speak to Charles Hogan's brother?' she had said at one point, as we took a riverside path into the village of Fontwell. 'He has a pet tarantula called Miggs. I do hope he doesn't turn out to be a degenerate.' I had bitten my tongue and tried to ignore her flippant tone.

'In shock?' Clara said. 'They're acting like a sheep's carcass was found at the side of the road. Something terrible has happened.'

I opened my eyes and said, with a weary lack of conviction, 'I suppose we shouldn't jump to conclusions.'

I crossed the room and got onto the bed alongside her. She smelt of talcum powder and eucalyptus oil.

Clara folded the newspaper and handed it to me. It was a copy of the *Evening Chronicle*. There was a large photograph of Rupert under the headline: *Human remains found on MP's estate.*

'Christ,' I said, taking the newspaper from her, and reading:

Human remains were found near a lake on the estate of Sir Rupert Drummond, the Home Office minister and MP for Dorset West.

Dorset Police said the body was likely to belong to an adult female, and had been there for several years.

A force spokesman said, 'As expected, the family is cooperating fully with the investigation and further searches of the area will be carried out over the next few days.'

The initial discovery was made by a member of the Drummond household. Officers have searched the area and found further remains in separate locations nearby. A police source said it was likely an animal had disturbed a body and scattered the parts.

In a statement, Sir Rupert said, 'My daughter, bless her soul, got married yesterday, and how proud we all were. The discovery on our estate has marred the occasion somewhat. We hope and pray there has been no foul play, but of course the lake is open for our constabulary to do what they need to do and find out the facts. No doubt we'll find out more in the coming days. My thoughts will now focus on securing the future of our country at the most important general election in my lifetime.'

I sank down to the pillow and stared up at a cluster of cobwebs on the low-hanging ceiling. A fat gull perched on the gable window, its black eye sunk deep in its socket.

Clara felt my forehead with the back of her hand. 'You're burning up,' she said.

I shut my eyes. A wave of nausea swelled from the pit of my stomach. She was right: something dreadful had happened at Merryvale Manor.

Chapter 13

Despite the police investigation, the Drummonds' focus remained on the general election. Over breakfast, the day's battle plan was pored over by Rupert and Channing, who took to the task with relish. Channing would bring up the day's agenda – an appearance at the county fair, perhaps, or lunch with the mayor in the Rochester Arms followed by a hustings in town. Rupert's lip would curl as he surveyed the day's lengthy to-do list, and he would question whether the second appointment just after midday was absolutely necessary, and whether it would be possible to skip the evening dinner with the chair of the business association, as he must keep some reserves in the tank.

This morning, three days after the wedding, Channing reacted to his brother's whinnying with greater peevishness than usual. 'You have two weeks of hard work if you want to remain a Parliamentarian,' he said.

'I command a five thousand majority,' Rupert offered in weak response.

'Four years ago you did,' Channing scoffed. 'Now they think you're a toff who doesn't give a fig about the price Farmer Giles can get for his sheep. And there is a small matter of a police investigation…'

'Yes, yes.' Rupert screwed up his nose. He knew he was in a tight race with the Liberal candidate. Simon Wingfield had worked as a labourer in a scrap metal yard before joining the Army. He had served in northern Europe during the Second World War, and later in Egypt and Kenya, with the Parachute Regiment. He now lived with his wife and four children in a townhouse in Dorchester. Most polls put the Liberals at least five points ahead, sometimes more. With the vote just a fortnight away, it was not looking good for my uncle, whose distant dreams of holding a ministry receded with every photo of Wingfield and his beaming family in the *Chronicle*, the former Para looking the very picture of health and happiness with his cropped silver hair and athlete's frame. In contrast, Rupert had done nothing over the years to disabuse the notion that he was a country squire who belonged to a very different era. He was a man whose will tended to bend the world in his direction, and whose appetite for life went far enough in charming others to negate his natural idleness towards improving the lives of his constituents.

Eva refreshed her cup of tea from the pot and slid a sheet of paper across the table towards her husband. 'It's for the hustings, darling,' she said. 'They are going to ask you questions, and you can't just waffle.'

Rupert read sombrely. 'Mr Hare wants to erect poultry houses, greenhouses and a piggery on land in Church Street, near the old chapel.'

Tom said, 'Mr Hare with the boss-eyes?' but the remark was ignored by Eva, who took a sip of tea and appealed to Channing with a tired glance.

Channing coughed. 'The Conservative council has inexplicably blocked permission for this man's little attempt at expansion. It's quite an issue in Upwey, as you'll find out this evening. At least a dozen jobs depend on it.'

'A dozen jobs, eh?' Rupert said, arching an eyebrow.

'Say you're on Hare's side, the side of the plucky farmer wanting to better himself,' Channing said. 'You'll take it up with the council even if it does have an impact on the view of the church from the High Street. We're not sentimental about that kind of thing. Remember the key message: Britain is working again, the Conservatives are on your side.'

'Most of the people have never had it so good,' Eva said.

Tom looked up from the newspaper. 'You don't believe that,' he said.

Rupert put on his spectacles and picked up a pencil. 'Mr Hare must have his piggery; the world must keep turning. Keep calm and carry on.'

'Then there's Rothan Radiators,' Channing went on, scanning his own notes. 'Tractor grilles, car springs, brake linings, that sort of thing. Old Rothan employs a handful of mechanics, but likes to see himself as the big cheese in the village. He's Labour through and through, and will no doubt be there. Don't get hostile. Smile, be stately. Most of the people have never had it so good, and that's because of people like us, steering the ship, hand at the tiller, rough seas or not.'

'Be patrician,' Eva said.

'Patrician,' muttered Rupert.

'This morning,' Channing continued, taking a cigarette from his tobacco box and looking at Eva for permission to light it, 'the guest of honour at the fair is Jane Corbin, the grizzled old dear from the telegraph and post office. She's valuable, give her your time.'

Rupert frowned. 'Good God.'

Eva said, 'She's just been awarded the Queen's medal. She's eighty-three, Rupert, and has run the place for more than sixty years.'

Channing lit a cigarette. 'We'll take Tom to the fair. He's good with people.'

'Especially old people,' Eva concurred, and she rose with a clap of her hands and a determination to kick-start the morning. There were people to see, letters to write, an election to be won. 'Come on everybody, show some enthusiasm. Number eleven Downing Street, how does that sound for an address?'

When she had left the room, Tom said, 'Has she lost her mind?'

'Your mother can get a bit carried away at times,' Rupert said, with sad understatement.

Mrs Kinney was clearing the plates from the table. She tutted when she came across Channing's half-extinguished cigarette butt. 'Those reporters won't go away, Mr Drummond. There's at least half a dozen of the buggers at the front gate.'

Rupert gazed over the top of his spectacles, a newspaper on his lap and a mug of coffee in his hand. 'They won't stop until they have a name,' he said.

Channing said, 'Look at you, you're all flaccid. Come on man, you need an injection of energy if you're to pull this over the line.'

Rupert said sadly, 'I think the hare has run its course, I'm afraid. There's a picture in today's *Gazette* of Wingfield with assorted war medals on his chest. In the same paper, there's a picture of police officers carrying out forensics at Merryvale.'

'A few old bones in the lake. They find bones everywhere,' Channing said.

Rupert licked his finger and turned the page. After a while, he said, 'We're missing about three thousand votes. Even without all this nonsense.'

'Door-knocking it is, then,' Channing said, and he looked across at Tom and me. 'I'm sure we can count on the boys.'

'We won't be knocking on any bloody doors,' Rupert snorted. 'No, a man must know when the race is lost. A few days ago, I thought we might scrape over the line, but now I'm thinking... well, I don't know what I'm thinking. Quite frankly, I need a good lie-down, or a holiday. I'm gazing at the end of days.'

'Oh, enough,' Channing snapped. 'You're not playing Hamlet, you're a member of bloody Parliament.'

'And I'm going to lose,' Rupert said. 'I'm going to be absolutely shafted up my backside by a Liberal.'

Tom said, 'People vote for a government, not personalities.'

The rest of us were silent for a moment as we tried to read what lay behind his statement.

Channing said, 'The hare has run its course. Bloody hell, man, those aren't the words of a statesman. What are you going to do all day? Sit around here getting fat?'

The door opened and Eva came back into the room, bearing a stony expression. She tossed a copy of the *Daily Telegraph* onto to the table. 'It's not going away, Rupert,' she said. 'Front page in the nationals yet again.'

Rupert read the newspaper, then passed it to me. The police had finished the search of the site with cadaver dogs. Human remains had been recovered from several sites in a small area of woodland. Detectives were combing through missing persons records and no line of inquiry would be ruled out. A spokesman for the coroner's office said an open pelvis and outwardly flared hip bones indicated the body belonged to an adult female. The high-heeled shoe had been cleaned and photographed. It was red leather, size six, and it had a distinctive starfish-shaped embellishment on the toe.

Rupert gazed out of the window. 'There are more important things than politics, really, aren't there? We should all retain some perspective. This represents a tragedy. Can we cancel the day's engagements?'

'No such luck,' Channing said.

Eva said, 'And there's another thing, I'm afraid. Charles has just phoned. They're coming home early. He wouldn't say why.'

Rupert lifted his eyes to the heavens. 'Please God, don't do this to me, Natasha. Not now.'

I reread the detail about the shoe. *A distinctive starfish-shaped embellishment on the toe. It was a high-end designer shoe, possibly custom-made.*

'Didn't Nat own a pair of shoes like that?' I said. Something about the starfish embellishment was familiar.

'She's owned lots of shoes,' Eva said, bringing a cup of coffee to her lips. 'It became something of an obsession when she was about seventeen. Do you remember, Rupert?'

The memory of me cowering under Natasha's bed surfaced with awful clarity.

I don't have any clothes for parties.

You've got some nice dresses.

I have plimsolls and sandals.

Oh, don't worry about that. I've loads of things you could borrow.

My uncle held a hand to his forehead. 'All the money we've spent on that girl, and she's coming back from honeymoon early.'

Channing placed a hand on Rupert's shoulder. 'Come now, the blue-rinse brigade abhors lateness.'

'Yes, come along, Benjamin, duty awaits,' Rupert said, stirring himself into action. 'Go and get ready. I'm going to command you both to be polite and wholesome to the old ladies.'

Eva observed me with a frown. 'You look like you've seen a ghost, darling. Is anything the matter?'

I was speechless, dimly aware of a rising sense of dread. It was implausible that those distinctive shoes had belonged to anybody other than Natasha. She had loaned them to Meryam. There was only one conclusion.

Tom got to his feet and rubbed his hands. 'Let's tear it up, then,' he said, squaring up to Channing with a big grin on his face.

Channing sent a playful jab to Tom's ribs. 'That's right, boy, we need you to charm every last vote out of them.'

'Got it,' said Tom. He put his arm round my shoulder. 'We'll make sure we drink lots of cider as recompense,' he said. 'How about it?'

I couldn't bring myself to say anything just yet. Instead, I forced a weak smile.

'Operation save the old fart is officially underway,' said Rupert, casting his eyes upwards in a feeble prayer.

*

As soon as we arrived at the county fair, Rupert was importuned by a silver-haired man who pulled out a timepiece from his smoking jacket and tapped it with his finger, forcing a smile that metamorphosed into a chuckle. He was Gerald, I learned, the chairman of the local Conservative Party, and he turned to me and Tom and said, 'He'd be late for his own funeral, would he not?'

We were ushered into a marquee where Gerald's wife was laying out leaflets on a wobbly trestle table. A few blue balloons bobbed at her feet. The men formed an informal circle and exchanged pleasantries about the campaign. The mood in Upwey, Gerald explained, was more febrile than they had first thought, and not everybody was yet convinced the economy had made a turn for the better.

Rupert nodded gravely and remarked that he was not taking any votes for granted. 'Indeed,' he said, 'in the coming weeks, I will explain to everybody from Upwey to Dorchester and back again that I care more for the nation's livelihood than I do mine own.'

Gerald's wife let out a whimper of pleasure.

Rupert went on, 'I hear Mr Hare is having problems with his plans for the piggery. I'm very much hoping to force some movement on that from the parish council.'

Gerald nodded his approval. Then, with an air of embarrassment, he said, 'Everyone is a little nervous about the impact of the... unfortunate discovery. What's the mood music with the police? A suicide? An accident?'

'Most probably a suicide,' Channing said, without evidence. 'Or a swimmer. There are wicked currents in that lake. It's twenty feet deep in places.'

Gerald raised an eyebrow. 'Swimming in heels, not very sensible, eh?' And he broke off the uncomfortable silence that followed with a chuckle and a slap of Rupert's back. 'I'm sure it will all blow over in time. Is there enough time? That's the question.'

Channing said, with disdain, 'There's plenty of time.'

Gerald's wife raised a balloon to her lips and blew feebly.

Rupert said, 'Let me help you with that, Mrs Breader – I happen to have very powerful lungs, despite all the piping. I was a distance runner at school, you know.'

'Well, I never knew,' Mrs Breader said, blushing. 'Come here, then, get those lungs to work on some of these.'

Tom tugged at my arm and we sneaked out of the marquee into a hive of activity. A group of men were erecting low-strung bunting in a wide circle where the dog show and military parade were due to take place. Along the perimeter, a few early risers had put up tables selling home-made jams and honey. The postmaster laid out prizes for the tombola, while a group of schoolchildren threw wet sponges at a game older boy who had volunteered his head for the stocks. Sinatra's 'Three Coins in the Fountain' played on a gramophone that had been rigged to the sound system in the centre of the arena.

'Pretty little England,' Tom said, as he took out a battered packet of Woodbines from his jacket pocket and handed me one. 'Isn't it dull?'

'Back to Cambridge soon.'

'Thank goodness. Are you OK? You seem rather distracted.'

I was beset with thoughts of Meryam. I pictured her flinging open the curtains at the vicarage and flooding the dusty little room with sunlight. There was the jet-black tattoo of a goddess on her upper arm, and the unbridled laugh that made Eva so uncomfortable.

'Playing politics feels rather trivial, I guess,' I said.

'The world goes on.'

We sat on the grass and smoked in silence as people arrived from Upwey, and further afield, from Friar Waddon and Bincombe.

Men and women in their Sunday best, with kids in tow. The smell of roasting pig battled for supremacy with the stench of manure from the surrounding fields. There were cheers when Gerald came over the public address system and declared the fair officially open.

Tom said, 'This Wingfield seems like an impressive fellow. Perhaps he's got more fight. Father seems rather resigned to losing, don't you think?'

I said, 'Did you read the newspaper this morning?'

Tom nodded.

'The shoes. Nat owned a pair like that.'

A few feet away, a young woman had perched on a bale of hay in anticipation of the falconry display. Every now and then, she sneaked a look in our direction.

Tom offered a wave. 'That's Ruth from the village. She tends the bar in the Anchor. Her old man copped one in the eye in Dieppe when she was just a baby.'

Tom called out towards Ruth, who motioned for us to join her. We went over.

Tom said, 'You're looking well.'

Ruth sucked a drink through a plastic straw. She had red hair and a peppering of freckles on her nose. She swung her legs back and forth and said, 'Just fine, thank you very much. How's posh school?'

'It's rather tedious, actually. How's your mother?'

'Miserable. Yours?'

'The same.'

Ruth eyed me up and down. 'This your brother? You feeling all right?'

'We're blood brothers,' Tom explained.

'Right-o,' Ruth said, and she used her arms to swing off the hay bale. 'So what's new?'

'Well, my sister got married,' Tom said, touching her arm to steady her. 'That was fun.'

Ruth said, 'Looks like you've lost a few pounds at posh school. You can see your cheekbones.'

'How sweet of you to say so.' Tom grinned.

Ruth's tongue darted over her top lip, then she pushed his hand away and said, 'Alan's brought a kestrel along. He's going to fly it in a minute.' She pointed towards the arena, where a balding man in a grey waistcoat was bringing the caged bird out of the back of a van. A crowd had gathered, with some taking up seats on the hay bales.

Ruth said, 'So you making scarce or what?'

Tom stared straight ahead. 'I'm here with Father. We're playing at politics.'

'We could go and drink some cider if you like,' Ruth said.

There was a murmur of approval from the crowd as Gerald announced the start of the falconry show over the loudspeaker.

'You look awfully pale,' Tom said to me.

I whispered, 'They *were* Nat's shoes.'

Tom shot me a sideways glance. 'I suppose there are many shoes in the world, and many people own the same pair.'

'You know who she lent them to, don't you?'

He shook his head. A yellow-beaked hawk opened its wings and took off into the sky. It soared above the field in a wide circle, then, upon its return, swooped down to take a morsel of food from Alan's fingertips. Then it was off again, gliding on the thermals above our heads, a dot in the sky. A small boy clutching a bunch of candyfloss pushed past me to get a better view. His mother followed, apologising to me with a roll of her eyes. The hawk returned to Alan's leather glove; its raptor eyes darted back and forth.

I turned back towards Tom and Ruth, but they had gone.

Chapter 14

The evening papers splashed on the post-mortem result. Blunt force trauma to the back of the head, the coroner said in a statement. There had been a break or rupture in the back of the skull casing, possibly caused by a physical attack, less likely a traumatic collision. There were indications that it was a depressed fracture, and broken portions of bone had been displaced inward. It was highly likely the fracture had led to haemorrhaging in the brain, crushing delicate tissue. On the balance of probabilities, he concluded that the woman had been hit on the back of the head with a heavy object, such as a hammer.

The phone in the hallway kept ringing. Every now and then Channing popped his head into the dining room and signalled to Rupert, who got up with a sigh, departed for a few minutes, then came back into the room, his demeanour becoming flatter as the evening wore on.

'The Westminster village is getting rather excited,' he said, as way of explanation. 'Never become a journalist, Ben, it's not a very nice profession.'

'The woman was murdered,' Eva said flatly, as if trying to come to terms with the awful reality of it. 'What else are the papers saying?'

Rupert wiped the sweat from his brow with a napkin. 'Oh, wild rumours, of the most pernicious sort. They've been door-knocking in Upwey, asking about any sudden disappearances, anything untoward.'

Natasha was fingering the carrots on her plate, dipping them in and out of gravy, but not eating. She had said very little since being dropped off by an ashen-faced Charles, who had insisted he had pressing business to attend to in London and would return within the week.

Channing entered the room and slumped into a chair. 'I've taken the phone off the hook,' he said. 'It never rains but it pours.'

'Whatever now?' Rupert said, and he repeatedly scratched at his mop of grey hair. 'It can't get worse, can it?'

Channing surveyed the faces in the room. 'Do we trust the girl?' he said, nodding towards Clara with quivering nostrils.

Clara was twirling her wine glass by its stem. 'Oh, it is a wise woman who can keep a secret,' she said, forcing an awkward smile.

Channing appeared to weigh up whether to proceed.

'Oh, come on, man,' Rupert bellowed.

'Tom was involved in a fight at the fair,' Channing said. 'He's been down the police station.'

Eva spluttered into her wine glass. 'He *what*?'

'Some sort of scrap with a villager,' Channing said, and he waved his hand dismissively. 'I'll sort it out.'

'Good God,' Rupert said. 'My son is brawling at the county fair, and my daughter has cut her honeymoon short. What the devil—'

Natasha lifted her gaze from her plate. 'Who gives a fig about my disastrous trip to St Ives?'

Eva silenced her with her palm and looked at me. 'Were you not looking out for Tom?'

'I didn't realise I was his keeper,' I said, blinking in the intensity of her gaze. 'He had buggered off somewhere.'

'Don't be sharp,' Eva said, not averting her eyes. 'It really doesn't suit you. Reverend Hardcastle visited earlier. He requested you go and see him tomorrow at the vicarage.'

'Did he say why?' I asked.

'You'll pay him a visit in the morning,' Eva said, and she resumed eating to signal that part of the conversation was over.

We finished dinner in near silence. There was the scrape of cutlery, the slurping of wine, and a few vague platitudes about the chicken divan and the tenderness of the broccoli.

When his plate was empty, Channing said, 'Tom's just being a young man, Evie – allow him that.'

Eva said, 'He's an extremely rude young man, that's what he is.'

Rupert touched his wife's arm and said gently, 'Tom's proclivities are best kept to himself.'

'Oh, it's nothing at all,' said Tom, who had appeared in the doorway sporting a sheepish grin and a black eye.

The grandfather clock struck nine. Tom gauged the temperature of the room and, quickly adopting a contrite tone, said, 'Sorry I'm late for dinner, but I ran into an old friend at the fair.'

'Some friend,' mumbled Rupert.

'What's wrong with your face?' Natasha said. As well as the black eye, there were two red lines running from his ear to his chin.

Tom took a seat and laughed it off. 'Oh, just a bit of argy-bargy, unfortunately. Nothing to worry about.'

'What sort of argy-bargy?' Rupert said, blinking.

'Oh, just some lads from Upwey, trying to front up,' Tom said.

Rupert let out a low rumbling sigh. 'You'll stay home until the election has passed. I don't want you—'

Tom scowled. 'Really? That's a rum deal. I'll just go back to Cambridge, then.'

'You damn well won't,' Rupert said, banging his fist onto the table. Everyone around the table froze.

Channing pulled out a case of cigarettes from his inside blazer pocket, fiddled with one between thumb and forefinger, and then put it on the table. 'Maybe it's time for a few home truths,' he said. 'Your father finds himself in a rather perilous position. There are two weeks to go until the election and the press are camped out on our driveway. The headlines are a daily nightmare; the polls are frightening. I think, in times like this, the Drummonds can, and should, conjure up a little Dunkirk spirit, eh? We'll go down fighting, if nothing else, and if that involves sticking together, and staying away from the heat of the press for a while, then let's do it for old Rupe, shall we? I think we owe him that.'

Tom gave a wan smile. He picked up his knife and fork and tentatively began cutting a piece of chicken. 'Yes, of course,' he said. 'I think we should be able to manage that.'

'That goes for all of you,' Eva said, with a false laugh. 'I don't want any more drama over the next fortnight.'

'We'll all be all right in the end,' Rupert said, reaching across and taking her hand. Eva raised her hand to his lips.

'My dear wife,' he said, planting a kiss on her fingertips.

Natasha made a retching sound.

Rupert broke into a chuckle. 'You must be questioning your choice of summer holiday, dear girl,' he said to Clara.

Clara smiled. 'Well, I can assure you it's far more entertaining than a week in Swindon with my parents,' she said. 'My father has become obsessed with building train sets. He sits in the attic all day working on the signalling. Mother thinks he's regressed to childhood.'

'What does he do, your father?' Rupert said.

'He's a socialist,' I said.

Clara kicked my leg under the table. 'He's a train driver,' she said. 'But he also does some work for the trade union.'

'Oh my giddy aunt,' my uncle said with a jolly smile, then raised his glass in Clara's direction. 'To each according to his needs,' he said. 'Do pour yourself some more wine.'

Chapter 15

The following morning, I left Merryvale early and headed for the village, taking the path through the woods. It was a cloudy and dull day, and the trees were shedding their first leaves of autumn. At the lake, there was a discarded piece of police tape wrapped round the trunk of an oak tree. I paused at the lake's edge. The water had stagnated; green algae coated its surface and the air was ripe with the scent of rotting cattails. A dozen or so moorhens bobbed past. A black-headed gull cawed as it swooped into view and landed nearby. Its head jerked this way and that, beady eyes settling on nothing. Had this bleak place served as Meryam's final resting place, her shattered body discarded in the murky water?

I skirted the lake's perimeter towards the gate that signalled the furthest point of the Drummond estate. From there, I picked up the path for Upwey, where nothing much had changed for centuries. Timber-framed buildings lined a cobbled high street. There was Ye Olde Nine Bells pub, the village shop, and the tearoom once owned by Mrs Chilvers. The pub landlord's old spaniel limped across the street towards the tearoom, where he would pick up scraps from the bins in the alleyway. I called his name – Forsyth – and he looked up, then continued his trek without recognition. As I passed the pub, a group of ashen-faced old men playing cards stared at me through the window. News in the village revolved around who had painted their front door a new colour, or grown the largest turnip ahead of the county fair. I had a longing to return to Cambridge and reconnect with people who faced forward, unshackled from their past. Clara and I would still be tucked under the sheets, urging each other to brave the cold and put the kettle on. Later, over toast and tea, we'd debate whether we should head out to the Ken Jacobs double bill at the Ritzy or join the boozy book club at the Pale Nag and Bear.

I paused outside the vicarage, took a deep breath, then knocked twice. A moment later, Jonathan Hardcastle peered through the letter box.

'Who is it?' he inquired, in that obsequious tone that always made him sound as if he was a courtier attempting to curry favour with an indifferent king.

'You wanted to see me.'

'Ah, Benjamin, yes,' he said, swiftly opening the door and ushering me inside.

The vicar clasped my hand and held it in a firm but clammy grasp. 'I'm very glad you came. I sensed a little hostility from you at dear Natasha's wedding, which saddens my heart. You're a fine young man. Remember, memories of our youth are easily distorted. If I remember, you had been through a very traumatic time. Losing a mother at such an age...'

'My aunt says you wanted to see me,' I said.

'Yes, come through.'

I followed the vicar through the dank hallway into the kitchen. Burnt pans and plates smeared with grease had overfilled the sink and cluttered most of the surfaces. Empty wine bottles lined the windowsill. A bowl of pungent tripe in a cat bowl on the floor turned my stomach. The vicar lit the stove with a match. 'I'll make us both a cup of tea,' he said. 'Forgive the mess. As you can see, I've become an old man.' A black cat circled his corduroy trousers, making urgent mewing sounds.

With his back to me at the sink, he filled a kettle with water. 'We were friends, back in the day, master and pupil, and I was hoping you might extend me a courtesy. I'm curious, you see, about this unfortunate discovery over at Merryvale. I mean, I've been reading the papers, so I know what's coming out of official channels, but, well, you're in the heart of it, the nerve centre, if you like, and I thought my old friend Benjamin might indulge in a little tittle-tattle.' He turned to face me, and his tongue darted out between his teeth. 'Just *what* are they saying?'

I scoffed. 'Excuse me?'

The vicar widened his eyes. His fingers tapped away insistently at the side of his thigh. 'The rumours, dear boy. Who was this poor woman? The villagers are saying you were the one to discover the body. Is there anything you can tell an old friend?'

A wave of revulsion came over me. 'There's nothing I'm prepared to tell you,' I said.

The kettle boiled, and the vicar poured hot water into a pair of stained mugs. 'Do you remember the French girl who tutored Natasha in the summer of fifty-nine?' he said.

My stomach muscles clenched.

The vicar handed me a mug of black tea. 'The milk's off, I'm afraid. I really must hop to the shop this afternoon. Anyway, you must remember the girl. She lived with me for a brief period. The most appalling house guest. A slob of a girl. Do you know, she lived out of a suitcase she'd placed on the floor? Never saw her hang a dress, or even use the chest of drawers. But I digress. You do remember, don't you? She would bring us lemonade.'

I nodded. 'Her name was Meryam.'

'That's right, it was on the tip of my tongue. Well, I know dear Meryam was dismissed from Merryvale by your aunt and uncle, no doubt for some indiscretion she thoroughly deserved, but there is something of a mystery as to what happened next.

Are you all right, Benjamin? You look remarkably pale-faced. Take a seat, please.'

'I'm fine standing.'

The vicar slurped his tea. 'You see, she left owing me a month's rent. I clearly remember the conversation. Young Tom Drummond had driven her over here to pick up her things before they made their way to the station, and she said to me she would send a cheque within the month.'

'So she made off with your rent money. That really doesn't surprise me.'

'Yes, I suspected she might, you see, so when she and Tom were loading some of her belongings into the car, I had a snoop in her handbag.'

'How decorous of you.'

The vicar shuffled towards a small wooden table in the corner of the kitchen and eased himself into a chair. 'I don't know what I was looking for, really – a forwarding address perhaps, some identification I could use to track her down if she fell foul of her promise to pay for her lodging. What I did find was altogether more interesting.'

'I don't want to know.'

'Oh, you do want to know, I'm sure of that.' The vicar reached down and attempted to scoop up the cat, but it squirmed from his arms and ran off. 'You see, it might offer you at least some insight into the Drummonds, which might embolden you to make the right choices.'

'I don't know what you're talking about.'

'Come and sit down.' He beckoned me with his finger.

I felt compelled to do as he asked. At my feet, there was a half-eaten fish bone that had been tossed onto a newspaper, presumably for the cat.

The vicar picked up a piece of paper from the table and handed it to me. It was a letter addressed to Rupert in Meryam's hand. 'I found what I was after,' he said. His breath smelt of whisky and sour meat.

I read the note.

Your hypocrisy on the terrace just now was quite something. She knows, of course, your dear wife. You know she knows. We had an arrangement and you must fulfil your obligations. You can send a cheque to 38B Chesterfield Street, St John's Wood, NW8.

The vicar's eyes narrowed.

'I don't know what this means,' I said.

'Oh, I think you do. I know the girl was using you as some sort of messenger. I'm not oblivious to what goes on under my roof.'

I jumped as the cat brushed past my legs and went out through the kitchen door. 'I should be getting back,' I said, but as I stood up my legs weakened and I was forced to hold on to the table for support.

'You're a bundle of nerves, young man,' the vicar said. 'But wait a moment, there's more. You see, I wrote to that address to enquire about my rent. There was no reply for several weeks, and then a letter arrived from Meryam's former landlord.' He paused, then, in a low, theatrical flourish, said, 'She never returned to St John's Wood… left the poor bugger short of a month's rent too.'

'It seems evident Meryam was the kind of woman who was not wedded to her plans,' I said.

The vicar's lips curled into a smile. 'That's one explanation.'

'The simplest explanation is always to be preferred. Good day, Mr Hardcastle.'

The vicar tapped a finger on the table and sucked in air through his teeth. 'It's my guess she never left Merryvale at all.'

'Pure speculation.'

The vicar wrenched himself to his feet. 'My guess is she was blackmailing your uncle over their little arrangement.'

'What are you suggesting?'

The vicar held his palms up. 'Nothing at all.'

I lost my temper. 'Then what on earth do you want? Did you really drag me over here to see if I could share some tittle-tattle?'

'Sit down, Ben,' the vicar said. 'I'll get some whisky from the cupboard and we'll drink to old times.'

The vicar went to the cupboard under the sink and rooted around for a while, before resurfacing with a bottle of Scotch. He came back, unscrewed the cap and poured a generous dash into my empty cup of tea, before doing the same for himself. 'Chin chin,' he said, knocking his back in one.

'What can I do for you, Mr Hardcastle?'

He toyed with the note from Meryam. 'For now,' he said, 'I'd just like you to make your uncle aware that I have something in my possession he would undoubtedly want back.'

I shook my head. 'And you had the nerve to say others indulged in blackmail.'

The vicar shook his head. 'I didn't say I wanted anything at all in return. I just want your uncle to know, if he wants to buy some property from me, I'm willing to accept any offers.' He gave a leering grin. 'Does that seem fair?'

Chapter 16

The town hall was three-quarters full, but, in anticipation of more arrivals, the clerk was busy unstacking plastic chairs at the side of the room and dragging them into rows. Rupert had been the last candidate to arrive, and was peering over his briefing notes at the top table. He was sitting beside Simon Wingfield, who had attempted to engage my uncle in conversation but had been met with weary replies until he had given up and turned to the Labour candidate on his left, a puckish little man with a thin moustache and a thick West Country accent.

I had taken a seat in the front row, alongside Channing, whose gaze darted around the room as he muttered about hidden agendas and members of the press who had infiltrated the meeting. He tapped my shoulder. 'That chap Vince Reilly with the ridiculous haircut from *The Times* is here. No doubt he's got bored of waiting outside Merryvale and has come sniffing around here like a shark following a trail of blood.'

I looked over my shoulder. At the back of the room was a shaggy-haired young man in a trench coat whom I instantly recognised.

'He was at Cambridge for a while,' I whispered to Channing. 'He's not entirely a bad sort.'

'He's a fucking rotter, that's what he is,' Channing said, with a scowl that suggested Vince Reilly should keep his distance.

At Cambridge, Vince had burst into the first seminar on medieval literature ten minutes late. He spoke in a chipper south London accent and wore a flowery shirt tucked into his corduroy trousers. When Professor Armitage told him, with solemn gravity, to come back next week, and to come on time, Vince had flashed a broad smile and said he'd rather not miss the rest of class if the professor didn't mind all that much. Despite the old man's mutterings about the discourtesy of tardiness, he had allowed Vince to stay.

In our first term, Vince joined the student paper and exposed a scandal about the college's investment fund shares, which led to his expulsion. In protest, his friends staged a sit-in of the English faculty that lasted thirty-five days. Vince, meanwhile, appeared not to care in the least; he took a job with the *Daily Mirror*, and had gained a reputation as one of the most talented young reporters in Fleet Street.

Channing said, 'Always sniffing around like a pig in a trough. People keep on feeding him, and he's got fat and drunk on the giddiness of it all.'

On the top table, the librarian, Glenda Jenkins, got to her feet and gestured for silence. When the noise diminished, she welcomed everybody to the hustings and introduced the candidates. Then followed a five-minute opportunity for each of them to set out their vision. The Labour candidate went first and blustered through his speech with some conviction. Then it was Rupert, who spoke well about the economy. 'To quote *The Times*, it has boomed,' he said. 'We are a nation on the up: four per cent growth year on year.' But it was Simon Wingfield who captured the imagination, with a passionate plea for reform. 'I hear what Mr Drummond says about the economy, and I'm not here to scupper that,' he explained. 'But that does not mean we don't need reform. We as a country are stale – our judiciary, our Parliament, our boardrooms, the corridors of Whitehall. We are crying out for change, for the old guard to take their hands off the tiller. And the Liberals can usher in these reforms. My head is not in the clouds like my Labour colleague to my left,' he went on, seeming to forget the man's name. 'I am an idealist without illusions.'

'Nice,' muttered Channing.

'Pithy,' I agreed.

Rupert indicated to the chair and, when Wingfield wound up, she motioned towards him. 'I just wanted to point out to my honourable colleague that the vast majority of us quite like the way we are,' he said. 'Where are all these people crying out for change?'

A man in the front row said, 'Hear hear.'

Rupert warmed to his theme. He turned towards Wingfield and affected a puzzled stare as if the words that had just come out of his opponent were the words of a madman. 'Do you feel stale, ladies and gentlemen? Do you want to scrap all the venerable institutions that have made this the greatest country in the world; that secured us victory in the most terrible war the world has ever known? Or do you want the government to sit back, steer the tiller, and let you get on with it all by yourself?' Rupert seized on the silence. 'You see,' he said, wagging his finger, 'your restlessness is not required. Nobody has ever had it so good.'

'Empty slogan,' the Labour candidate said.

Wingfield looked rattled. He stumbled over his reply at first, before it began to flow. 'You may say that, Mr Drummond, but it is nigh on impossible to sense the winds of change locked up in your ivory tower. I live in this town – I meet people every day. Not just these good folk here this evening, but people the length and breadth of Dorset. They're not saying they want things to remain the same.'

Rupert left a dramatic pause, before he said, with a thunderous roar, 'Not *the same*, dear fellow. Four years of consecutive growth. I didn't say they wanted it the same. Their wallets are getting thicker, their children will lead healthier and more fulfilling lives, their grandchildren even better lives than them. That's what good folk care about: the dinner on the table, the roof over their heads.'

Channing said, under his breath, 'Keep rattling him, be a dog with a bone.'

Rupert was in no mood to lose the momentum. He said, 'Mr Wingfield, you speak so much of your love of Dorchester.' He unfolded a piece of paper he had pulled from his inside jacket pocket. 'I understand you spend a substantial amount of the year in Oxfordshire, do you not? I believe your solicitor's office in Dorchester is closed on Fridays, and you don't open again until Tuesday morning.'

There was a murmur of disapproval.

Wingfield gave a wry smile. 'Cheap stunt, Mr Drummond. My elderly parents reside in Oxford, and, due to ill health, I do visit them on weekends. I don't see that that is any of your business.'

'Not my business,' Rupert replied. 'But the business of your potential constituents, surely?'

Channing kept glancing over his shoulder in the direction of Vince, who was waving his hand in the air as the chair opened up questions to the floor.

Glenda pointed in his direction. 'The man in the flowery shirt?'

Vince stood up and said, in a clear voice, 'Can you update us on the police investigation, Mr Drummond?'

Rupert gave a worried glance at Channing, then he replied, 'This is a hustings, dear fellow, about constituency issues. Nobody wants to hear about matters that have no bearing on—'

There were a few grumbles from the crowd, then someone said, 'No bearing? You must be having a laugh, mate.'

The Painter family in the back row, who all had Wingfield stickers fixed to their lapels, snorted in derision.

Glenda Jenkins banged a small mallet on the table. 'No shouting out,' she said. 'Now, who else had their hand up?'

Vince said, 'I'd urge Mr Drummond to answer the question. He's not said anything publicly for four days. What is his response to the post-mortem examination? There are lots of unanswered questions.'

Channing stood up and said in a loud voice, 'We will not be answering any questions on what is a matter for the police and an active investigation. We have said all we can. We will do everything in our power to help the detectives find out what happened to that poor woman, and we hope a family who must be grieving the disappearance of someone dear to them will one day before too long find closure.'

Without looking at Channing, Vince said, 'Do you have any theories as to—'

Rupert said, 'Absolutely none at all.'

Channing said, in his most indignant tone, 'This is not a press conference, sir. This is a political hustings for the people. Please give way.'

Vince refused to sit down. He said, 'Have you spoken to the police, Sir Rupert?'

Rupert's face flashed with anger. 'Certainly I have, as a matter of course.'

'Under caution?' Vince persisted.

Mrs Jenkins said, 'Would the member of the press please leave the room?'

A wave of discontent rippled through the crowd. People shuffled their chairs and spoke to their neighbours. One woman shouted, 'Same old Tories. Think they can get away with anything.'

Wingfield sighed and said, with a reluctant air, 'Many of us are aware of the rumours surrounding this young lady, but let us remind ourselves of our responsibilities. We do not know the truth of these rumours, and no polite debate should entertain them. That said, my honourable friend obviously has questions to answer in due course.'

Rupert had turned a shade of scarlet. He turned to the Liberal candidate and said, 'A new low, Mr Wingfield. How dare you give credence to the scurrilous tittle-tattle of simple folk.'

There was a defiant wheeze from an elderly man in the front row, who got to his feet and started wagging his finger in the direction of the top table. 'Simple folk ain't gonna give you their vote, that's for bloody sure.'

'Simple folk – you should be quite ashamed of yourself,' the Labour candidate said. 'Coming here from your ivory tower and—'

Rupert was shaking his head, and with a nervous smile said, 'Of course I do not in any way believe the wonderful people of this ancient county are in any way simple. I was merely highlighting the fact that gossipers do a lot of damage to people, to their families, to their reputations.'

'Retract that comment,' the old man said, and he removed his tweed cap and threw it on the floor in disgust.

'Sir, please sit down,' Rupert said. 'Does anybody here want to talk about the issues that matter to them? Sit down – you're making a spectacle of yourself.'

'How dare you?' the man hissed. 'You are the spectacle, sir. You have turned this village into a circus, and you are its ringleader.'

Mrs Jenkins brought her mallet down on to the table three times. The room fell silent. 'Quite frankly, I'm not going to preside over a rabble. Now, can everybody compose themselves, and we will resume the business of the day.'

The hustings closed an hour later. Rupert never recovered the goodwill of the audience. In fact, his performance had bordered on incompetent as he forgot the fine details of the constituency issues he had been so well primed on.

Later, back in the car, he wound down the window and stared grim-faced at the passing fields. 'I'm not entirely sure that went very well,' he said, at one point, to nobody in particular. Channing drove at high speed down the badly lit country roads until we reached the front gates of Merryvale.

Chapter 17

I found Tom on the verandah when we got back. He had opened the bifold doors and was sitting on the steps with his flip-flops on the wet grass. He had wrapped a blanket round his shoulders and was clutching a half-empty bottle of red wine. A pile of discarded cigarettes lay in a pile at his feet. A gentle breeze blew a sweet scent from the star-shaped flowers in the hanging baskets.

'The moon looks very yellow tonight,' he said, when he saw me approach. 'Yellow and sickly, like it's not quite right.'

I took a seat next to him and accepted the bottle. 'Things are happening,' I said, taking a swig of the full-bodied Malbec, which seemed to bring on an instant melancholy feeling. 'I have a feeling in the pit of my stomach that won't go away.'

Tom looked at me. 'Things are *happening*. That's one way of putting it,' he said, with a snort. He put a hand on my arm and held it there. 'Listen, I've been thinking about what you said, and I suppose you must be right.'

'About Meryam?'

Tom nodded. He undid the top button of his cotton shirt and said, 'God, I feel flushed, and rather strange. I was probably the last person to see her. Have you considered that?'

I looked at him. He still managed to look handsome, even with his face flushed and his eyes tired and puffy. Clara said he looked like a First World War poet, a raffish officer who stumbled about with a constant puzzled expression, as if he didn't have the faintest clue where he was and why he was doing it. I thought of him following his father into politics, but no, that wouldn't do; he would do something more idle, in sunnier climes, where the pressures of employment were outweighed by the evening martinis and a string of glamorous women. A diplomat, perhaps, or a foreign correspondent? Wherever he landed, it would most probably come easily, a route to success lubricated by wealth and privilege. For, quite frankly, who could resist Tom Drummond? The raffish wink, the unmistakable chink of money in his voice, and the easy manner in which he made those in his company feel good about themselves. He almost seemed to relish the anticipation of all the pleasure that was left to come, as if he was saying, 'Well, it's been fun so far, but this is just the start.' And yet, this evening, as he sat there staring at the night sky, his demeanour had changed into something more introspective and brooding.

Tom puffed out his cheeks. 'What a terrible mess,' he said.

'They're going to find out who she is sooner rather than later.'

'I suppose they'll find out sooner if you tell them.'

'I have to tell them.'

'You don't *have* to do anything,' he said, taking the wine bottle and filling his glass. 'You have to do what's right for everybody.'

'Not what's right for her?'

'Yes, of course,' he said, his voice betraying his agitation. 'But there are obviously things to weigh up. No decision is ever simple. Listen, I've thought about that night a lot, it was something I deeply regret, but hear me out, it's not what you think.' He hesitated and took a deep breath. 'OK, we didn't go to the train station at first. We went to a few pubs in Dorchester and got sloshed. It was her suggestion. She was a funny girl, you know, good company. She was slagging off Mother no end for dismissing her – she was making me laugh. One thing led to another... we got some food, went to another pub, and the night soon got away from us.' He shook his head slowly from side to side. 'It all seems rather hazy after that. We might have had a row or something, but all I know is it ended in a parting of ways. She went her way, I went mine. This is where I black out a little. The memory's just gone, and it's not coming back. I must have found my way back to the car and slept it off in the back seat because that's where I woke up. Meryam wasn't with me.'

'What happened to her?'

Tom scratched the side of his head and a few flakes of dandruff came to nestle on his shoulder. 'That was it,' he said. 'I woke up in the back of the car and she wasn't there; I never saw her again. Presumed she went back to Paris, got knocked up and lived in the suburbs with her two sprogs. Or she became a dancing girl, and was lusted after by every man who entered the Moulin Rouge, but she never let them touch. Or she retired to the countryside, where she wrote epic poetry.'

'Don't be facetious, Tom.'

'I'm sorry,' he said, as his glass slipped from his hand and smashed into several pieces on the stone step. 'Bugger, I've had too much to drink. I should go to bed. Are you sure this wine isn't spoiled?'

I touched his wrist. There had been something else on my mind. 'Do you remember coming into my room?' I said gently.

Tom looked at his feet. 'Cousin, listen to me. I didn't hurt Meryam.'

'You were confused. You said you thought you'd got into trouble.'

'Like I say, it was a proper blackout, Ben. Those hours have gone.' He rocked back and forth with his knees hugged to his chest. 'Look, your imagination will lead to a brilliant novel one day, I'm sure of it. Hell, maybe you'll even write transparent pen portraits of your family, and we'll all fall out, despite recognising the genius of your work, but listen to me, your imagination is running away with itself if you think I'm capable of—'

'OK,' I said, levering myself up from the steps. 'Let's go to bed.'

As I helped Tom to his feet, I thought of Clara, who I had left alone in the attic since leaving for the hustings, and a heavy feeling came over me. We'd spent a fractious week since the wedding night, sniping at each other over petty things. I wanted to be with her and tell her that I was sorry; that she was the brightest and most decent girl.

Tom said, 'I know I'm not a paragon of virtue, but really – I wouldn't stamp on an ant, you know that.'

He grasped my shoulders and said, 'Obviously, I won't tell you what to do, but there's something else, old boy. That business the other day when I came back late from the county fair. Well, I got into a bit of trouble. I went down to the river with that girl. You know, the one from the Anchor? She seemed game, we had a little kiss, and then suddenly all hell broke loose. One of her husband's friends turned up and grabbed me from behind. Took a great big scratch at my face as he did so. Then we were rolling on the floor, taking shots at each other. At one point he had me, but somehow I turned him over and socked him one. I hit him pretty bad. Bosh, right on his nose. He went out cold, so I hauled him to the river and splashed his face with water until he came round. He wasn't happy, kept bleating that I'd broken his nose and he was going to press charges. I'm hoping it will blow over, and that the press don't get wind of it, but there's half a dozen of them in Dorchester sniffing around for more scandal at Merryvale, so I just don't know.'

I looked into his watery blue eyes. 'Wouldn't stamp on an ant?' I said.

Tom scoffed. 'It was self-defence. All I'm saying is I don't want the police to put two and two together and make five. I'm not a violent person.'

'I don't know what you're asking me to do.'

He puffed out his cheeks. 'I just think it would be easier if the police don't make an identification. It would just be easier all round.'

'*Easier*? For who? For her family?'

Tom looked away. 'She said she didn't have any family.'

'She had a boyfriend.'

'Oh, come on,' Tom said. 'Nobody has come looking for her, have they? She was a nomad, drifting around Europe breaking hearts.'

I stared at him in disbelief.

'You have a very accusing look, which I don't like one bit,' Tom said, his eyes narrowing. 'Anyway, I'm not going to stand here and protest my innocence. I know what happened that night and you don't know anything.' He crossed the verandah, his flip-flops slapping on the floor. Stopping at the doorway, he said, 'Father *will* lose the election if this story keeps on giving. All dreams of becoming a minister shattered for good.'

I knelt and picked up the fragments of shattered glass from the steps. Dark clouds drifted across the night sky. A large red fox darted across the lawn. It froze, turned to look at me for a moment, then ran away in the direction of the woods.

When I turned to go inside, Tom was gone.

Chapter 18

The next morning, Clara and I made love in my creaky childhood bed. It was careful and sleepy and slow, and when she came she made a brief, urgent shriek, which made us both giggle. Afterwards, she lay across my chest and told me she was going to reveal something 'super exciting' to everybody over breakfast.

'You must tell me now,' I insisted. 'I'm getting sick of surprises.'

'No,' she said, rolling off my chest. 'You'll try and persuade me otherwise. Now fetch me a towel, would you? I can't believe among all this opulence I'm sharing a bathroom with your cousins.'

Downstairs, Rupert was in ebullient form as he dished out breakfast from a greasy frying pan. He had borrowed the chef's hat and stretched a tiny apron across his paunch. 'It's Mrs Kinney's day off so I have done bacon and eggs,' he said, dropping a rasher on to my plate. 'I guarantee you'll never eat better than this next meal.'

Tom stopped scoffing his slab of white toast for a moment to observe his father. 'What's got you so cheery?'

'Oh, you know, what do they say about sitting in the gutter and looking at the moon?' Rupert said, taking off his hat and wiping away beads of sweat from his brow.

'Looking at the stars, you philistine,' Natasha said.

Channing tossed *The Times* across the table towards Tom and me. 'Good thing you're a glass-half-full man, because it's not going away.'

We scanned the front page. *Search intensifies to identify murder victim in MP's lake.*

Clara buttered her toast and said, 'They still have no idea who this poor woman was?'

Natasha gave her a withering look. 'I presume that's quite hard to know when you've got nothing but a scattered collection of bones.'

Clara reached for the jar of jam. 'Dental records, items of clothing, identifiable breaks or fractures,' she said. 'You can see how much they've learned from a forensic examination of her skull.'

'Quite the detective,' said Natasha, folding her arms across her chest.

Rupert said, 'The national polls are looking more tolerable, despite all this brouhaha. Have a look at page three.'

Tom turned the page and studied the report. 'So they're saying a three-point swing to the Liberals. I don't understand.'

Channing snorted. 'That would still mean a thirty-odd majority for the Tories. We're not dead in the water just yet.'

Eva lifted her napkin to her lips and said, 'The electorate are very fickle out here.'

Rupert made a circuit of the table, dishing up fried eggs. Pausing behind his wife, he said, 'They won't vote Labour down here. They're all rural types. As big-C as they come.' And he kissed Eva on top of the head and said, 'Fabulous bloody woman, you worry too much.'

Eva's eyes rested on me. 'What do you think, Ben?'

When I had finished chewing a mouthful of bacon, I said, 'I have to be honest and say that I don't feel like talking about the election right now.' No one said a word. 'I'm sorry,' I went on. 'I don't mean to be a killjoy.'

Eva cast her eyes down and said softly, 'We're just trying to focus on some good news amid all the gloom.'

My uncle scratched at his nose and dipped his eyes. 'The election is not going to be postponed, and we cannot be left dawdling at the starter's gun. No, we must win votes, and win them we will.'

'I just wish we were showing more respect, that's all,' I said.

The Drummonds stared at me.

'Not really for you to say, though, is it, young man?' Channing eventually said, with a sneer.

'Oh, it's just a temporary commotion,' Rupert said, with a wave of the hand.

Clara said, 'I must say, even with everything that's going on, I can't remember the last time I was so spoiled. I could get used to this, Ben.'

Rupert banged the table with his fist. 'There's a hint for you, master Benjamin.'

Clara blushed. 'Oh, I didn't mean that at all. I won't get married. I don't believe in it as an institution, I'm afraid.'

Rupert rolled his eyes and said, 'I wish our daughter was of the same opinion. It would have saved me the better part of four grand.'

Eva, unable to hide her disapproval, said, 'You've found quite the radical, Ben.'

Clara felt the eyes of the table upon her. 'Let me clarify – I absolutely love weddings, just not the anticipation of my own.'

I squeezed her hand under the table. 'Actually, Clara wanted to say something to everybody over breakfast. She says it's super exciting, and I have no idea what it is.'

Eva rolled her eyes. 'If this is what I think it is, there *will* be a wedding. There will be no question about that.'

'No, no, not that,' Clara said, waving her hand. 'Besides, I don't want children either, you see.'

Eva swallowed. 'Do these ideas prosper at Cambridge? Is that where you get them from?'

Natasha said, 'Mother, let's hear what Clara has to say. I'm all ears.' And she placed her elbows on the table and leaned her chin on her hands.

Clara cleared her throat. 'Well, Ben's rather put me on the spot by building this up into something it's not, but you see, I do have some exciting news. I know it's been a difficult week for everybody, but I hope this might make you smile.' She pulled out a piece of paper from her trouser pocket. 'I think I may have found your ancient mask.'

We stared at her blankly.

She waved the letter and grinned. 'The Ooser.'

'What on earth are you talking about?' said Natasha, exchanging a look with her mother.

'You see, when I learned that your fabulous treasure had gone missing,' Clara said, 'I thought, well, surely something like that must have been insured. And so, a month ago, knowing we were coming down here, I thought, well, if it was insured, it may have been placed on the art loss register.'

'I'm sure we checked all eventualities at the time,' Eva said, and looked at her husband. 'Didn't we, darling?'

Rupert shrugged. 'It was a long time ago. I think we just thought, well, that's that. It was a very ugly thing... but go on.'

'If something is registered, and if it later turns up at auction, it can be traced,' Clara said, but the excitement had gone from her voice. 'So I wrote to the register to see if the mask had been sold. And it turns out, well, it *was* sold at Dorchester auction house in 1959.'

I squeezed her knee under the table. 'That's kind of you to go to so much trouble.'

Rupert lifted a steaming cup of coffee to his lips. 'Yes, how frightfully thoughtful of you. Our very own antiques sleuth.'

Tom said, 'Mother thinks the mask brings the house the damnedest luck.'

Channing was watching Clara intently. 'Let her finish,' he said.

Clara blushed. 'I'm really sorry if I've done anything out of turn. I thought it would be a nice surprise. It was bought by a dealer from Dorset called John Perkins. I wrote to him, told him I would be coming down this way, and he wrote back. You see, he bought the mask for his wife, but she hated it, and now he keeps it in a box in the attic. He was quite alarmed at the thought that it was stolen property.'

Rupert said, 'Well, my dear, they do say there were plenty of Ooser masks in circulation. It might be a different one.'

'Not quite true,' Clara said. 'It was very specific to this region. There are only a handful or so in collections that we know of.'

Rupert had put on his spectacles and turned his attention to the newspaper. 'Very kind of you, dear girl, to go to such lengths,' he said, as if that was the end of the matter.

'I'd like to see it again, if nothing else,' I said.

Natasha said, 'Don't you think it's a bit odd to be meddling in our affairs?'

'It's hardly meddling,' I said.

'I think, perhaps, we will let Mr Perkins keep his Ooser,' Eva said. 'I'm not quite as superstitious as my son makes out, but a mask that was used for such mischief can't bring good fortune to a household.'

Channing nodded. 'Wholeheartedly agree. I'm afraid we don't want it back.'

Clara's lips had pursed into a tight grimace. 'Very well,' she said, and I had a sudden fear she was about to burst into tears.

'It's been with us for centuries,' I said. 'It's a piece of family heritage.'

Tom said, 'It's ghastly.'

Clara said, 'Mr Perkins says we can have it for nothing, and he bought it for a song. I was really hoping to see it, you see, for my research.'

Rupert looked at Channing, then back at Clara. He said, 'I'd rather let sleeping Oosers lie, young lady, but will defer to my wife.' He stretched his arms above his head and yawned. 'Now then, what's on the agenda for today? And what's a man got to do to get a pot of coffee refilled in this house? First things first, I'd like to speak to you this afternoon, young Benjamin. In my study at two, if you please.'

Clara squeezed my hand under the table. She whispered, 'Well, that was a bloody disappointment.'

Chapter 19

'Not asleep, not asleep,' Rupert said, and he jerked his head back from the desk and gazed around with startled eyes, which eventually focussed on me and softened. 'Caught me out indulging in Spanish practices,' he said, chuckling to himself and rubbing his eyes. Bess, who was curled up under the desk, dragged herself up and came towards me, her tail wagging.

'What are you doing here?' I asked the dog as she licked my hand.

Rupert said, 'Don't tell anyone, but we've developed a mutual understanding. She taps her little paws at the door when I come in to work. Not the only family member who relishes the quiet of the study. It's also rather warm, hence we both keep falling asleep. Come and sit down – we haven't had a proper chat yet since you got back.'

I took a seat on the other side of the desk. Rupert pulled out a bottle from a drawer and two glass tumblers. 'This is a twelve-year-old blended Scotch,' he said, pouring the amber liquid into a pair of glass tumblers and then sliding one towards me. 'Another secret of the study, and, seeing as it's gone two o'clock, it's perfectly acceptable.' He put his finger to his lips. 'Just don't tell your aunt.'

'Lips sealed.'

Rupert swirled his drink and took his first sip with a satisfied sigh. 'So, good to be home?'

'It's always a pleasure to be back,' I replied, but my eyes were drawn to the portrait of Sir Edward Drummond hanging above my uncle, the contemptuous stare.

'Yes, the comforts of home, I always think so,' Rupert went on merrily. 'When I'm on the train back from London, it's like I'm racing away from hell towards paradise.' He paused, then said, 'Perhaps I exaggerate.'

'You said you wanted to see me?'

'Ah yes,' Rupert said, as if he had forgotten. 'Listen, if I'm not mistaken, I believe you've become increasingly worried about... the situation. You've made a few observations over breakfast to the effect that we're not taking things seriously. I can assure you that's not the case. I've had several chats now with the investigating officer, and we'll do our damnedest to find out what happened to the unfortunate woman. And of course, you feeling upset is totally understandable. It *is* upsetting' – and he reached for another word – 'it's sad, terribly sad, and of course there are no immediate answers. But your aunt thinks, considering the circumstances of Natasha's wedding, which was meant to be a celebration, but we now have this rather odd situation in which the bloody fellow seems to have cut the honeymoon short, and that's a worry to her, but she thinks, you see, that it's the first time you three children have been back home together for a while, and of course you now have this marvellous young lady with you, and Evie just wants you all to have a good time, so what I'm asking... what I'm saying, I suppose, is could you lose some of the negativity? It does rub off, you know.'

I gripped the sides of the chair tight. 'I guess I'll try to be merrier, then. Was that everything?'

I went to get up, but Rupert stopped me with his upturned palm. 'No, there was something else, actually,' he said, casting his gaze down.

'If it's about the mask, I must say I thought everybody was rather rude. Clara had gone to a lot of work, and she felt thoroughly deflated.'

My uncle's once cheery face had become bloated; red capillaries networked across his bulbous nose. He said, 'Is the girl oversensitive? That's a warning sign, take it from me. She also doesn't want children, which I have to say is another red flag, isn't it?'

He looked for a sign of agreement, but I remained stony-faced. 'You said there was something else?'

Rupert scratched at the grey stubble under his chin. 'Now, don't see this as a breach of confidence, but Tom mentioned to me you have a theory about the identity of the dead woman. Is that right?'

'He had no right to tell you that,' I said.

Rupert stood up and began pacing the room with his hands clasped behind his back. He said, 'We are one ecosystem, are we not? We do things in the wider interest of the Drummonds, which is a great sacrifice at times, but that's what we must do. I'll be honest with you, Benjamin: the spectre of the election is hanging over me like the Grim Reaper himself. I feel, you see, that it's my last chance of reaching a great office of state, of doing something that might ink me into the pages of the history books, in some small way. I don't want to sit around Merryvale drinking myself silly. This theory of yours. The French girl. *Really?*'

'Meryam,' I said. 'Everyone seems to have forgotten her name.'

'Yes, Meryam something or other,' he said, with such insouciance I felt a sudden compulsion to hurl the tumbler in his direction. What had she been to him? What was the illicit arrangement they shared? *She knows of course, your dear wife. You know she knows.*

'She never got back to London,' I said, jutting out my chin. It was time to throw some grenades in my uncle's direction.

'And you know this *how?*' he said, with furrowed brow. He got up and started pacing the room.

'It doesn't matter.'

Rupert's face turned crimson. 'Of course it fucking matters,' he said, and he danced a little jig of rage on the spot. 'I don't want you snooping about behind my back.' He went to his desk, picked up the whisky and poured himself another generous splash.

'What harm would it do if we were to give Meryam's name to the police? They must be going through dozens of missing persons reports. At least they could rule it out.'

Rupert knocked back his drink, recovered some composure and slumped back into his chair. Eventually, he said, 'That seems like the logical thing to do, but let's think about it a little more, shall we? We are making a massive presumption on very little. The result of that, I'm afraid, would be to give the press another cudgel to batter me. They are having a field day already. Tom says you're saying something about a shoe?'

I let out a weary sigh. 'It *was* her shoe, Rupert.'

'Well, I'm afraid I am of the opinion that a shoe is just too flimsy a piece of evidence for me to bring down merry hell upon my head. Your aunt would never forgive me.'

'This is unbelievable,' I said, shaking my head.

'Natasha says she simply doesn't remember whether they were hers.'

'There seems to be a contagious amnesia.'

Rupert tickled behind Bess's ear. 'Good girl,' he said softly. 'You wouldn't bring merry hell upon your head so close to an election, would you? No, no, you would not, would you? You're a sensible beast.'

'I don't want that either.'

Rupert flashed a facetious smile. 'I'm glad we are on the same page,' he said, reaching for his spectacles to signal an end to the meeting. 'Let's be a sensible beast and keep it that way, shall we?'

I stood up to go.

'Just one thing, Ben,' Rupert said. 'You were very young at the time, but the full story is that she turned out to be rather – how best to say this – an indelicate woman. She was not very regular, if you know what I mean. It was a terrible mistake on my part to hire her.'

'We all make mistakes,' I said, with a false smile.

My uncle's anger had been replaced by desperation. In a beseeching tone, he said, 'Even if it was her, even if at the greatest stretch it happened somehow to be the girl we hired years ago… Well, none of us had anything to do with her unfortunate demise, of course, so none of us deserve to get smeared. Sometimes you just have to let bygones be bygones. Do you understand what I'm saying?'

'Let bygones be bygones,' I repeated.

Rupert mustered a weak smile. 'Yes, for the sake of the family. Now, go away and think about what I've said.'

'There's one more thing from me, actually,' I said. 'I saw the vicar earlier today. He wants to let it be known that he has a letter from Meryam in his possession. He says it's addressed to you.'

Rupert froze. 'What else did he say?'

'That's everything.'

My uncle let out an involuntary groan. 'Is this what I think it is?'

'You'd best speak to him.'

He banged his fist on the table. 'The despicable shitter,' he said. 'That man's a cancer in a fucking dog collar.'

Outside, I steadied myself against the wall and took several deep breaths. It was clear my uncle was actively seeking to obstruct a murder investigation. Perhaps he was telling the truth, and he was so frightened of losing the election that his judgement had been clouded beyond reason, or perhaps he was terrified that the true nature of his relationship with Meryam would emerge. It didn't matter. The police needed to know her name.

Chapter 20

In the Black Sheep pub in Dorchester, I avoided the lunchtime crowd by finding a table in the snug where a frosted window separated me from the outside world. The pub was infected by a general feeling of drab melancholia. Men in ill-fitting suits huddled over their newspapers at the bar, turning every now and then to their neighbour to comment on the weather or the football results. The barmaid scraped the contents of the ashtray from my table into a metal bin and wiped the table with a bleach-soaked cloth. I sipped at a frothy pint of pale ale and waited.

Five minutes later, Vince Reilly slid into the chair opposite me and placed a pint of Guinness and a packet of peanuts on the table. 'Thanks for coming, man – suspected you might bail,' he said. From his briefcase, he took out a notebook and a pen. 'How's tricks? That hustings was lively, weren't it? First time I've seen that Wingfield fella, but he's odds-on to win next week. He must know it, old Rupert Drummond. He's toast.'

'You're not one for formalities, Vince, that's what I like about you,' I said, breaking into a smile.

Vince scoffed. 'There's something about your uncle, though. He's got stamina. Not a lot of common sense, but stamina. Or is it just a sense of entitlement? He doesn't just think he's going to win, he *expects* to win.' He finally paused, swept his blonde hair back over his ears and took a sip of beer.

'I don't think he does, actually.'

'How so, fella?'

'He's despondent. He looks old.'

Vince opened the peanuts and stuffed a handful into his mouth. 'Guess you would too if a corpse turned up in your garden two weeks off an election.'

'That's another thing I like about you, Vince. You don't hold back.'

Vince chewed while he spoke. 'You still with that redhead?'

'Clara.'

'That's it. Going well?'

'She said to say hello. How are you, Vince? Hope you're enjoying this pantomime down in the West Country.'

Vince wiped foam from his upper lip. 'Makes a change from Westminster. I tell you, Fleet Street is more closed shop than Cambridge, mate. It's not been easy.'

'No, I don't imagine it has.'

An old Alsatian trotted over, looking for scraps under the table. I patted its warm flanks.

Vince cocked his head to the side and gave me a curious look. 'So, I'm obviously intrigued to know what all this is about, then.'

'If anyone sees me here...' I said, looking over my shoulder. Deep down, I knew it was not the type of establishment any of Rupert's acquaintances would frequent – this was not the Conservative club, or the Regency Hotel; it was a dingy place in a forgotten backstreet – but I was still nervous.

Vince lifted his pint to his lips and took a sip, leaving white froth on his upper lip. His tongue snaked out and licked it off. 'Relax, my friend,' he said, sliding a packet of cigarettes across the table. 'You're all tense. Have a smoke, sit back, drink your beer – let's talk about football or anything else for a while. I've got no agenda. Sit back, man, and smoke my cigarettes.'

He lit one himself, then went on, 'Everyone in Fleet Street is all over your uncle. All over him like a rash. There's two reporters holed up in Upwey, three in Dorchester, at least half a dozen free-lancers having a go. Honestly, I've not seen anything like it, mate, at least since Keeler.'

I took a cigarette from the packet, lit it, and enjoyed the delicious first rush of nicotine. 'What are the cops saying?'

Vince breathed smoke out from the corner of his mouth. 'They think the woman was connected to the household in some way, that she was known to them. A guest, a visitor.'

'How so?'

'The shoe. High-end, distinctive, designer. You don't pick them up in Woolworths, do you? The Drummonds used to have parties every other weekend, everyone dolled up in their glad rags. It just makes sense, doesn't it? This woman was not baking bread in the village.'

I took a deep breath. 'I shouldn't be here with you. It's a huge breach of trust for the people I care most about in the world.'

Vince tapped his fingers on the table. 'I mean, you did give me a call, mate. What's on your mind?'

I looked over my shoulder again. The men around the bar had moved to a table and were setting up a game of cards.

'It's just you and me, pal,' Vince said.

'Look,' I said, deciding I needed to take the plunge. 'This is not about attributing blame, OK? It's about identification. It's a lead, nothing more, but it's where you should be looking.'

'You might spit it out one of these days,' Vince said, grinning.

I spoke in a hurried voice. 'There was a tutor who left under a cloud in the summer of 1959.'

Vince sipped his Guinness. 'OK,' he said.

'Her name was Meryam Martin. She taught Natasha French for a few months.'

Vince was looking at me blankly. 'And what makes you so sure she's the bag of bones?'

I told him about her friendship with Natasha, and the twins' joint party for their seventeenth birthdays. I told him about the shoe with the crystal starfish embellishment, how it had belonged to Natasha, but she had loaned it to Meryam, who had nothing to wear.

We sat in silence for a moment.

'So there you go,' I said. 'She was staying with the vicar of Upwey, Reverend Jonathan Hardcastle. He's an unsavoury character. You should look closely at him.'

'Fucking hell, mate, you serious?'

'A hundred per cent.'

Vince seemed unable to take it all in. He stared out of the frosted glass and sucked on another cigarette. After a few minutes, he said, 'So why did this Meryam girl leave under a cloud?', his pencil poised over the notebook.

'There was an argument. She was dismissed by my aunt. We never heard from her again.'

'That's it?'

'That's mostly it. Just check her out, Vince. See if she was reported missing – see if there's any trace of her.'

Vince had folded his arms across his chest. 'Not a huge amount to go on,' he said, shaking his head.

'St John's Wood. Her last London residence was there.'

'That's better,' said Vince, scribbling it down. 'Anything else?'

'She had a boyfriend called David, a film critic for *The Times*.'

'A film critic for *The Times*,' Vince repeated. 'You really think it's this girl, don't you?'

When I got back to Merryvale, Eva was sitting on the verandah gazing at the garden as dusk fell. There was a small bowl of olives on the table, and she was picking at them with a cocktail stick in the way her daughter always pushed food around her plate without eating. She looked tired and unhappy. 'Charles Hogan hasn't telephoned once,' she said, beckoning me to take a seat. 'That's very poor form. Until we know otherwise, I will have to accept Natasha's reason for coming home early. The man has pressing business; he has to work; he'll be back soon. But of course it seems very odd to cut short a honeymoon after a few days, and the appearance of it is just ghastly.' She wrapped a shawl round her shoulders. 'And can I take what Natasha is saying at face value? The truth is, I'm not sure I can. Do you know, as a little girl, she was so cheeky? By far the best little person you could ever know, so curious and bold.' She took a sip from her wine glass, then said, 'For all our faults, Rupert and I have never been bitter. We are hugely appreciative of what we have. It's one short life and all that. The question is, what is she making of hers?'

'She doesn't know what she wants out of life. I think she's depressed.'

Eva waved her hand at me and, with a note of hysteria, said, 'Oh goodness, everyone's depressed, darling. We just learn to live with it.'

We sat in silence for a while, watching the horizon turn a glowing red as the sun descended behind the trees. A large crow landed on the lawn and hopped back and forth, looking for worms. A shadowy shape emerged from the woods and began the ascent up the sloped lawn towards the house. It took a moment for us to realise it was Cresswell and Bess returning from a walk. He waved in our direction as he crossed the lawn and headed for the cottage. A memory came back: Meryam saying she had been followed into the woods by a man with a black dog.

Eva dabbed at her eye with a tissue. 'My father used to pretend he could forecast the weather by taking a deep breath of fresh air. Then he'd say, "It'll be dry tomorrow, perhaps with some rain in the evening," or something like that. Silly, really, but it always made me laugh.' She placed her hand on my forearm. 'If there's something you want to talk to me about, then you know I'm here for you.' She reached for her wine glass and brought it to her lips. 'The bottle's in the kitchen, if you want to partake.'

I declined.

Eva held the stem of her glass between thumb and forefinger. 'Mr Cresswell has tended our land for more than ten years, but I don't think I could tell you three square facts about him. I couldn't tell you what brand of tobacco he prefers, or whether he drinks Irish whiskey or Scotch. Isn't that astounding? It feels like a moral failure on my part.'

'You're in a wistful mood tonight, Evie.'

'Should I have done more to fit in? I've always had the sense the villagers feel Rupert is some sort of intruder here. His family has lived here for a hundred and fifty years, but despite our largesse I don't think we'll ever be accepted. Do you know, when your uncle and I married, we held an open day at Merryvale, for anyone to come? Come and see our Gainsborough, the Hudson, the Shackleton. Come and see the Ooser. And do you know how many people took up the invitation?' She held three fingers aloft. 'The only people that both-ered were Mr Hardcastle, the queer English teacher from Malting Crawley, and an old drunk killing time before the pub reopened. Ungrateful, the lot of them.' She paused, then continued in a quieter voice. 'That's one thing we've not brought you up to be, is it, darling?'

'You know how grateful I am.'

She pressed the back of her cold finger onto my cheek. I got a waft of her breath – red wine and tobacco – as she leaned in to inspect me, pushing the hair from my face. 'We're all so proud of you,' she said. 'Who would believe you were the nervous little boy who accompanied me on the train journey from Paddington? You really must get a haircut soon, though, darling – this kind of thing just won't do, even if it is quite *à la mode* at Magdalene.'

She sat back, lit a cigarette and smoked in silence. After a few moments, she said, 'The reason I ask, darling, about being ungrateful, is that Rupert has informed me about this theory of yours.' Her tone had become brisk and efficient.

'In what sense—'

Eva cut me off. 'I'd like you to keep this theory to yourself,' she said, blowing smoke from the side of her mouth. 'I can't see any good coming from airing it.'

'It's the right thing to do,' I said, stunned by what I was hearing and aware that, somewhere in Dorchester, Vince Reilly was probably phoning the news desk in London with my tip-off.

'The right thing for who?' Eva said, tilting her head. A V-shaped blush had appeared from her neck to her breastbone. She waggled a finger in my direction. 'It's funny, because you never showed much care for the French girl back then, did you? I seem to remember you concocted a little story about her planning to whisk Natasha off to London.'

'You didn't believe me?'

'Of course I didn't believe you,' she said, scoffing.

'Then why...'

She spoke slowly, enunciating each word. 'I wanted the bitch gone.'

The crow hopped towards us, cawed a few times, then took off into the night. Eva rose from her chair, flicked her cigarette into a pot of devil's ivy at her feet and went into the house. At the doorway, she paused, looked back and said, 'And I don't want her coming back, is that clear?'

Chapter 21

Elizabeth Perkins had brought us a plate of cheese and cucumber sandwiches – slices of brown bread neatly cut into four squares – with a pot of Earl Grey and some biscuits. We were sitting on a lime-green leather couch opposite a round walnut-top table. Japanese art adorned the silk panelling on the walls. A large abstract painting of spots, lines and circles hung over the fireplace.

We had spent the morning driving to the Perkins' clifftop cottage on the outskirts of Lyme Regis. Our host was an elegant woman in her mid-sixties with light blonde hair, which fell long and loose over a white chiffon shirt. 'I am so sorry to keep you waiting,' she said softly. She perched on the edge of the window seat, rousing a long-haired white cat with a round face. 'Oh, Clemence, you are such a grouch,' she said, stroking the cat's arching back. 'He sits there all day, never wants to be disturbed. How's the tea?'

'Delicious,' I said.

Mrs Perkins brushed the cat hair from her hands and said, 'My friends, we are having a little trouble upstairs. My husband is in the attic, but it is like a junkyard up there and he can't find the mask anywhere. He thinks perhaps he might have chucked it out.'

Clara's face crumpled. 'Oh, no, you can't have.'

Mrs Perkins gave a sympathetic smile. 'You are very keen to be reunited with this mask, I can see,' she said. 'My husband is a hoarder, a trader, an aesthete. He picks up stuff from auction all the time. Most of the time it drives me mad, as we don't have the space. Then, just sometimes, he comes home with a gem.' She pointed at a vase on the windowsill, which appeared to glow mint green. 'One such success.'

'You have a beautiful home,' Clara said.

'Thank you,' Mrs Perkins said. 'I'm afraid it was made uglier by that mask. John tells me it was used for punishment beatings. Is that right?'

Clara said cheerfully, 'It was how a village policed morals. It's more common than you might think, actually. All over Europe, and further afield. Ancient tribes probably had something similar. But in this little part of sleepy England, they had the Ooser. Don't step out of line because the Ooser is watching. They thought that, as people started to lose the certainty of their faith, there needed to be other ways of enforcing morality.'

'He's the devil?' Mrs Perkins said.

'Sort of, but then others think its traditions may be pre-Christian. That it's somehow linked to the Celtic horned god of fertility. I'm not sure I subscribe to that. It seems rooted in Puritan England to me. The theory is the Church needed something more than priests to keep people in check.'

Mrs Perkins dunked a biscuit into her cup of tea. She pointed to the adjacent room. 'We used to hang it in the dining room,' she said. 'John thought it was funny to tell guests the Ooser was hovering over them in judgement. Most people thought it was just a silly joke, but one time, about a year ago, his younger sister Sara and her husband Francois were dining with us. Lovely couple, she's a ceramicist, he stuffs animals. They have a four-year-old girl with cerebral palsy. Anyway, John had cooked boeuf bourguignon and asparagus. We were drinking red wine, but not excessively. It was a very pleasant evening, but Sara was distracted. She said she knew it was silly, but she couldn't shake the feeling the Ooser was staring at her. I was sitting opposite her, and

I could see she was affected. She kept looking up at it. At one point, she went to use the bathroom upstairs, and when she came down, she said, "So it's not enough to have one ghastly mask in the house, is it?" We didn't understand what she was talking about, and she said, "The mask hanging in the bathroom. It gave me a horrendous fright when I looked in the mirror."' Mrs Perkins wore a pensive smile as she recalled the memory. 'Of course, there's no mask in the bathroom,' she said. 'The poor woman's mind was playing tricks on her. But after that, I told John to put the damn thing in the attic.'

'Oh, creepy,' Clara said. 'Some sort of anxiety hallucination, no doubt.'

'And then you get in touch,' Mrs Perkins said, 'and tell us the mask was stolen, when we've had it sitting in our house all this time. I was angry at John because he never asks any questions at auction houses. He's not – how do you say? – very discerning. Anyway, he insists he saw all the correct documentation at the time. He said it was sold as part of a lot from a country house in Dorset, along with a couple of paintings.'

I leaned forward. 'How do you mean?'

Mrs Perkins said, 'He says the sale was all above board.'

Clara and I exchanged glances.

'Whoever told you the mask was stolen, my dear?' Mrs Perkins said.

There was a loud clattering sound from upstairs.

Mrs Perkins hurried to the door and called to her husband. There was a muffled reply. 'Have you found it?' she said.

Clara popped another quarter of sandwich in her mouth and chewed. 'Please, *please* be up there,' she said, crossing her fingers.

Mrs Perkins came back into the room. 'He'll be down shortly. He's got one last place to look.'

Clara pulled an anxious face.

I said, by way of an explanation, 'Clara's writing about the role of folk customs in social control. She was hoping the mask would bring some inspiration.'

We were interrupted by a large man with a bushy black beard and a balding head. He used a handkerchief to mop sweat from his brow as he came into the room. 'Nada,' he said, throwing up his hands. 'It can't be up there. I've searched every damn box, and I'm afraid it's not there.'

'Oh, John,' Mrs Perkins said. 'These people want so very much to see it.'

Mr Perkins said, 'I can only apologise. I was sure it was there, absolutely certain as buggery.' He went to the window and lifted it open to a cool sea breeze.

'You're absolutely sure?' Mrs Perkins said.

Mr Perkins said, 'I can only think I must have chucked it out in the rubbish. I'm sweating like a basted pig, you know.' He turned to face us. He was wearing a waistcoat stretched over his paunch and a red bow tie. 'I do apologise, young man. I hear it was something to do with your studies.'

'*My* studies,' Clara said. She seemed close to tears.

'Well, if it does show up, I'll drive it up to you myself. How about that?' He appeared to observe Clara's disappointment. 'I can go up there again, but damnit if I haven't emptied every box. It was in frightful condition. It had a great crack running from the top of its head. We were worried to hang it up because it was close to collapse. And it was starting to smell. God knows what of, but it was bloody unpleasant. Hey, Elizabeth, did you tell these two about the mask following my sister to the bathroom?' He chuckled to himself.

I said, 'Thank you for your efforts. We won't ask you to go back up.'

Clara said, 'Maybe we could help with just one more look?'

I placed my hand on her knee. 'I think Mr Perkins has done more than enough. Let's get going, before they send out a search party.'

We thanked the couple for the afternoon tea. As we gathered our things, Mrs Perkins was muttering to her husband that he should have located the mask before we made the journey, and he responded with gruff but sincere apologies once more. There was nothing more to be done.

In the car, Clara said, 'Do you think Mr Bow Tie wanted to keep it for himself?'

'No, he was a hundred per cent genuine.'

'At least your family won't be disappointed. They clearly didn't want the damn thing back anyway.'

I turned on the engine, looked over my shoulder and started to reverse down the steep driveway.

Clara reached for her seatbelt. 'Oh, hang on a sec,' she said.

Mrs Perkins was running towards the car. I wound down the driver's window as she approached.

'We haven't found it, I'm afraid, and dear John is ever so embarrassed, but he has found something that may be of interest.' She held out a piece of paper. 'The receipt from the auction house.'

'Thank you, Mrs Perkins,' I said, taking the piece of paper and handing it to Clara. 'Do give us a tinkle if the Ooser rears his ugly head.'

She went back to the house.

Clara made a confused little whimper as she read the receipt. 'I think you'll want to see this.' She bit her bottom lip. 'Mrs Perkins was right: the mask wasn't stolen.'

I turned off the engine.

Clara handed me the receipt. It showed that John Perkins had paid twenty pounds for the mask from Stoneyhouse Auctioneers in Dorchester. The date was 18 July 1959.

'Why would they do that?' Clara said.

I reread the receipt. 'Sorry, I don't follow.'

'Look at the seller, Ben,' Clara said, pointing at the signature. 'It was sold by Mr C. Drummond.'

Chapter 22

Rupert, dressed in a navy suit and blue tie, addressed the handful of staff who had gathered in a line in the dining room. He was proud of the unwavering support he had received over the past five years, and was grateful to every one of them for the roles they had played. 'Mrs Kinney,' he said, stopping in front of her and smiling fondly, 'you have put up with the worst of me, and yes, I include the mess I make when I smoke my pipe. Mr Cresswell,' he said, moving down the line and grasping the gardener's hand in a firm handshake, 'you have maintained Merryvale to the finest standards, and you have done so for more than ten years without mustering more than a dozen words. It is a remarkable dedication to taciturnity.' There was a ripple of nervous laughter from the young women who stood in blue cotton uniforms with their hands clasped and heads slightly bowed. Rupert shook each of their hands in turn – 'Noreen, Jane, Sarah, Magda, thank you all' – and, when he had finished, he declared the rest of the day a holiday. 'I'm afraid you won't receive such generosity if I lose my job in a few hours' time,' he said in an attempt at jocularity that fell flat with his audience.

Mrs Kinney clapped her hands. 'Well, go on then, girls, before Mr Drummond changes his mind,' she said. The women left the room in a burst of excited chatter.

Clara had watched the scene unfold from her space at the dining table. When they were gone, she whispered to me, 'It still makes me laugh that you said you were middle class. Your family has *ser*vants.'

I smiled. 'You should meet the De Veres from Templeton Hall.'

'I really don't want to meet the De Veres,' Clara said, gritting her teeth. 'The Drummonds are quite enough for anyone.'

From across the table, Eva said, 'They say whispering is ruder than loud mouths, don't they?'

Clara brushed her fingers through her hair and blushed. 'I was just saying, it's incredibly exciting to be in the bunker, so to speak.'

Eva said, 'And a serpent in the midst? It's incredibly exciting for us to have a Labour supporter with us on election day.'

'Mr Baxter is the socialist,' I said.

Clara corrected me. 'A daughter takes after their father, as they say.'

Eva waved her hand. 'Oh, I'm just amusing myself, darling. If my husband's party keep on electing grey old Etonians, I am not in the least bit surprised when young people drift away. The country is changing.' She turned to Rupert on her left. 'And you, my dear, are certainly not.'

'Rubbish,' my uncle snorted. 'I am a man attuned to the needs of our country's young people. Aren't I, boys?' He ruffled Tom's head. 'No old fuddy-duddy, me.'

Natasha, who sat at the end of the table with her wet hair wrapped in a towel, said, 'You know nothing about any of us, I'm afraid.'

'Someone's awake at last,' Eva said.

Rupert stretched and yawned. 'Well, I'm doing my best, darling, and never stop doing your best just because someone doesn't give you the credit you deserve.'

Eva wrapped her arm round his waist. 'We'll have to go and vote soon. Are the children coming?'

Rupert said, 'My little snooks will get dressed and come to Upwey, won't you?' He put a hand on Natasha's shoulder and massaged it lightly.

'Will the press be there?' Natasha said softly.

'It's quite possible, I suppose,' Rupert said, affecting a nonchalant air. 'But who gives a fig?'

Natasha shook her head. 'I don't want to be in the papers – I've got hideous spots.'

'Nonsense,' Eva said, leaning over to study her daughter. 'It's a tiny patch. Nothing we can't conceal. And anyway, the press have got bigger fish to fry than our little drama. It's a September general election, darling, and all the half-decent reporters have been called back to London.'

Channing burst into the room with wild eyes. Throwing a copy of *The Times* onto the table in front of Rupert, he said, 'I wouldn't be so sure of that.'

Rupert removed his glasses from his breast pocket and read the front page. 'Fucking parasites, the lot of them,' he grumbled.

'What is it, darling?' Eva said, and she tried to reach for the newspaper, but Rupert batted her hand away. A moment later, he looked up and fixed his gaze upon me. A vein above his temple pulsed.

Channing said, 'It's quite evident we have a canary, Rupert.'

Rupert removed his spectacles and looked out of the window. It was an overcast day and the branches of the trees, now bare of leaves, danced in the breeze. 'Not the best timing, I have to say,' he said, with a sigh.

'Have you seen this?' Channing said, pushing the newspaper across the table towards me. 'Your reporter friend has run with your theory.'

Under Vince's byline, *The Times* had run the headline: *French tutor theory in body in lake probe.* The report said police were pursuing a line of inquiry that the victim was Meryam Martin, a French national who had worked as a tutor at the Drummond household. She had been living in St John's Wood in London when she was recruited by the Drummonds in 1959. There was a quote from the chief inspector of Dorset Police appealing for anyone who knew of her whereabouts, or who had information, to contact them in strictest confidence. *I would like to reiterate that we have no official suspects in this case. However, we have been given credible information concerning a possible identification of the victim and are pursuing every line of inquiry.*

'"We have been given credible information,"' Channing scoffed. His hands curled into fists as he paced the room.

'Perhaps we shouldn't ignore what's staring us in the face any more,' I said, lowering my gaze.

Rupert scratched his forehead. 'Tom swears to me he took her to the railway station and sent her on her merry way.' His gaze darted around the table. 'Where the hell is he? Is the blighter still in bed?'

'He's out running,' Natasha said.

Channing folded his arms and looked at me. 'Credible information,' he said. 'You couldn't make it up.'

'Fuckity fucking hell,' Rupert said, bringing his coffee cup down on the table with a thud.

Eva crossed herself. 'Dear God,' she muttered.

Rupert's knuckles whitened as he gripped the mug. 'Benjamin, may I have a quiet word in my study when you've finished your breakfast?' he said.

'It's simply been staring us in the face,' I said, but my voice came out reedy and thin.

'Son of a bitch,' said Channing, as he left the room. 'You've always been an envious little shitter.'

Clara looked at me with gritted teeth. 'What's going on?' she said, a note of panic in her voice.

'Not now,' I said. 'Finish your croissant.'

Rupert was sitting on the piano stool when I entered his study. He played a few minor chords, then spun the stool round to face me. His thatch of grey hair had been smeared with hair product and the top two buttons of his shirt were undone, revealing the top of his hairy chest. 'I don't get any better, do I?' he said, smiling. 'I've only been learning this bloody thing for six years now.' He stood up, motioned towards the chair at his desk with a flick of his hand. 'Sit down, Ben.'

'I've picked up the guitar only once since we've been at Magdalene,' I said. 'I don't have the temperament for it.'

'We're not a musical bunch, are we? Your aunt can't sing a note, and Natasha insisted on those violin lessons for years, but she couldn't play for toffee. Tom got as far as the screech of a recorder.'

He sat down in the swivel chair and clasped his hands together. 'Now, it seems like only five minutes ago I'd implored you to be a sensible beast. It seems you didn't take my advice.' He flashed a facetious smile.

'I don't think we're fully cooperating with this investigation,' I said.

'Tom tells me this reporter chap went to Magdalene,' Rupert said.

'He did.'

'And he was kicked out?'

'Yes, something like that.'

Rupert said, 'I'm going to tell you a little Westminster story, if you can suffer it. In the months before last year's reshuffle, people close to Alec told me I was a dead cert for transport minister. Ernest Marples was in the shit with all the bloody station closures – nobody liked him, nobody would have missed him. Now, I may not show my ambition nakedly, but this proposition excited me greatly. My grandfather was a peer, my father served as the first aviation minister, and, well, it dawned on me that this might be my last chance to become a minister of state. Making sure the trains run on time: hardly a glamorous job, is it?' He scoffed, opened his desk drawer and pulled out his pipe. He tapped it on the desk and tobacco fell out. 'Glamorous or not, I wanted it with every ounce of my being. The morning came to pass. People got the call and came and went to Downing Street with a spring in their step, swinging their briefcases in front of the press pack. But Marples kept his job, and I, well, I remained a backbencher whose sole achievements were still cheering up the blue-rinse brigade at county fairs and objecting to the extension of the bingo hall in Dorchester on the grounds that it contravened the conservation order in the High Street.' He smiled ruefully and lit his pipe.

I said, 'That seems like a harsh assessment.'

'Does it? Well, it's my assessment, and when a man comes to the end of his life and looks at his paltry list of achievements, that's quite rightly the only assessment that counts. I found out, a few weeks later, why Alec had decided against my promotion. He thought I indulged in what the Scots call "clishmaclaver".'

My expression was blank.

'We call it idle talk,' my uncle went on. 'Can I say the Prime Minister was wrong in his assessment? No, I cannot. I am a man who likes to grease the conversation, as they say, with titbits I've heard. Late at night in Strangers' Bar, dishing the dirt on men I've loathed, besmirching the name of twits like Marples. It's all rather fun, playing the game like that. Do you know what I'm saying, Ben?'

'I'm sorry to hear you were overlooked.'

Rupert lit his pipe and inhaled. 'Well, I was in a dreadful sulk for a while, and then, after much ruminating, I realised it was probably the correct decision. You see, who would knowingly let into their inner circle someone who fails to protect the sanctity of that circle? Someone who exposes the inner circle to unwanted intrusion.'

We sat in silence for a minute while Rupert smoked. After a while, he said, 'There are snappers all over the place, Benjamin, and the phone hasn't stopped ringing.' He wiped a fleck of spittle from the side of his mouth with his shirtsleeve and eyed me with disdain. 'We're trying to fight a fucking general election, and what I'm asking you, what I need to know, is this: are you here to help or hinder?'

I stood up to go. 'I should imagine, in the circumstances, that any information would help the police. Even tittle-tattle.'

Rupert said, 'My advice would be to think long and hard about the story I just told you.'

At the door, he called my name. 'And one more thing,' he said. 'Your aunt and I have agreed it would be better during this difficult time if you cut short your visit and returned to Cambridge.'

'We're due to stay another week,' I said, unable to hide my surprise. 'Clara wants to drive down to the Jurassic Coast.'

Rupert scratched his nose and looked away. 'Your aunt feels very strongly about the situation, and I'm afraid I agree,' he said. 'Tomorrow, once the election is out the way, you'll drive back.'

'This is what,' I said, 'some sort of *pun*ishment? It's still three weeks until the start of term.'

Rupert gave a dismissive wave of his hand. 'We want you out of Merryvale.'

I turned away from him and grasped the doorknob. A foolish part of me thought he was talking in jest.

I turned the handle. 'Rupert,' I said, 'I've only wanted to do the right thing.'

'We want you out of Merryvale,' he roared, 'and you can take your red-flag-waving piece of skirt with you too.'

Later that morning, after I had gone back to bed and buried myself under the blankets, I thought again of the advice my mother had given me. *We are not who we think we are, Benjamin*, she had said, *but we are condemned to be who we think we are.* She always had cold hands, my mother, and red, blistered fingers, but in my attic room, hiding from the world with my head buried in the pillow, I longed for the touch of those fingers on my cheek.

Chapter 23

It was inevitable, after the *Times* front page, that the police would return to Merryvale to ask questions. My turn came in the study that afternoon, as voters across the country went to the polls and my uncle sweated over his political future. Detective Inspector Hillcroft was a slight, agitated man with a neat black beard and a habit of running his tongue over his front teeth as he thought. Sitting in Rupert's armchair, with a notebook on his lap, he gave me a long preamble about the circumstances of our talk, which, he insisted, was an informal interview, and certainly nothing to be alarmed about. 'This woman was a strange gal, bit of a bohemian,' he said, handing me a photograph of Meryam. 'She'd been living in London in various bedsits. Wrote to her elderly father she was going to the south-west to teach, and he never heard from her again. Poor bastard died last year, still not knowing. He was a professor of chemistry at a university in Paris. Single dad – nice man by all accounts.'

In the photograph, Meryam was sitting on a picnic rug in a park. It must have been somewhere in London as you could see the high-rise buildings in the skyline. There was a bottle of champagne between her knees, which she was attempting to uncork. She was laughing with an open mouth, head tilted back, some private joke with the person behind the camera.

I handed it back to Hillcroft.

'Striking young woman, wasn't she?' he said. 'What do you remember about her?'

A dull ache had spread from my temple to my forehead. I reached for a glass of water from the coffee table and took a sip. 'I'm afraid she wasn't here long. We didn't really get to know her.'

'Yes, I understand she went away under something of a cloud. What do you remember about her departure?'

'Not much,' I said.

'Your uncle remembers. He said there was a disagreement. Do you remember what it was about?'

'No, I don't. Well, she had grown close to Natasha. I think my aunt considered her a bad influence. She was older than her, you see, and different.'

'Different?'

'She was different, yes, more worldly.'

Hillcroft ran his tongue over his teeth. 'Your aunt has given us the date she left the household,' he said, licking his finger and turning the page of his notebook. 'Your cousin Tom was asked to drive her to the railway station in Dorchester. Two members of staff have confirmed Meryam was in the vehicle with Mr Tom Drummond when it left the premises. Why do you think she never got on that train?'

'I have no idea,' I said, unable to hold eye contact. Instead, I scanned the rows of books lining the case from floor to ceiling and thought of Clara, upstairs in the attic, working on one of her own.

Hillcroft coughed into his fist. 'There are other witnesses too. Somebody witnessed Tom and Meryam in a pub in the town. They remember because they were inebriated and intimate.' He narrowed his eyes and said, in a deliberate tone, 'They were making a scene.'

I stared at the rug beneath my feet; its red and beige triangles seemed to shimmer and vibrate.

'Mr Butler?'

'I'm sorry,' I said, shaking my head. 'Could you repeat the question?'

'I just said they were making a scene.' Hillcroft tapped a pencil on his notebook in a little rhythm. 'Your cousin and Meryam stood out like a sore thumb.'

'Yes, well, I suppose that sounds like Tom.' I offered a weak smile, but was met with an impatient stare.

After a pause, the detective said, 'Tell me about Tom.'

'What do you want to know? He's terrible at maths and science, has the concentration span of a flea. He prefers to be outdoors, doing anything really, as long as he's not confined to a library or classroom. He was the best cricketer by far at St Francis's, and he's also a brilliant fly half.'

'I meant how would you describe his personality?'

I thought for a moment. 'He's affectionate, tactile, courageous. He'd stand up for you if you were in trouble. I'm sure he would be the first to volunteer if another war broke out. He's very loyal to his family, but also to his friends. He can be very funny, in a dry sort of way. Listen, Inspector Hillcroft, there's really nothing in his character that has ever indicated to me he would be capable of doing something... that he would be... there's just no suggestion at all.'

The detective's tongue darted over his top lip. 'You are aware that he was involved in a fight at the county fair. Broke a man's nose and left a poor girl in tears. The unfortunate chap was going to make a complaint, but he's withdrawn it. Your cousin is fortunate he wasn't charged with assault.'

I steadied my shaking hand. 'It's rather desperate to extrapolate from an act of self-defence to suggest he was involved in murder.'

Hillcroft sucked on the end of his pencil. 'Tell me, have you ever seen him be violent towards women?'

'Absolutely not.'

'Just towards men?'

'He says it was a misunderstanding.'

Hillcroft exhaled as he scanned his notes. After a pause, he said, 'You do know it's a very significant crime to withhold information on an ongoing criminal investigation.'

There was a rap at the door and Eva came in without waiting for a reply. 'Excuse me, Mr Hillcroft, but I'm wondering just how much longer you'll be. There is always much to be done on election day in our household, and I really must speak to Benjamin.'

The policeman's posture stiffened. 'Before I go, Mrs Drummond, I was wondering if you'd had time to think over the question I posed earlier. Did you ever have a conversation with your son about the night Meryam left your household? Did you not, perhaps, reprimand him when you heard reports of impropriety?'

Eva gave the detective a waspish smile. 'Detective, there are lots of things a mother doesn't know about her son when he is in the process of becoming a man. I prefer, in some circumstances, to leave my children to learn from their mistakes. I believe the lesson runs deeper if they do. Now' – and she clapped her hands twice – 'I'm afraid I really must press you to end this conversation for now. Mr Cresswell is waiting outside the salon and will escort you to your car. I do hope my family has been accommodating today. It's a frightful business, and we will do everything we can to aid your investigation.'

'Well, I can't ask more than that, Mrs Drummond,' the inspector said, wearing the puzzled look of somebody meeting my aunt's iron will for the first time. He slipped his pencil and notebook into the breast pocket of his jacket. For a moment, he appeared to contemplate risking another question; instead, he shook both our hands briskly and left the room.

Eva had retrieved a bottle of Scotch from the drinks cabinet and was pouring a generous splash into a tumbler. 'What a wretched little man,' she said, with a roll of her eyes. Then she sat back in the chaise longue and kicked her black heels off. She crossed one leg over the other and rubbed at her heel. 'What did you say to him?'

'He was asking lots of questions about Tom.'

'What kind of questions?'

'About his character.'

'And what did you say?'

'Nothing but praise.'

'Nothing but praise,' she repeated slowly, and she looked up to the ceiling and let out a dry laugh. 'I suppose the damage is already done, is it not?'

There was something unguarded about my aunt at that moment. She was usually so sleek and prepared, but there, on the chaise longue, with her black hair looser and her lips free from scarlet lipstick, she resembled a tired woman in late middle age worrying about her son.

'Is it true you want me gone?' I said, resisting a wave of emotion that constricted my throat.

Eva swirled her tumbler and knocked back the contents. She let out a groan of satisfaction and said, matter-of-factly, 'Did you speak to that journalist?'

I nodded.

Her dark eyes widened. 'You *did*?'

'For the sake of that girl.'

Eva sucked in air through her teeth. 'Many years ago, I told you what kept this family together. Sticking together, no matter what. Clearly, in this instance, you decided you knew better, and that's unacceptable to me, it's unacceptable to Rupert. You'll go in the morning. Make it before breakfast.'

Chapter 24

Rupert and Eva came back to the house just before midnight, displaying a levity of spirit that caught us off guard. In the vestibule, before removing his overcoat and hat, Rupert gripped Eva by the shoulders and kissed her hard on the mouth, his hands reaching down her back to clutch her backside. Eva pulled away, wiped her lips with the back of her hand and tottered towards Tom, Clara and me on high heels.

'Children,' she said. 'Why are you all looking so miserable? We may be on the brink of defeat, but conjure your Churchillian spirit,' and she attempted to throw her arms round us all.

'Mother, have you been drinking?' Tom said. 'You smell of whisky.'

'Oh, my sweet disapproving boy, come into the salon and let's see what's happening. Our beloved country seems destined to vote for its own ruin.'

Channing and his girlfriend Caitlin came through the door behind them. He was singing the 'Internationale' in an exaggerated bellow and swinging his cane. Caitlin clutched a bottle of unopened champagne.

'You four must have been quite a sight at the count,' Tom said.

'Why pose as a moraliser, darling? It suits you not,' Eva said, ruffling his hair.

Caitlin waved the bottle. 'I will kiss the bloody daylights out of the chappie that can open this,' she said. And she pursed her thin lips and twinkled her eyes at Channing.

Tom took the bottle from her. 'I would be much obliged.'

'My hero,' she replied, kissing him on the cheek. And then she saw Clara and threw open her arms and said, 'My wedding pal, come and give me a hug.'

Clara, bleary-eyed from a nap, attempted a weak smile as she took in the scene before her.

'Where's Natasha?' Eva said, noticing her daughter's absence for the first time.

'She's sleeping,' I said.

Channing stopped singing and said, 'Fuck me, if we had a vote for every hour that girl spends in bed, we'd romp home, wouldn't we, Rupe?'

Rupert shook his head in exaggerated despair and said, 'Do you know she's talking to Eva about divorce? She's claiming the marriage is unconsummated.' The two men began to chuckle, then to shake with laughter, until Eva chided them to stop.

Channing wiped a tear from his eye. 'Dear God,' he said, 'our very own Anne of Cleves.'

'Poor bloody girl,' Caitlin said, rubbing her gloved hands together for warmth. 'I warned you that bloke was a cold gentleman.'

Rupert said, 'We've found the only banker in Dorset who won't get his willy out of his pants. It's enough to make a man despair, eh, Channing?' And the two of them broke into another bout of prolonged laughter.

'Stop it, you silly men,' Eva said. 'Let's all go into the salon and watch the country throw away its future. Where's Tom with that bottle? Do we not have any staff on tonight? I told Mrs Kinney we'd be up late. We need some sandwiches, at the very least.'

The party gravitated towards the salon, where the first results were being declared on the BBC. We drank champagne and talked politics. Channing's attempts to put records on the gramophone were thwarted by Rupert, who stood before the black and white television in the corner of the room and relayed the news in a series of agitated outbursts.

'Have we wasted thirteen years of power?' he said, to anyone who would listen. 'You see, the damned thing is that people may own their own homes, they may have fridges and vacuum cleaners and all sorts of jolly nice things they never had before, but Britain's share of world trade has fallen off a cliff. We are a nation in sad but inevitable decline.'

'Oh, enough maudlin twaddle,' Channing said. He had retrieved a loaf of bread and a large slab of Cheddar cheese from the kitchen. 'Anyone want a sandwich? Tom, fetch the pickled onions, will you? And the pork pie in the fridge, and a bloody knife that works.'

Richard Dimbleby and a panel of guests went to the first televised announcements just after two in the morning. The Tories held Cheltenham, followed by Billericay and Exeter.

Eva sank back into the couch, crossed her long legs and sighed.

Rupert peered ever closer to the screen, as if he could barely believe what was unfolding.

Clara whispered to me, 'Not another five years of this lot – are people fucking mad?'

The telephone rang. Channing ran out of the room, clutching a sandwich and a glass of champagne. When he reappeared a few minutes later, he had redone his top button and adjusted his tie.

Rupert turned to face him, wearing the alarmed expression of a little boy being called out of class by the headmaster. 'Is it time?' he said.

'They're an hour away. We should get going.'

'Oh God,' Eva said, putting her hand over her mouth.

Rupert knocked back his drink. 'Come along, Tom, put a dinner jacket on, the bell tolleth.'

Clara and I watched the television in silence. Ever since Natasha's wedding night, our relationship had soured. We didn't notice it at first, but as the days passed we had withdrawn from each other, inch by inch, until we found ourselves either side of the chaise longue, unable to look at each other, let alone break down the divide through touch. 'What's going on, Ben?' she said, in a flat monotone.

'I don't know, darling. I'm sorry there's a distance between us.'

She gave a rueful smile. 'I didn't mean between us. I meant your family. You might have noticed they've just waltzed off to the count without you. You might also have noticed your aunt and uncle can barely look at you.' She shuffled up alongside me and clasped my hands in hers.

I clenched my jaw, determined not to show any emotion. That was a cruel and stupid thing to say. Though she had been welcomed into Merryvale with open arms, she had been unable to drop her own prejudices.

Clara gently circled my palm with her index finger. 'You're different here,' she said.

I resisted the urge to pull my hand away. I didn't want this small gesture of intimacy; I wanted to be alone.

I stared at the television. 'We'll drive back to Cambridge tomorrow,' I said.

Clara let go of my hand and nodded. 'That seems a good idea.'

After a while, she said, 'Are you coming to bed?'

I shook my head. 'I'll wait for the result.'

I sat alone in the dark in front of the screen. The reporting became more frantic as it emerged Labour was heading for a knife-edge majority. The television studio buzzed with excitement and tension. Dimbleby kept adjusting the mic in his ear and saying things like, 'And the latest we are getting is that the Prime Minister is in Downing Street with his aides discussing the possibility of a hung Parliament. Would Mr Douglas-Home do a deal with the Liberals? That is a scenario the country faces as we emerge into a new day.'

One of the guests, a politics don from Sussex University, spilled a cup of tea in excitement, and the camera panned to an unsuspecting and tired-looking hack from *The Times*, who came to the wicket in the nick of time and said, 'Richard, what we are witnessing may not be the death of the establishment, but it is without doubt the day the nation chose modernity and cocked a snook at the old order.'

I must have fallen asleep, for when I woke up, Natasha, in her dressing gown and slippers, had curled up beside me on the chaise longue. She smelt of peppermint and cough medicine.

'What's happening?' she said. There were tiny black hairs on her earlobe from where she had recently cut her hair.

'They think Wilson's won it.'

'They *do*?'

'It's very close. One or two seats in it.'

'What about Father?'

'I don't know.'

The screen flickered with static, then the picture reappeared. Dimbleby scrutinised the top lines from a piece of paper recently thrust in his hand.

The camera flicked to Robin Day. 'Well then, where are we, gentlemen? I think people out there are wishing that they had taken the bookmakers' offer of thirty-three to one for no party with a clear majority. We may be in a situation where the Liberals are holding the balance. And here's the result for Manchester Cheetham, which has been held by Labour. Flying Officer Lever. On a two per cent swing, less than there has been in other parts of the north, though it was of course a seat that swung exceptionally far to Labour at the last election, right against the national tide. Well now, that Manchester result brings us up to date, but we have had an almighty flutter of them in the last hour.'

From the hallway came the sound of Rupert's booming voice. A moment later, he burst into the study with Eva, who fumbled for the light switch in the wrong place and cursed when she couldn't locate it.

'Are you drunk, Mother?' Natasha said.

'Yes, darling, blotto,' Eva said, unbuttoning her fur coat.

Rupert tossed his jacket and tie on to the back of the armchair. Rubbing his hands together, he said, 'So, there's life left in the old dog yet. Didn't see it coming, did you? Nope, neither did I.'

Natasha sprang up and threw herself into Rupert's arms. 'You won?'

'The people of Dorchester are not so stupid as the rest of this daft country,' Rupert said. 'They know what side of the bread their butter is spread.'

Eva had retrieved a bottle of whisky from the drinks cabinet and was pouring it into glass tumblers. She said, 'Benjamin, aren't you going to offer your congratulations?'

'Yes, yes of course,' I said, getting to my feet and offering my hand. For a moment, I thought Rupert might not accept, but then he loosely clasped my palm and said, 'I know you didn't mean to cause such a commotion, but it's over now. Somehow, I've secured five more years.'

Eva handed Rupert a glass of whisky. 'What we said still stands, doesn't it?' she said.

'Yes, it does,' he replied. 'I'm afraid your aunt thinks it still does. I'm willing to let bygones be bygones, but—'

Eva spoke over him. 'We think a period of contemplation back at Cambridge would do you good. A break from Merryvale, a break from us.'

Rupert shrugged. 'All part of life's merry dance. Take care of yourself, Benjamin. This is your aunt just sort of...' But his words trailed off.

'Just sort of what?' I said.

'Teaching you a lesson, I suppose,' he said sheepishly. 'We shouldn't really be talking to reporters, not at a time like this.'

The next morning, I walked through the woods and stood near the lake, its surface rippling gently in the breeze. A gull swooped and arced, letting out a single caw as it disappeared beyond the trees.

I undressed. My body was thin and pale and insignificant.

I tried to grasp the totality of the place, the depths of the water, the metallic green surface, the surrounding trees, the gold- and rust-coloured leaves, but nothing felt concrete; everything was merely a reflection of what was real.

If my body lay at the bottom of the lake, I would be mourned for a little while, talked about from time to time over breakfast, perhaps even recalled fondly as a nice young man who had showed a hint of promise; but my absence would not be grieved, and nobody would carry forward the pain of my loss.

Benjamin, I said to myself, and even the name suddenly felt like a simulacrum. There was nothing to me: nothing to be missed and nothing to be feared. 'Benjamin,' I said again, this time out loud, and the syllables seemed to break free from the beating heart of me and float away.

I stepped forward until it was deep enough to plunge into the cold water and swim amid the reeds and leaves.

Act IV

Chapter 25

It was always obvious when Clara was holding something back. She would fret and mutter to herself, and seemingly be on the verge of saying whatever was on her mind; but then she would bite her bottom lip and say something anodyne instead, a light comment to take the sting out of the growing tension. There would always come a tipping point, however, and so it came, as she was making bacon and eggs in a frying pan over the stove. With a greasy spatula in one hand, she turned to me and, with a pained expression, she said, 'You don't see it, do you? You're sitting there writing a letter to your cousin the moment we get back. It's always Natasha this, Tom that, as if there's anything interesting about them at all.'

'It's just a letter.'

'*My* God. They've just... cast you aside like an old glove.'

Last term, as we came towards the end of our first year at Cambridge, we had moved into an Edwardian terrace in Dove Row with a solemn girl from north-west London called Rebecca Friend. Clara and I shared a sparsely furnished double bedroom at the back of the house, where patches of green mould spread across the walls and ceiling, however many times we scrubbed them clean. The bedroom overlooked a narrow strip of land that had been cultivated by the previous tenants into a makeshift allotment. Runner beans wound their way up their climbers, rows of spiny gooseberry bushes lined either side of a pebbled path, and a small, scrubby patch of earth somehow brought forth parsnips and potatoes. We had spent the summer months exploring beyond the city, sometimes taking our bikes out to the hamlet of Clayhithe and whiling away the afternoon in the riverside garden of the Axe pub. At sunset, we'd go back home to make love on our creaky mattress, all too aware that Rebecca Friend was the other side of the thin partition wall, peering down her wide-rimmed spectacles at her maths books.

Clara turned back to the stove and flipped the bacon rashers. The oil cracked and spat from the pan. Her hunched shoulders quivered.

I said, 'If it wasn't for my aunt, I would have ended up in care. I certainly wouldn't be here at Cambridge.'

Clara said, 'But the moment you become an inconvenience...' She turned the hob off and turned to face me. She had moist eyes and a trembling lower lip. 'I'm on your side,' she said, cupping her hands together in front of her chest. 'But I'm afraid they're not.'

I was overtaken with anger. 'And there I was thinking you might show a degree of gratitude.'

'*Grat*itude? What are you talking about?'

'To the Drummonds. For putting you up, for making you feel welcome, for wining and dining you.'

Clara's eyes widened. 'You have the most cramped room in the house,' she said, tossing the spatula into the cluttered sink and crossing the kitchen floor. 'There are mice in the gables and it's damp. But yes, they've got decent wine.'

And then I was following her out the room and up the stairs, yelling that she had no right to be so sneery and, anyway, what had she ever done to merit climbing on the back of such a high horse?

Clara swivelled round at the top of the stairs and held aloft her index finger. 'You simply cannot be taking your family's side on this. They've just kicked you *out*.'

I palmed her hand away. 'That's a gross distortion.'

'And what's more,' she said, warming to the theme, 'they're secretive, and they're liars, and they think they're above the law. And yet... and yet... the people of Dorset want their representative in Parliament to be a Drummond.' She threw up her hands in exasperation. 'I mean, if that's not enough to make one want a revolution, I really don't know what is.' And with that, she ran into the bathroom and locked the door. A moment later, she called out, 'I'm having a *very* long bath.'

Standing on the landing with a pensive smile was Rebecca Friend. 'Is everything OK?' she asked.

'Everything's fine, thanks, Rebecca,' I said. 'There's some bacon and eggs downstairs if you like.'

In the bedroom, I lay on the bed and stared at the woodchip ceiling. It was true that the Drummonds had rescued me from a miserable fate, but they had been unable to save me from a permanent feeling of dislocation that had begun when my mother took her own life. Since then, I had experienced life like a stream of images at the cinema: someone's story was unfolding, that was true enough, but my role was to watch and observe; it was not for me to share the intimacy of the characters on screen.

Memories from my childhood resurfaced. There was the time I was perhaps three or four, and my mother was pulling on a pair of black stockings over her slender legs. She smelt familiar – powdery pink soap, cinnamon and mothballs – but her voice had changed; it was more fevered and urgent. *Mummy has to go now. Betty will come and sit with you. I'm going to a restaurant to meet a friend.* Who had she been going to see? Was it Uncle Billy, with his side parting and stench of cheap cologne? Or perhaps an American airman on a fleeting trip from the States? A risky little rendezvous with the woman he briefly knew during the war? Of course, I never asked. I just read my books, as old, kindly Betty snoozed and dribbled in the armchair, a brown blanket rising and falling on her large bosom.

When she got out of the bath, Clara came into the bedroom in a dressing gown with a towel wrapped round her head. She had smeared a coconut-scented cream over her face. 'I'm going out to see George and Marilyn,' she said. 'You can come if you like.' Marilyn was George's new girlfriend: a loquacious New Yorker who studied modern drama and played the trumpet in a jazz band at weekends. Clara pressed her lips together and dabbed at her face with a piece of cotton wool.

'I need to work,' I said. It was partly true, I had an essay for my Middle English class to write within the fortnight, but I was in no mood to start.

Clara said, 'You mean you're going to lie here in the dark and sulk?'

'Stop, please.'

'Or finish your letter to dear cousin Natasha? By the way, has her divorce come through yet? I mean, cutting the honeymoon short underlines my central point, does it not? Just who *does* that?'

We found it difficult to cease hostilities when an argument broke out, going back and forth until one or both of us grew too weary to carry on. That evening, I was the weary one. I couldn't face George and Marilyn, or Clara, or anyone for that matter. Above all, I didn't have the energy to fight.

I rolled on to my side and closed my eyes. Clara's footsteps sounded as she went back and forth from the bathroom. When she was finally ready to go, she leaned over and planted a kiss on my cheek. 'Are you asleep?' she said softly.

'No.'

She pressed my hand in hers. 'Darling, it's been hard for you, I recognise that, but you've been in a tremendous funk ever since the wedding. I need to ask you, and I won't ask you again, but is there something you're not telling me?'

I should have lifted the burden and told her everything. I should have told her about Tom's behaviour that night when Meryam left the house, his confused appearance in my bedroom. I should have told her about the pressure the Drummonds had put on me not to disclose Meryam's name to the police. Instead, I said, 'There's really no need to be envious of my friendship with Natasha, you know. It brings out the worst in you.'

Clara removed her hand from mine. I closed my eyes and silently willed her to leave.

'She brings out the worst in *me*?' she said quietly, and with such an air of stunned disbelief that I clenched my muscles tight as if it was possible to curl up into a ball so tiny I would never have to be seen again.

Chapter 26

That night, a frost settled over our relationship that proved difficult to thaw. Over the next week, Clara seemed to avoid my company as much as possible. She spent the majority of her time at the library, or with her study group. In the evenings, she went to meetings of the Socialist Student Federation in the basement of a dingy pub with George and Marilyn. She came back late, and fuelled by red wine she would tell me about the impending dismantling of the social order.

'We've both been quite square, you know,' she said, in the bedroom one evening while wriggling out of her jeans.

'I don't know what you're talking about,' I said, putting down my study book.

'What would you say if George kissed me?' She unfastened the strap of her bra, threw it on to a pile of clothes and gazed at her reflection in the full-length mirror.

'I don't know.'

'He didn't – you don't need to worry – but he looked at me in a certain way, so that for a moment I thought he might kiss me. I wouldn't have minded; neither would Marilyn.'

I picked up my book and pretended to read. If she was trying to provoke me into a reaction, she wasn't going to succeed.

Clara was standing naked in front of the mirror. Suppressing a little whimper, she said, 'It was nice to be looked at like that.'

I went to the bathroom and stared at my reflection in the mirror above the sink. I thought if I stayed there long enough, a feeling would surface: a pang of envy, perhaps, resentment or rage. But sometimes the more you look into your eyes, the more evident the emptiness becomes.

After that night, I didn't see Clara for days. I spent most of my time at the kitchen table, attempting to finish my essay on the development of Middle English. I read impenetrable books about the evolution of the language, the elimination of grammatical case and the simplification of verb inflection. I discovered how the Northumbrian dialect had evolved into the language of the Scots. I tried to understand how the evolution of language showed how our ancestors thought; I wanted to glimpse the linguistic structure that brought them into being.

The more I tried to focus on the task, the more my thoughts returned to Merryvale. I had expected a letter or a phone call from my aunt, in which I imagined she would say sorry, that she had overreacted, but that nevertheless family fidelity was an important lesson to learn, and it went without saying that of course I would be welcome back at the house whenever I wanted. But the letter had never come, and, as the days passed, surprise turned to anger. I thought of an intoxicated Rupert and Eva on election night, spinning each other around the study and congratulating each other on a job well done, and then I thought of Meryam's father, the chemistry professor, who had died not knowing whether his daughter was alive or dead.

Two weeks after the row with Clara, Professor Alicester called me in to his cluttered office. Books and papers covered every available surface. There was a soggy half-eaten tuna sandwich and a satsuma on a paper plate in front of him. He motioned for me to sit, then scratched his balding scalp in agitation. He took a cigarette from a brass case and lit the tip. After a few inhalations, he said, 'You are an interesting young man,' and he let the thought hang in the air as he took a sheaf of paper from a ring binder in front of him. 'There are plenty of interesting young men who never do anything of note in their lives whatsoever. Do you know why that is? It is because they are undisciplined in their thinking.'

I nodded.

'The task was to write about the Great Vowel Shift,' he said. 'The discovery of Otto Jespersen, the Danish linguist. He's not mentioned once in the three thousand words you have written. What you have managed is a rambling essay about determinism and the development of consciousness through the Middle Ages. It's all rather interesting, I have to say, but it's an absolute fail.' He slid the ring binder towards me. On the first page, he had scribbled multiple comments in red ink.

'I wanted to enlarge the brief with some personal thoughts on language, sir,' I said.

The professor stubbed out his cigarette in a glass ashtray. 'This is not a diary, it's an academic essay. Listen, are you under any particular strain?'

'No, sir.'

'Are you being truthful with me?'

'Absolutely.'

'There are strange elements in this essay,' he said. 'Elements that one might be concerned by. It is extremely ill-disciplined, dare I say incoherent, in brief passages.'

'I've been very tired.'

Professor Alicester took off his spectacles and placed them on the desk with a weary sigh. 'You're Sir Rupert Drummond's ward, aren't you? We're aware the family has been under some degree of public scrutiny, and it is my duty to make you aware of the college's policy on extended illness. You can apply for a break, if you like. It might be possible to delay your studies. You would have to see a doctor, of course. I would advise you to tell him you are thoroughly washed out. I am happy to make a recommendation of approval to the board. I would hate to see a young man with promise fail when such an option is readily available.'

I gave a polite smile. 'I'm not ill, but thank you.'

'The spotlight on your family has been affecting you?' The old man had the remnants of a kindly face beneath a craggy exterior.

'I lost focus. It won't happen again.'

'Last year, you happened to be a model student, and I have good reason to believe this is just a blip. There are some remarkable insights in your essay, despite a lamentable lack of structure. You suggest the mind is unknowable, and, by doing so, make a rather solipsistic judgement that all people are essentially unknowable. But we do have Thomas Aquinas as a guide. We are all human, the great man said, and so have certain goals inherent within us, but we have the intellect to steer us through. If you want to know how the medieval mind thought, then that is our best estimate.' The professor blinked and held a handkerchief to the corner of his eye. 'You must excuse me, I have the most appalling stye.' He inspected the handkerchief and placed it back down on the desk.

There was a knock at the door, and a secretary came in holding a large brown envelope. She placed it on the professor's desk and left. He put it to one side and lifted his eyes in my direction once more. 'I believe this envelope contains a report from Professor Beauchamp concerning your attendance of his series of lectures on Civil War literature. I am led to believe your attendance has been very poor during these first weeks of term.'

'I am thinking of quitting the class. My interests lie more in philosophy.'

'You can't just quit without discussion or agreement.' For the first time, Professor Alicester sounded irritable. He squeezed his middle finger and clicked a knuckle.

'May I resubmit the essay, sir?'

'I am of the opinion that you need a thorough break from your studies,' the professor said. 'At least until this business with your family is over.'

'This business has nothing to do with me,' I said, feeling a flush of colour in my cheeks.

'I want to give you some breathing space while the investigation runs its course,' the professor said. 'Take some time out, Butler. See a doctor, say it's stress. Come back and see me in a month. Don't read any more pseudo-philosophy. Show some agency yourself, pull yourself together, go and see your family. Go for a morning walk and read a few trashy novels. Come back next term and put all this behind you. All right?' He motioned towards the door.

I stood up to leave, but had to grip the side of the desk to steady myself.

The professor stood up and offered his hand. 'Life throws up challenges from time to time. You have my very best regards.'

'Thank you, sir.'

The professor gave a curious smile. 'You know,' he said, 'sometimes it is necessary to cut ties, to go away and reinvent ourselves. Have you seen this morning's newspapers? I should advise you to read them.'

On the way home, I stopped at the newsagents, and returned to the house with copies of *The Times*, the *Telegraph* and the *Daily Mail*. They all ran with a picture of Tom when he had captained the Cambridge cricket team to victory against Durham the previous summer. He was raising a flute of champagne in the clubhouse, his blonde hair a little wild, his blue eyes twinkling with mischief, despite a nasty-looking shiner engulfing his left eye. And they all had the same scant information, though those few details were enough to merit a sensational front-page splash.

Dorset Police arrested the son of the MP Sir Rupert Drummond on suspicion of the murder of Meryam Martin. Tom Drummond, 22, was being questioned by detectives at Dorchester Police Station. The body of Miss Martin, a French national, was identified through dental records. The Drummonds declined to comment.

Chapter 27

The restaurant, situated in a cobbled side street, had a faded art deco glamour: all shiny leather, mirrors and chandeliers. I sipped nervously at my beer in a corner, watching waiters carry plates of Dover sole and venison steaks with the affected air of bored children. Outside, November had brought a bitter cold spell, and flurries of snow showers had covered the pavement in grey sludge.

After twenty minutes, Rupert came in, wearing a dark grey flannel suit that appeared a size too small for his growing bulk. He was carrying a briefcase and an umbrella, which he shook free of snow. He didn't see me at first, as his gaze jumped from table to table; then he caught my eye and, sporting a wide smile, approached the table, dropped his briefcase and opened his arms. 'Dear boy, how marvellous it is to see you,' he said. 'Are you keeping well?' As he sat down, he clicked his fingers at a waiter and signalled for a wine menu. 'They do the most fantastic Domaine de Chevalier here. Red all right?'

'Whatever you suggest,' I said, and despite myself I found myself smiling. It was good to see the old bounder, I had to admit.

Rupert sank into his surroundings with a satisfied sigh. 'It's quite a feat to get a table here, you know? The last time I was in Cambridge, Tom and I had a superb nosh-up. Forgive me, but I can't remember if you were there?'

'My birthday.'

Rupert screwed up his brow. 'Bloody hell, my memory these days. I've seen the doctor and he doesn't think I'm going doolally just yet, puts it down to stress, which is more palatable because at least I can do something about that. I'm in London most of the week, which your aunt doesn't like at all. She thinks I'm having a string of affairs, but the truth is I'm as knackered as a workhorse.'

The waiter, an avuncular figure with a domed head and pencil-thin eyebrows, returned with a bottle of wine and opened it at the table. He poured a splash into Rupert's glass and waited for him to taste. Rupert groaned appreciatively. 'You'll enjoy this, Benjamin,' he said. 'I won't tell you the price; you'd only weep.' He forced a weary smile. Beads of sweat glistened on his forehead.

'Chin chin,' he said, raising his glass. 'I really didn't want to be late, so I got a train from Kings Cross after the afternoon session in the House. Some interminable old toff droning on about the Road Safety Bill. I was grateful to get away.'

'It's nice to see you.'

Rupert's face softened. 'Indeed, and you too, my boy. Now, what's new?'

'Where to start?' I said, letting out a sigh. 'Well, my tutor has asked me to stay away from class, I think Clara is sleeping with my old housemate, and I can't stop thinking about Tom.'

Rupert wore a weak, pensive smile. He reached for my hand and gave it a lukewarm squeeze. 'Things have rather taken a turn, haven't they? One of those periods in life when you just want to say fuck it all to billy-o and slink back to bed with a stiff drink, but we can't do that, young man. We're not quitters.'

'We?'

Rupert's eyes narrowed. 'We Drummonds. You're just as much a part of this family as you ever were.'

'It's not felt like that,' I said. I had spent the weeks since Tom's arrest pacing the streets of Cambridge in my parka, the hood pulled up. I found the non-student pubs where I wouldn't recognise anyone, and sat alone at a table. Over pints of brown ale, I trawled my memory for indicators – the slightest portents – that Tom was capable of such a violent crime.

Rupert picked up a menu and studied it. 'It's been a jolly rum time for all of us, you know. Evie is struggling. You know she can be a terrible grouch in the winter months when her melatonin and her serotonin and whatnot fall through the floor. In fact, I've been looking into getting her a solarium, if only for my sanity.'

'I'm sorry to hear that,' I said, but my body stiffened. Not a letter, or a phone call.

Rupert's finger traced down the menu. 'She's lost a lot of weight, spends a lot of her time in the salon on her own. She's terribly worried about Tom, of course, but she's definitely feeling your absence too, you know. She'd love to see you.'

I pursed my lips and blew out air. 'She knows where to find me.'

Rupert lifted his gaze. 'Look, Ben, I don't think cutting short your visit over the summer was the right thing to do, and it made me very uncomfortable, but what's done is done. It was never meant to be a permanent ban from Merryvale. Your aunt and I are not in the business of banishing people from court like a pair of Russian potentates. It's important now to rebuild. Shall we work on that?'

'I wrote to her, you know,' I said, my voice trembling. I had been determined not to show any emotion, but the last few months had brought a loneliness more acute than in the aftermath of my mother's death.

Rupert grimaced. 'She's had a lot to deal with. She's distraught about Tom.'

I shook my head slowly. 'I wrote to Natasha too. Not a word in reply.'

Rupert scratched his neck. 'Your cousin, unfortunately, continues to create drama. The marriage, I have to say, has turned out to be a rather peculiar affair. This Charles Hogan fellow has fallen short of all our expectations. Throw in Tom and we have what my father would call "a great clutter".' He lifted his wine glass to his lips and took a sip, then shook his head and said, 'I myself would call it a bloody shambles.' He wiped his palm across his forehead. 'Quite frankly, it's taking its toll on all of us. Not least my bloody ticker.'

An attractive woman in a burgundy cocktail dress was ushered to the table next to ours. Rupert stole a look, then glanced back at me with a crafty grin, which I refused to reciprocate.

He said, 'Let me be straight with you, Benjamin, I thought it was a harsh lesson your aunt imposed on you. For me, family is everything, and if mistakes are made, then, well, we learn to accept each other's foibles and move on... Your aunt takes a more unforgiving view, but listen, she's softened, and I believe she will be in touch very soon.'

The waiter appeared alongside Rupert to take our order.

'What would you recommend?' I said, picking up the menu.

'You look like you would benefit from a chateaubriand,' Rupert said. 'You're looking rather peaky, I must say.'

We ordered two steaks. When the waiter departed, Rupert wrung his large hands together and said, with a sigh, 'I'm afraid there has been a development.'

'I'm all ears.'

Rupert spoke in a lowered tone. 'I'm sorry to say Tom has now been charged. The papers haven't got wind of it yet, but it'll only be a matter of time. We've been lucky enough to secure the services of Sir Anthony Brasshouse, a top-rate barrister, slick bastard. He's convinced the case will fall apart. I think we can all agree Tom made a mistake in going on the lash with the girl that night, but he's not done her in, on that everybody is most clear. The case is purely circumstantial. Sir Anthony doesn't even think it will progress into the second week. My theory is that it was that disreputable old bastard, the vicar. That poor drunk girl, having missed the train after larking about with Tom, made her way back there. She needed a bed for the night. He may have tried something, she resisted, and the rest...'

The waiter reappeared with our steak and chips. Rupert tucked his napkin into his shirt and rubbed his hands together. 'Bloody lovely,' he said.

We ate a while in silence. The food appeared to energise Rupert; the colour returned to his cheeks. 'So, there's another thing. Sir Anthony would like to call you as a character witness,' he said, masticating on a piece of steak. 'All you've got to do is get up on the stand and tell them what a decent sport Tom is.' He put his cutlery down and cradled his hands.

I stared at him in stunned silence.

Rupert said, 'Ah yes, I know what you're going to say. I know Tom stumbled into your room that night garbling nonsense.'

'Yes, he was confused.'

Rupert said in a hushed tone, 'Tom was blotto, and when he's blotto he often says silly things. I don't know where he gets it from, but I've told him when this is all done he must maintain a period of abstinence. Get himself in order, stop fucking up.'

'He said he'd got himself into trouble.'

'Yes, he did. He *had*. He was supposed to take the girl to the station and come straight home, not go on the razzle with her. But the point is, if the prosecution got wind of this, they'd have a field day. Two plus two equals five, you know the rest. If you're cross-examined, you won't make mention of it, all right?'

I let out a derisive scoff. 'So that's what this was about? I didn't suppose it was actually a peace mission.'

Rupert waved a dismissive hand. 'No, no, no, don't be like that. This is about healing a wound that everybody, in their own way, is feeling very deeply, and that's your *absence*. That's why I'm here, to sort out this mess, to sort out our disagreements. I am trying to prevent my family from collapsing in on itself. If there's one thing I'm good at, it's keeping a sense of perspective, and this has all got wildly out of hand. It's all completely insufferable. What we'd like you to do is take the stand and tell the jury Tom is a man of integrity and decency.'

I put down my knife and fork. 'He had mud on his face.'

Rupert banged his fist on the table. 'You'll kill him if you say what you saw,' he said, and then he let out a gasp and put his hand to his chest.

'Are you OK?'

Rupert took a few deep breaths, and when he had composed himself he said, 'I'm perfectly fine. Listen, don't make me a disappointed old man. I was hoping this would be a positive meeting to help reintegrate you into the family.'

'You had an ulterior motive,' I said.

My uncle piled chips onto his fork and shovelled them into his mouth. 'Of course, your reintegration back at Merryvale would very much depend on the choices you make going forward,' he said.

I stared at my half-finished steak, with a sense of nausea rising from my stomach to my throat.

Rupert knocked back the rest of his wine and said, 'I've not led a blameless life, Ben, and I haven't, nor ever will, reach the heights I hoped to reach. I'm also vain, insecure, and sometimes thoroughly depressed. All that I freely admit. But that is the sum of it, that really is the sum of it. I've done my best to raise three children and send them into the world prepared and happy. Tom's privilege in life has rather gone to his head, and for that too I can only blame myself. But, I believe, with all my heart, that he is a good man, and that he will mature and grow into an even better one. He has his faults – we all do – but I did not bring up a boy who would kill a young woman. I did not do that.'

He reached down for his briefcase, pulled out an envelope and handed it to me across the table. 'Sir Anthony has obtained a witness summons from the court. It would be in contempt of court to ignore it. But I know you won't let any of us down, not least your cousin.'

There was not much more to say. When we had finished our meals, Rupert looked at his watch and said he had to dash to the station to make the last train back to London. There was important business in the House in the morning. It had been lovely to see me, he said, and we should all let bygones be bygones. He settled the bill and then he was gone.

Through the window, I watched him hail a taxi. He bent to pick up his briefcase, then took three uneven steps forward towards the kerb. Before he got inside, he turned back and lifted a hand to his temple in salute. It was what he used to do when he would drop me off at boarding school. 'Sergeant,' he would say, 'I am to remind you of your absolute duty to show willing. Once you do, everything will follow.'

When I got home, Clara was lying on her back on the sofa in the gloom of the living room. A Joan Baez record played on the record player. There was an empty bottle of wine on the coffee table and a half-smoked joint in the ashtray. Next to the ashtray, a candle flickered. She sat up when she saw me, and held her hand to her breastbone. One strap of her red dungarees had slipped off her shoulder. 'Oh Christ, you gave me a start,' she said. 'I thought you were out tonight.'

'Rupert had to catch an earlier train.'

She adjusted her strap. 'Still in the doghouse?'

'I've been shown a way out, if you can call it that. Are you OK? You look flushed.'

'We're celebrating – hope you don't mind. George popped round with some news. He's been awarded the Eric Gregory award.'

I gave her a blank look.

'For his poetry.'

The toilet flushed upstairs.

Clara gritted her teeth. 'It was just a spontaneous thing. We really didn't expect you back.' She picked up the smouldering joint from the ashtray and sucked at the end. 'OK, cards firmly on the table,' she said. 'I'm sorry, but I am attracted to George.'

'Oh.'

Clara fidgeted. 'I mean, before the wedding, I felt very different about you.'

'So what's changed?' I felt a rising sense of panic that made my ears ring. Years later, my therapist would identify an acute fear of rejection. She would say other people perceived me as inauthentic because I lived behind a mask, and that I perpetuated the cycle of rejection by failing to commit to my true self.

Clara said, 'Spending time at Merryvale was fun, but I'm afraid it just confirmed some fears I had.'

'What fears?'

'I don't believe in your family's right to inherited wealth, for a start. I think your uncle only sits in Parliament because of his privilege, and I think your cousins are snobs.' She hesitated, then said – almost with a hint of apology – 'And the worst thing is I'm worried you might be one too.'

I snatched the bottle from the table and took a swig of cheap, vinegary wine.

The staircase creaked under someone's footsteps. A moment later, George came into the room wearing a pair of underpants and a white vest. He had broad feet and rugby-player thighs. 'Oh,' he said, spotting me.

'I'm sorry,' Clara said. 'You do understand, don't you? We're just very different people.'

I nodded. At last, I thought I did understand. I existed in a liminal space, not one nor the other, and it was a terribly lonely place to be.

Chapter 28

The Crown's lawyer, Robert Harris, had thin silver hair and round spectacles. He stood before the jury without notes and held aloft a photograph. 'May it please your honour, and ladies and gentlemen of the jury, the defendant Thomas Percy Drummond stands before you accused of murder,' he said. 'Take a good look at this young woman, for her cruel and untimely death is the reason we're all here today, and nothing, in the next three weeks, should sway you from your task, which is to obtain justice for this woman, and for the people who knew and loved her. The judge has already explained to you this will be no easy task. You will be at the centre of a circus; you will be torn this way and that; you will be trying a young man whose family is well known, and the press will no doubt label it a sensation. But put all that aside, and remember why we are here.

'Five years ago, this young woman was killed at the hands of the man sitting in the dock. We are going to show you incontrovertible proof that the defendant, born with all the advantages available to him, through a rash act of unconscionable cruelty, snuffed out her young life.' He paused and handed the photograph to the foreperson of the jury, a woman in her sixties with white hair tied up in an immaculate bun. She took the photograph and studied it with an inscrutable expression. 'Please pass it to your fellow jurors, madam,' Mr Harris said. 'That woman's name was Meryam Martin.'

I was sitting on a wooden bench in the packed public gallery that overlooked the court. Next to me, in a black trouser suit, Eva peered intently at the proceedings below. She had greeted me at the security gate with a pensive smile and a peck on both cheeks. 'Hello, stranger,' she had said, without irony. Now she clasped the backs of her knees and silently tapped her foot. Every now and then, she turned to Rupert for reassurance, but he just stared straight ahead, his round face sombre and seemingly disbelieving of where he was and why.

In the centre of the courtroom, Tom stood in the dock, his hair neatly combed into a side parting, head slightly bowed, hands clasped together. From our vantage point in the gallery, he appeared diminished: his stature smaller, his lustre stripped. He looked up every now and then and sought out a familiar face, a reassuring glance from his parents.

Mr Harris lingered in front of the jury and said, 'First, we have to take you back to the events of that summer and introduce you to the principal characters you will encounter during the course of the trial. The Drummonds, as you may or may not know, reside on a country estate known as Merryvale Manor. The estate covers some thousand acres, and comprises three main parts – the house and adjacent cottage, a garden, and an area of woodland, in which can be found a large natural lake, where some of the remains of this young woman were found. I present a map to the jury as item B, your honour.

'On 20 June 1959, Meryam Martin was employed by the defendant's father, Sir Rupert Drummond, to serve as a French tutor for his daughter, Natasha Drummond. Miss Martin was twenty-five years old. She was originally from Orly, a Parisian suburb, where she lived with her elderly father, now deceased. It is believed she arrived in the UK in 1957 and had been residing in several addresses in London, most recently St John's Wood.

'When interviewed by Mrs Eva Drummond upon her arrival, she claimed to have been under employment in the Fitzrovia area of London, working as a nanny to two small children of a family called the De Blooters. Suffice to say, the references she provided to Mrs Drummond are believed to have been forged. There was such a family, but the unfortunate parents died when a bomb landed directly on the roof of their house in 1942. Their two children were staying with a family in Penzance at the time, where they remain.'

Mr Harris moved to the front of the dock and pointed at Tom. 'I will now familiarise you with the character of the defendant Thomas Drummond,' he said. 'He is twenty-two years old. He graduated from Magdalene College, Cambridge, and is currently a postgraduate student at Clare College. His father is Sir Rupert Drummond, a Member of Parliament, and his mother is Eva Drummond. Thomas has a twin sister, Natasha, and a cousin, Benjamin, who was adopted by the family following the death of his mother – Eva Drummond's sister – in the summer of 1959.

'Your honour, and members of the jury, I will tell you now that much of the Crown's case is circumstantial. Now that is not to say that circumstantial evidence should be seen as guesswork; rather, each piece of evidence corroborates the conclusion of the others, leading you to the only outcome it will be possible to support, namely, that the defendant took the life of Miss Martin, that he sought to cover up the fact, and that he prevented her lawful burial by abandoning her lifeless body near a lake on the grounds of his father's estate.

'Before I continue my opening statement, your honour, I would like to address the jury directly. Thomas Drummond, as you will come to see, is a handsome and articulate young man, who, before these unfortunate events, had a bright future, one in which he might conceivably have flourished. His family is held in similarly high esteem. They have money, power, a certain way of doing things, which you may find seductive. What you must deal with are the facts, and nothing more than the facts. You will come to see that this young man's self-confidence and determination to secure his elevated position at the top of society were principal factors in leading him to do what he did. You will come to see that Miss Martin had no such position. She was taken under the wing of the Drummond family, with none of the privileges the family members enjoyed. She was vulnerable, a woman alone in a foreign part of England in a country with which she was only partly familiar. She had an elderly father who she hadn't seen in years. She was, you will come to see, virtually invisible, and so, when she vanished, nobody really endeavoured to locate her. Nobody shed a tear.'

My throat tightened. Meryam had appeared so self-assured compared to my timid fourteen-year-old self that I had been unable to see she was vulnerable, or alone.

Mr Harris said, 'Secondly, I would like to say to the jury that some of the evidence concerning what happened to that young girl, alone as she was in that large house, populated by strangers, will no doubt be harrowing. Her injuries were severe, her body treated like a piece of rubbish to be tossed away. But we are presenting this evidence in order for you to understand the severity of the crime. I pray you harden your hearts a little and listen dispassionately.'

Mr Harris had retrieved a sheaf of paper from the clerk and was scanning it through his round spectacles. He said, 'For reasons not immediately apparent, the bountiful Drummonds chose not to house Miss Martin in their capacious home, but instead arranged for her to lodge at the vicarage in Upwey, a small village situated around three miles north of Merryvale. You may consider this to be indicative of a certain disregard towards the people they employed.'

Tom's counsel, Sir Anthony Brasshouse, got to his feet for the first time. He was a large man with a bushy black beard and a mass of unkempt hair. He spoke in a loud baritone. 'Request for the comment to be struck from the record, your honour. Ridiculous speculation. There are multiple reasons why Miss Martin...'

The judge said, 'He's right, Mr Harris. Strike it from the record.'

Mr Harris raised an eyebrow. 'Indeed,' he said. 'For whatever reason, Miss Martin resided at the vicarage. She was not happy there, and wrote to a male friend in London about her acrimonious relationship with her new landlord, a certain Reverend Jonathan Hardcastle. In that letter, Miss Martin wrote, "I am starting to fear this has all been a terrible mistake. I am staying in a village a long way from anywhere. I miss you and I miss London. The girl I am teaching is fun, but precious. She has a twin brother, who can't take his eyes off me. He makes me feel uneasy. The summer will be over before long, I suppose. I'll call you when I'm back."'

Mr Harris removed his glasses. 'For the record, the twin brother Martin refers to in her letter is the defendant.'

Tom screwed up his nose and said, 'I'm awfully sorry she felt like that... that puzzles me.'

The judge gave him a castigating look. 'There'll be absolutely no speaking on your part, Mr Drummond, unless you are on the witness stand. Do you understand me? Absolutely none at all. Pray continue, Mr Harris.'

'It soon became clear that a combination of Miss Martin's eagerness to return to London, and friction between her and Mrs Drummond and the rest of the staff, was making her position untenable,' Mr Harris said. 'She was a fish out of water. A woman who had lived in Paris and London, who was well known among a certain bohemian set in the capital. She was not best prepared for a more tranquil life at Merryvale Manor.

'And so, one day, the inevitable occurred. Meryam Martin was asked to leave the Drummond household. Witnesses will testify as to why that was the case. Quite frankly, it remains a matter of some dispute, not least between the members of the family. What we do know is that there was a rather unpleasant and sudden falling-out, and that this led to Miss Martin's dismissal during a heated discussion on the verandah at about five o'clock on the eleventh of July. She had lasted in her tenure less than three weeks.

'Eva Drummond wanted the young woman out of the house immediately. There was a train from Dorchester to London Paddington, due to leave at seven thirty that evening, and it was agreed that Thomas Drummond would take his father's car and drive Miss Martin to the railway station with her belongings. She never made that train; indeed, she never left this quiet corner of England. For later that night she would be murdered, and by the following morning her body had been abandoned on the Drummond estate, where it would lie undiscovered for the next five years.'

Eva covered her mouth with her hand. Her face was gaunt and smeared with foundation. 'I'm not sure I can do this,' she whispered in my direction.

Rupert stared at his hands.

Mr Harris said, 'For now, picture the defendant, this confident and brash young man. He is in the car with Miss Martin, a woman he found sexually attractive, a woman whom he had sought to impress since her arrival. A woman who says she was frightened of him.'

Sir Anthony said, in his booming voice, 'Your honour, that is really quite unacceptable. Mr Harris is playing with the facts in the manner that a sixth form debating society would blush at.'

The judge said, 'Mr Harris, frightened is interpretive to say the least. I believe the letter said the young woman felt uneasy.'

Mr Harris conceded. 'Your honour, I strike the comment from the record. The defendant is alone in a car with Miss Martin. They never got to the railway station. Mr Drummond drove Miss Martin to Dorchester where he parked his vehicle at the Quiet Woman public house in Ironhead Lane, just a few minutes after six o'clock.

They took a table in the corner and ordered beer and whisky. The landlady of the establishment, Mrs Sarah Lightfoot, had never seen Miss Martin before, but she was aware of Thomas Drummond. The pair became increasingly drunk, and Mrs Lightfoot began to feel uncomfortable about serving them more alcohol, as they were attracting attention. At one point, Mrs Lightfoot was retrieving glasses from their table when she overheard Miss Martin say something about missing her train. She became panicked and began to gather her things. At that point, Mr Drummond put his hand across her arm, which caused Miss Martin to fall back into her seat. Soon after this, Miss Martin and Mr Drummond left the pub together and went back to the car. Mrs Lightfoot watched through the window, as she was worried Mr Drummond was too inebriated to drive. She recalls the vehicle jerking forward out of the car park, but, just before it reached the road, Mr Drummond got out and went back into the pub. He was agitated and said his friend had missed her train and needed somewhere to stay. It so happened that Mrs Lightfoot had had a cancellation earlier that afternoon. She was anxious about letting Miss Martin stay there, but she was also worried about the pair driving while under the influence of alcohol. In her police interview, she said she was disturbed by the manner in which these two young people were engaging with each other. They were, in her words, "acting physical".

'The couple had been upstairs for about an hour when Mrs Lightfoot went upstairs to check on what was happening. She objected to her establishment being used for a casual encounter. At the door, she heard voices, but nothing untoward, and so she went downstairs again.

'Shortly before ten o'clock, she was back behind the bar when the defendant and Miss Martin reappeared. They walked through the pub without saying a word. A few moments later, a car engine started and the pair drove off. It was the last she saw of either of them.

'Where the couple went next is the subject of some speculation. One witness has come forward to say they stopped at the Flask and Spittle pub in the centre of town and asked if they were still serving food. The proprietor of the establishment does not recall seeing the couple, and the Crown has decided not to call the witness.

'The next sighting of the couple is in Lulworth just after midnight. Lulworth is a coastal village around ten miles from Dorchester. A local man, Leonard Mcallister, was taking his spaniel for a short walk before retiring for the night. There was a blue Vauxhall Victor in the car park near a path that leads to the cliffs. It was unusual for Mr Mcallister to see a vehicle there at that time of night, and he remembers feeling unnerved, not least because of the calibre of the vehicle. He approached the car but there was nobody inside. There was a discarded bottle of whisky on the grass and some cigarette butts. He took a note of the number plate of the car because he was concerned it had been stolen. The Crown can confirm the vehicle was registered to Sir Rupert Drummond. Mr Mcallister saw nothing further suspicious in the area, nor did he hear any voices. He returned to his cottage around twenty minutes later. The next morning, he went back to the same spot, but the car had been driven away. He telephoned the police to report what he had seen. A note was made by the acting sergeant. Sir Rupert was contacted, but had nothing to report, and nothing further on the matter was pursued.

'The final, and key, sighting of the vehicle occurred just after dawn. A lorry driver called Pat Godfrey was returning from London. He had driven for six hours straight and was looking for a lay-by so he could shut his eyes for half an hour. There is a spot he usually heads for on the A515 because it is rarely used. The lay-by is about three miles from Lulworth, and approximately two miles from Upwey. Mr Godfrey was surprised to see a sky-blue Vauxhall Victor in the lay-by. He pulled up alongside and got out of his cab. The defendant, Thomas Drummond, was asleep in the driver's seat. He woke with a start when Mr Godfrey rapped on the window. He described the defendant in a statement he has given to police as dishevelled, drunk and scared. Mr Drummond started the car and drove away at high speed. Mr Godfrey did not recognise the defendant and had no evidence a crime had been committed. He forgot about it until the recent coverage surrounding the defendant and the charges he now faces. It is the Crown's contention that the body of Miss Martin was in the boot of the vehicle as Mr Drummond drove away.'

Eva took out a handkerchief and blew her nose. 'Wake me up from this nightmare,' she said quietly to me. She reached for my hand.

Mr Harris paused in front of the jury. He said, 'At some point, between the hours of midnight and dawn, the defendant attacked Miss Martin with a blunt object. It may be that she spurned his advances; it may be he discovered something about Miss Martin that enraged him. We will speculate as to what that might be when we present our next witness. The truth is we will never know what triggered this cruel and impetuous young man to do what he did. What we can determine is that the defendant spent a wild night with the victim, and after that night, Miss Martin vanished into thin air. Her elderly father never heard from her again; neither did any of her friends. They all came to the conclusion that this independent and daring young woman had ended one chapter in her life and moved on to another. Indeed, she was a free spirit who tired easily of people and places. They all presumed they would receive a postcard from her six months hence, from Spain, or the United States, where she often spoke of going.

'In fact, her battered body was driven to Merryvale Manor in Sir Rupert Drummond's car. There, just after dawn, Tom Drummond removed Miss Martin's body from the boot of the vehicle, and, it is our contention, he used a wheelbarrow, or some other means, to transport the body across the lawn and into the woods that form the perimeter of the estate. From there, it is a short ten-minute walk to the lake, where Miss Martin's body was found.'

Mr Harris returned to his team of solicitors and retrieved another file of papers. He walked back to the jury.

'Miss Martin's body was disposed of near the lake,' he said. 'Your honour, I ask the jury to look again at item B, map of the grounds of Merryvale Manor. You will see the lake is of substantial size. The River Lyce runs through it, and on to the Solent. The waters of the lake are famously deep and clear. It was and remains a popular bathing ground for the nearby villagers of Upwey. In the north-west corner of your map, you will see an access gate, which is where the villagers came and went. The defence will suggest this opens wide the list of possible suspects. We will refute that claim. During the summer of 1959, the gate was closed to the public. The summer before there had been a dispute between the Drummonds and the family of a young man who had got into difficulty swimming there, and had claimed Sir Rupert bore some degree of liability for the safety of visitors. While that dispute rumbled on, Sir Rupert, quite understandably, blocked off access.

'Miss Martin's body was submerged in cold, deep waters. Due to the buoyancy caused by decomposition, it would have been inevitable that the body would have resurfaced, probably within a few weeks or a month of being left there. That did not happen. And that is because the defendant had committed an unspeakable act of mutilation on the corpse, piercing the bowel and intestines with a sharp object to block the accumulation of gas. This would have helped enormously in assuring the corpse remained where it was, at the bottom of the lake.'

There was a collective intake of breath throughout the court-room. Tom looked down at the floor between his feet. Eva squeezed my hand.

'Such grotesque mutilation would not have prevented the body from rising for long,' Mr Harris said. 'At some stage, Meryam Martin's body would have resurfaced, and it is the Crown's contention that, when it did, Tom Drummond retrieved the body and buried it under a fallen oak tree, just a few yards away. We will prove that the defendant Tom Drummond is guilty, ladies and gentlemen, and we will prove that to you beyond any reasonable doubt.'

Eva put her head in her hands and let out a sound like a fox with its leg snapped in two by a trap.

Chapter 29

'Mary Rogers, Stewardess of the *Stella*, 1899,' Eva said, taking off her sunglasses and reading the inscription on the tiled panel. We were under the canopied memorial to self-sacrifice in Postman's Park, a small green space in the City of London. She went on, 'Self-sacrificed by giving up her lifebelt and voluntarily going down with the sinking ship.'

'I hope whoever she gave her lifebelt to was worth it,' I said.

Eva put her sunglasses back on and touched my wrist. 'You're still angry with me, aren't you?'

'Let's just think about Mary Rogers for a moment.' I moved my hand away. 'We should say a little prayer of thanks or something.'

Eva gave a sad, closed smile. 'I don't give a shit about Mary Rogers.'

'I know,' I said. 'But I don't want to talk. I just want to get a drink.'

'You have every right to be angry,' she said, pinching the bridge of her nose with thumb and forefinger. Eva's high cheekbones, which once gave her face symmetry and poise, now looked sunken and gaunt. Grey hairs had emerged among the roots of her black hair. She was growing old, I thought, my closest blood relative.

I swallowed a lump in my throat; I was not going to show her how rejected I felt. 'I thought you might write,' I said.

Eva let out a little whimper. 'That's unforgivable of me. Come, let's stroll a little.'

We followed the path out of the park and walked down St Martin's Le Grand towards St Paul's. It was a bright afternoon with a fresh breeze.

'When I was in my early twenties,' Eva said, 'I used to have so much free time. I used to visit all the museums and galleries. I felt like I was educating myself, you know. Your mother and I didn't have much schooling. For a while, I used to always think, I must better myself, I must read this book, or go and see that play. After I married Rupert, I had such crippling anxiety about time passing by without my having done anything of significance. When the twins were much younger, we'd go on holiday and I'd line up all these things to do – these godawful little museums in the middle of nowhere, manned by some old woman. Nobody enjoyed them.' She chuckled to herself. 'Natasha used to sulk, desperate to go to the beach. Rupert was always thinking about getting back to the bar. Tom, I suppose, had a natural curiosity. He always appreciated new things.'

We stopped outside a pub called the Shakespeare with a yellow and blue tiled frontage and window baskets blooming with pink begonias. 'Shall we?' she said, dipping inside. A few minutes later, we were sitting on leather stools at the bar with a couple of gin and tonics and a bag of peanuts. My aunt popped a handful into her mouth and slid the packet towards me.

'Now, I have to say this, Ben: what I did was frightful,' Eva said, and she lifted her palm to forestall any interruption. 'I just felt very defensive about Tom when that poor girl's body was found, and the stress of the election, and the media sniffing around, the bloody police investigation... it all got too much and I made some bad decisions.' She circled a plastic stirrer through her glass, then lifted the drink to her lips and sipped. 'Do you know, when I was a younger woman I had the strange notion I had the talent to become a novelist? I wrote these silly little books about a head girl at a school in Stroud who played at being an amateur sleuth. She was called Bronwyn, I seem to remember. Anyway, nobody wanted to publish them, and that was perfectly fine, the right decision no doubt.' She paused to light a cigarette. Closing her eyes, she took a deep inhalation and breathed out smoke through her nostrils. 'So then I took up jewellery-making. Rupert and I had just got married, and he used to work long hours in the City. Sometimes, he would stay there most of the week, only returning to Merryvale at weekends. I was twenty-eight, in this grand old house with too much time on my hands. I did a course in Dorchester with a bunch of old women, and learned how to make a few trinkets. It didn't last. You know how the women can be in that part of the world; they're all insufferable bores. I should have done something more exciting, taken a lover, got a divorce and moved to Milan or Paris. I should have been bolder, but then the bloody war broke out and all dreams of boldness were indefinitely on hold. Rupert was conscripted in 1940. His first post was north of the Arctic Circle, in a Norwegian town called Bodo. He wrote to me from there to say he was perfectly safe from the Nazis, and that the only threat was the cold and the lack of a good meal. A week later, the Luftwaffe destroyed the town. Two British servicemen died. Rupert escaped with a third-degree burn to his calf. He was sent home to convalesce, and that was the end of his war. I think he served seventy days in total, never fired a bullet. When he was able to walk again, they sent him down a coal mine in Penzance.'

'Rupert has the most unabashed luck,' I said, signalling to the barman for two more gins.

'Oh, he does, darling,' Eva said, waving her cigarette towards the ashtray.

'They seem like happy times,' I said.

'When Rupert was convalescing, we had the most remarkable second honeymoon. The world was falling apart, but we were perfectly content in our little bubble. We emptied the wine cellar and listened to the wireless, hearing the buzz of the Lockheeds overhead. We were happy. Rupert was desperately worried about Channing, who was somewhere in Abyssinia fighting the Italians, but his attention was soon captured by the arrival of the twins, our little wartime babies.

'When the twins came along, that was the end of my wanderlust. I placed the stupid unpublished Bronwyn novels in a cardboard box in the attic. I gave up all my silly hobbies. I stopped dreaming of a new life in Paris or Milan. Now I had a family to raise – I had Merryvale. From then on, my family became my art. I would be the best at that, I decided. I would be the bloody best at that.'

'You've been good to us all,' I said.

Eva's voice thickened with emotion. 'We were all very happy for a while. I loved motherhood so much. I wanted more children, another two at least. We tried, God knows we tried, but it wasn't to be. I reconciled myself with that. And that's why, dear Benjamin, you were such a gift to me. A gift to emerge from appalling tragedy, but a gift nonetheless.'

She paused to sift through her handbag, and brought out a small envelope. On the front was scrawled her name. 'Open it,' she said, handing it to me. Inside was a handwritten note in my mother's handwriting.

My dearest sister, it read. *Please give the boy what I've been singularly incapable of delivering. Call it love, if that's what you can muster. At the very least, give him a home. Yours, Margot.*

I sucked in air through my teeth. 'Ever the expressive, my mother,' I said.

Eva managed a faint smile. 'When I read that note, I promised to bring you into our family and make you my own. I'm so sorry if I failed you.' She sipped at her drink and tilted her head towards me. 'Now, enough about me, how have you been?'

I scratched the back of my head and sighed. 'I've been asked to stay away from college for a while. At least until the court case is over.'

'How terribly unfair.'

'It's fine.'

'At least you can spend more time with that wonderful girl. Please tell me you're keeping her close.'

'Argh, Clara,' I said, shaking my head.

'Oh, what happened?'

'She's seeing somebody else, my ex-housemate.'

Eva's features softened. 'For goodness sake, you young people,' she said, rolling her eyes. 'You're in and out of each other's beds like there's no tomorrow.' She stubbed out her cigarette and clutched my forearm. 'Come back to Merryvale for a while. Natasha misses you awfully. When Tom's acquitted, he'll be coming home too. Let's regroup as a family.'

My aunt had been manipulative and cruel, but for the first time in many months it was as if the bricks lined up on my chest had been lifted. I wanted to go home.

Eva cupped the back of my head and pulled me close for a hug. 'I told you we're made of strong stuff, darling. We sail through choppy waters.'

Chapter 30

The rest of the first week of the trial saw the prosecution call several witnesses to confirm their timeline. Mrs Lightfoot, the pub landlady, gave a testimony that was damaging for the defence. She was an expansive witness who interspersed her narrative with barbed comments about Tom's behaviour, both on the night in question and on previous visits. He was a reasonable young man, she explained, until he had a drink, and then he turned arrogant and mean. She had seen him in the pub with several women, she said, over the years, but that night something had been different. The atmosphere was charged, she said, and dangerous. She'd had a good mind to call his father because she felt something bad was going to happen.

In cross-examination, Sir Anthony made a good job of belittling her reliance on instinct and pushed her on the evidence. 'They were just two young people enjoying a drink, were they not?' he said. 'Nobody else has come forward to back up your supposition that this happy evening was about to erupt into violence. That's what people do in your pub, isn't it? Have a drink, and, if the flirting spills over, they get a room. I'm sorry if that behaviour offends you, ladies and gentlemen of the jury, but it is the decade we are living in, for good or for ill.'

Next, Leonard Mcallister described finding Rupert's car near the cliffs. He was an old and cantankerous witness who clearly felt it was of little use him being there. When Sir Anthony asked him whether there were signs of a violent struggle, he shrugged and said no. 'Nor did you hear anything untoward,' the barrister said. 'An argument perhaps, some screams, the sound of a woman being battered to death. You lived less than fifty yards away, but you heard nothing.'

'That's right.'

'No further questions, your honour.'

Later, Pat Godfrey gave a tetchy statement that confirmed he had found Tom asleep in the Vauxhall Victor, but ventured nothing further.

'You had no reason to assume he had just committed the offence of murder?' Sir Anthony asked. 'Was there any blood on the defendant, for example?'

Godfrey folded his arms across his chest. 'He was drunk as a skunk, and sitting in a motor vehicle when he shouldn't have been,' he said.

'I asked you whether you had any grounds to believe the defendant had committed murder? Was there any blood on the car, for example? Could you see anything suspicious in the vehicle?'

'I weren't peeking around to be honest, just making sure he was alive. He weren't fit to drive a car, I know that.'

'Can you answer the question, Mr Godfrey?'

The witness shook his head. 'No blood as far as I can recall,' he said.

Sir Anthony dismissed the witness and said, 'Does that not strike you as strange? This man is accused of committing a violent crime in the heat of passion, and dragging the battered body into the boot of his car. And yet, nobody who saw him after the fact recalls seeing any blood on his car, or on his shoes, or on his shirt, or on his jacket. Once again, we are seeing the prosecution's wild suppositions fall down when placed under any sort of scrutiny.'

The following morning, the coroner Dr Peter Grainne stepped onto the witness stand for the prosecution and was sworn in by the usher. Mr Harris asked him about the post-mortem findings that had already made their way into the public domain through the newspapers. Meryam had been struck on the back of the head with a heavy object that had fractured her skull. Her partial skeletal remains were found scattered in several places near the lake on the Drummond estate. This was most likely caused by scavenging activity by animals. Recovery of her skull enabled identification through dental records.

Mr Harris bowed his head and took a theatrical deep breath. 'We move on now to an unspeakable act of cruelty committed by the defendant on the corpse of this young woman. We outlined in our opening statement how it seems there was an initial attempt to dispose of Miss Martin's body in the lake, and that her bowel or intestines had been pierced to remove any bloating and ensure the corpse did not float, as is usually the case after two or three days in most cases.'

'Objection, this is pure speculation,' Sir Anthony said, throwing up his hands. 'There was no bowel left, your honour.'

Mr Harris gave him a tetchy look. 'You've anticipated my next question. Mr Grainne, how do you explain this theory?'

Mr Grainne gave a pursed smile. 'We noted that several ribs had been broken and that this would indicate the individual responsible had attempted to damage the abdominal cavity.'

Under cross-examination, Sir Anthony rounded on the coroner. 'Dr Grainne, you are a Fellow of the Chartered Institute of Legal Executives,' he said, in his booming voice. 'You also have ten years' experience of being a medical doctor. You inspected the evidence and the pathology reports concerning the remains of Meryam Martin upon their discovery last year in your official capacity as Chief Coroner of the South-west.'

'I did.' Dr Grainne spoke quickly in a clipped monotone.

'And you determined that in all likelihood she had been unlawfully killed?'

'That is correct.'

'Can you explain how you came to that belief?'

'That is due to the stress fracture on the back of the skull. There had been a break or rupture in the back of the skull casing, most probably caused by a physical attack.'

'Most probably?'

'Yes, most probably,' Dr Grainne said. 'The wounds would be consistent with blunt force trauma caused by a fall from a high place or a motor vehicle accident. The fact that the body was disposed of in such a manner leads me to believe the injuries were caused by a third party.'

'But you cannot be sure of that?'

Dr Grainne raised his eyebrows. 'There are not many things in my field of which you can be one hundred per cent certain. We work in probabilities. So what I am saying to you is that to a high degree of probability the injuries Miss Martin endured were caused by a third party, most probably from a blunt object.'

Sir Anthony barely concealed his contempt. He bared his teeth in a half-smile and said, 'But the body was in such a state of decomposition, nothing other than the stress fracture to the skull gave you indications of foul play?'

'That is correct. There was not a lot to go on, I'm afraid.' Dr Grainne clasped his hands together over his lap. 'But there was considerable evidence in the form of her shattered skull.'

Sir Anthony paused and put his hand to his chin. 'The Crown has said a very strange thing, Dr Grainne. They have suggested the corpse was initially submerged in water and that it remained submerged because the body had been mutilated in such a way as to resist the accumulation of gas. Is that something you've ever come across in your career?'

'No, it is not. Well, not directly.'

'You've heard of this, though?'

'I've heard it's possible. Most bodies float, some don't. There are multiple variables. Preventing the accumulation of gas from the body would certainly be one of them.'

Sir Anthony said, 'I should imagine it would require some specialist knowledge of the human body, of the nature of decomposition, some fairly advanced biology as to what happens when a corpse is placed in water.'

'I would tend to agree with you.' Dr Grainne looked towards the prosecution bench for reassurance.

Sir Anthony said, 'Do you think a teenage boy would be equipped with such knowledge?'

'I'm not privy to the young man's learning.'

'But you can speculate as to whether you believe that would be likely? So I ask you again, you have never come across this practice in all your years of dealing with criminality, yet the Crown posits this young man would know what to do to ensure a corpse did not float? Do you think that's probable?'

Dr Grainne gave a thin smile. 'Like, I say, sir, I'm not privy to the young man's learning. I have no criteria from which to judge the probability.'

'No further questions, your honour.'

Later that afternoon, continuing to make the case for the prosecution, Mr Harris stood in front of the jury with a leather-bound notebook. 'Your honour, I'm passing before the jury for inspection three notebooks that were seized from Merryvale Manor, shortly after the defendant's arrest. These are volumes of a diary in which the defendant has made various observations about the world. There are regular entries for the years 1957 to 1959. To give you a flavour of this, on 3 August 1958, Mr Drummond writes, "Spoony opened the batting, which was always going to be a disaster. I told Parker he'd be out in the first over, and he was. I scored 34, quite respectable seeing as I hadn't played all summer." And in another entry, on 2 January 1958, he writes, "Top rate NYE party. Snogged Celia, but she wouldn't go any further and told me to leave. Kicked up a stink at first, but went back to Checks and drank with the boys until dawn. Played a little poker."'

Mr Harris sighed as he flicked through the pages. 'It goes on like that, fairly regularly, sometimes daily, at least three or four times a week. Month after month, year after year. The defendant records his boyish exploits, nothing we need to bother ourselves with here, but then, well, there finally is something of interest.'

Sir Anthony stood. 'Your honour, I object to this...'

The judge considered a moment. 'I will allow Mr Harris to continue.'

'Thank you, your honour,' the prosecution lawyer said. 'I was saying that, amid the defendant's banal observations, we finally come to something interesting: the arrival of Meryam Martin. Here, in full, is an entry from 24 June 1959. This is what Mr Drummond felt inclined to write. "I am wrestling with intense feelings over M. She's not a beauty by any means, but she makes me faint with desire. We went swimming this afternoon, and I was on the shore watching her walk down to the water's edge in a two-piece, and I had to put a towel over my lap. She thinks I'm some sort of dunce too. Maybe because I seem to lose the ability to speak when she's near. Had a dream I was sitting astride her. She was lying down on her front and I was licking the back of her neck. Strange or what?"'

'Your honour, I am afraid I have to raise another objection,' Sir Anthony said.

The judge shook his head. 'I will allow the line of questioning to continue. These are the direct thoughts of the defendant on the victim. The jury should hear them.'

'Thank you, your honour,' said Mr Harris. 'We move on a few days. The entry reads, "Life goes on. Meryam goes on. Torture goes on. I think I need to get away from her and go back to Cambridge early. Never have I jacked off so many times in a week."'

There was a murmur of laughter from the public gallery. Eva tutted and turned to look at her husband, who stared impassively ahead. Tom sat perfectly still with his hands on his thighs.

'And that is that, members of the jury,' Mr Harris said, the hint of a smile on his lips. 'There are no further mentions of Meryam Martin. In fact, after the last night Miss Martin spent alive in the company of the defendant, he never wrote another entry.' The QC thumbed open the notebook. 'Not a word. It seems after that night Tom Drummond gave up all pretence of being the next Samuel Pepys. He put down his pen and didn't divulge any more thoughts. Now, we know that he saw this young woman as an object of desire. We know he was quite infatuated with her. He spends more than nine drunken hours in her company, hours of which remain unaccounted for. And yet, and yet, ladies and gentlemen of the jury, he never mentions her again. Even stranger, he decides that fateful night is the cut-off point for writing anything at all. It is up to you to draw your own conclusions as to why that might be.'

Tom took to the witness stand and was sworn in. He shifted his weight from one foot to the other.

Sir Anthony said, 'Mr Drummond, you were attracted to Meryam Martin, is that right?'

'Yes, sir.'

'You were how old?'

'I turned seventeen that summer, sir.'

'Do you remember being attracted to many young women at that time of life?'

'Yes.'

'Miss Martin in particular?'

'I wouldn't say in particular. It was a long summer.'

'Did you ever overstep the mark? Do anything to make her feel threatened?'

'No, sir.'

'Did she ever spurn your advances?'

'No, sir.'

'Did you ever – excuse my language, your honour – jack off when thinking about her?'

Tom nodded. There was laughter from the public gallery. The judge grimaced, but said nothing.

Sir Anthony said, 'Is that a yes, Mr Drummond?'

'That's a yes, sir.'

'Do you understand that to be a crime under this jurisdiction?'

'No, sir.'

'That is because it certainly is not. Why did you stop writing about Meryam Martin in your diary?'

'She went away. There was nothing more to say about her. I was ashamed. I had got drunk. It was not my finest hour.'

'But in no way did you harm Miss Martin?'

'No, sir.'

Sir Anthony let the exchange sink in with the jury, then he said, 'We're now going to go over the night Miss Martin left Merryvale Manor. The prosecution has laid out an account of that night, which is based largely on the testimony of three witnesses: one who saw you at the pub, another who saw your father's parked car at the cliffs, and then, finally, another man who saw you asleep in the car in a lay-by later that morning. There are quite a few gaps, so let us start at the beginning. You agreed to take Miss Martin to the railway station. You changed your mind and went to the pub. Why was that?'

Tom took a deep breath and began to speak in a clear and confident tone. 'That was my fault. I was bored that summer, and

Miss Martin was charming and funny. I thought it would be fun to drink with her and talk to her a little. We hadn't had much opportunity, you see.'

Sir Anthony said, 'You got on well, didn't you?'

Tom nodded. 'We talked about what we wanted out of life. She made me feel quite humble, and she made me think about a lot of things I was doing wrong, and about my assumptions. Nobody had really talked to me like that before.'

Sir Anthony said, 'You then had sexual intercourse with Miss Martin after taking a room at the pub?'

'That's correct, sir.'

'On whose instigation?'

Tom paused. 'Well, it was just… I suppose it was me. I said to her, "They have rooms here, you know?" And she said something like, "Well, you have the money, not me," and so I went and asked about availability, and then we were there in the room and one thing led to another.'

Sir Anthony took a few paces towards the dock. 'You left the room later that evening. Why did you leave the pub? Why not just go to sleep?'

Tom said, 'Miss Martin became animated. She asked me to drive her back to Merryvale because my father owed her money. We left the room and went to the car, but I knew I couldn't turn up back at the house with Meryam. That would have been unacceptable to my parents.'

Sir Anthony stood in front of Tom, his finger stroking his beard. 'What did you choose to do?'

Tom said, 'The plan was to get something to eat and sober up, but nobody was serving food. We drove to Lulworth. It's a place I know well, so I thought I'd show it to her. She said she loved the sea.'

Sir Anthony scanned his notes. 'What happened next, Mr Drummond?'

Tom took a deep breath and glanced up at the public gallery. 'It's all a bit of a blur, I'm ashamed to say,' he said. 'We sat by the cliff and looked out to sea. We drank some more, smoked some cigarettes. I think I must have passed out. When I woke, it was in the early hours of the morning and I couldn't see Meryam. I panicked because I thought she might have fallen, so I started calling her name, and I scrambled up the hill towards the car. That's when I saw her. She was trying to open the driver's door, but it was locked. She was very insistent in asking me to drive her back to Merryvale. In the end, I just agreed.'

Sir Anthony said, 'Why did you stop in the lay-by on the A515? You were only three miles from home.'

'I thought I was going to cause an accident,' Tom said. 'I was falling asleep at the wheel. I told Meryam I needed twenty minutes to shut my eyes and then we would be on our way. She seemed OK with that, but, when the lorry driver woke me up, Meryam had gone.'

'And did you see Miss Martin again?'

'I did not.'

'And you have no idea what happened to her?'

'I do not. I presumed she had found a lift back to London. Quite frankly, I didn't give it much thought.'

'What happened when you got home?'

Tom hesitated.

Sir Anthony prompted him. 'Was anybody home?'

'My parents had been very worried,' Tom said. 'They had taken my mother's car out to look for me. The rest of the household was asleep, as far as I could tell. It was just before dawn, a faint light, a few birds stirring. I knew I was in deep trouble. I wanted to lock myself away in my bedroom and never come out.'

'Did anyone see you return home?'

'I believe the housekeeper Mrs Kinney may have seen me.'

'You have sworn an oath on the Bible before this court. Did you in any way harm Miss Martin that night?'

'I did not.'

'Mr Drummond, are you responsible for the murder of Miss Martin?'

Tom shook his head. 'I am not.'

'No more questions,' Sir Anthony said.

That night, from my hotel room, I called Clara at Dove Close. She answered in the clipped 'Hello' she only used when answering the telephone.

'I don't know why you do that,' I said, smiling.

'My telephone voice? I don't know either. It just sort of brings it out of me.' She laughed.

'How's George?' I said.

'You don't want to know about George,' she replied. 'He's perfectly fine, as always.'

'And you?'

'I'm fine. I've been following the trial, of course.' In the background, the Rolling Stones blasted from a record player.

'Have you got people round?' I said.

'Just a few. I'll probably have to go soon.'

I hesitated. 'I just wanted to ask you something.'

'Go ahead.' Someone called her name.

'It's just... what would you do if you knew something about somebody that could either be very damning, or it could be entirely explainable, and of no consequence at all? Would you just say it anyway and be damned with the consequences?'

There was a pause on the line. Clara called out to somebody that she would be there in a minute.

'Clara?'

'Sorry, yes, I was thinking. Look, I don't know why you'd want my advice, but whatever it is, of course you need to say it in court. It's not for you to play judge and jury.'

Chapter 31

By the fourth week of the trial, everybody was exhausted and our nerves were shot to pieces. My aunt and uncle had paid for me to stay in a five-star hotel set near the northern bank of the River Thames, a short walk from St Paul's Cathedral. My morning routine was to join them at eight for breakfast. Over a boiled egg, a slice of brown toast and a black coffee, we would dissect the previous day's proceedings, and anticipate what was to come. 'There's a young man on the jury with a rat's face,' my uncle would say. 'I believe he's got it in for Tom. I keep looking at him.' And Eva would roll her eyes and tell him to stop trying to predict what everybody was thinking. 'The outcome will not rest on whether a man resembles a rat, darling,' she said. After breakfast, we walked through narrow streets, passing the livery halls and guilds of the city's merchant past, until we arrived at the familiar dome of the Old Bailey, with the gold-leaf figure of Lady Justice on top.

On the second day of the fourth week, I was called as a character witness. Sir Anthony, also looking more ragged and red-faced than he had a month ago, explored my relationship with Tom. I said he had been a rather intimidating presence when I first joined the family as a timid teenager, but over the years we had grown as close as brothers. I told the court Tom was generous with his time, loyal and warm-hearted.

'This is a young man,' Sir Anthony concluded, 'with no previous convictions or cautions and no allegations of reprehensible behaviour. A brother, a friend, a son. It beggars belief, does it not, that Tom Drummond was capable of concealing another character, something monstrous and dark?'

As he cross-examined me, Mr Harris stepped close to the witness box, hands folded behind his back. 'Now, Mr Butler, what I am going to ask you next is really rather crucial,' he said. 'We know the defendant went on a night of excess with Miss Martin. She was never seen again until her remains surfaced at Merryvale Manor, years later. Tom, however, *was* seen again. He returned to Merryvale in the early hours of the morning. You had the attic bedroom directly above his on the third floor, is that correct?'

'That's correct.'

'You must have been aware that he had gone missing and that his parents were incredibly worried. Did you see or hear anything unusual? Did you, perhaps, hear him return home?'

I shook my head.

'Please give me a verbal answer, Mr Butler.'

'I don't recall,' I said.

The barrister gave me a quizzical look. 'I'm sorry, can you clarify?'

Tom closed his eyes and waited for my next words. The trial was finely balanced. The prosecution case was circumstantial, but the fact remained, Tom had been the last known person to see Meryam alive. I had witnessed some of the jurors look at him with contempt, this spoiled young man who had been handed everything on a plate, but who had tossed the plate away.

I took a deep breath.

The doors of the public gallery swung open. Natasha, dressed in a navy-blue suit and sporting a pair of dark glasses, looked briefly around the courtroom, then took a seat next to her parents.

Mr Harris said, with a little irritation, 'Are you all right? I asked you a simple question. Were you aware of the defendant coming home?'

If the Drummonds hadn't adopted me, I would have become a junior clerk at an accountants' in Holborn, married to a vaguely unhappy woman called Wilma or Mary, and we'd have lived in Ealing and gone to the pictures on Saturday afternoons. We'd probably have had two kids, perhaps raised enough money to move further out into the suburbs. I would have lived the life of my mother.

'I was not aware of Tom coming home,' I said. 'I'm a heavy sleeper.'

Mr Harris said, 'When did you next see the defendant?'

'I don't remember exactly. I believe it would have been the following afternoon, when he had slept it off. I don't remember anything unusual about his demeanour.'

Mr Harris gave me a puzzled look. When he addressed me again, he spoke in a raised voice. 'Mr Butler, it is the Crown's contention that your cousin Tom had just perpetrated a grave crime. He had killed a young woman and disposed of her body. Are you seriously telling this court you noticed nothing unusual in his demeanour?'

Tom lifted his head from his hands and looked at me with defeated eyes. He shook his head slowly.

I glanced at the Drummonds in the public gallery. Natasha gave the slightest nod of her head and offered a weak smile.

'There was nothing strange about his demeanour. I can only presume, sir, that he had not committed the offence for which he's charged.'

Mr Harris frowned. 'I didn't ask you to speculate. You do know that the wilful and intentional act of withholding information under oath is an indictable offence?'

'I do.'

'You do understand that if the Crown Prosecution Service considers you to be committing an act of perjury that potentially changes the material outcome of this case, you may face charges?'

'I completely understand.'

'So, I will ask you again. Was there anything about Tom Drummond's behaviour the following afternoon, or in the ensuing days, that raised your suspicions? Anything he said to you? Anything he did that you would deem unusual? Did he make any unexpected trips to the lake?'

'Nothing at all, sir.'

I experienced an unexpected release of all tension. What I had seen and heard in the attic five years ago was not enough evidence to ruin a man's life. I had done my bit, and damn the consequences.

Chapter 32

Sir Anthony got to his feet and adjusted his wig. He approached the jury and said, 'Ladies and gentlemen, you may be forgiven for wondering just why you have spent so many weeks in this esteemed courthouse. What the prosecution have laid before you in evidence can variably be described as flimsy, insubstantial and derisory. This young man standing before you in the dock has been charged with the most heinous of crimes. The Crown now turns to you and asks you to make a very serious decision, one that will put him in prison for a very long time. They should not ask you to make such a decision lightly; in fact, they should send you into the jury room convinced, beyond reasonable doubt, that Mr Drummond was guilty of the crime of murder. It must be no doubt apparent to you by now that the Crown has failed to do so.

'We are here to judge the case against the defendant. We know Tom Drummond was tasked with driving Miss Martin to the railway station to catch a train to London. The pair, no doubt attracted to each other and being young and impetuous, stopped off at a pub and got drunk. They then hired a room, and, as Tom Drummond has testified under oath, they had consensual sex. Remember, ladies and gentlemen, you are not judging the morality of the young man in the dock. He is, by his own admission, short of the maturity he no doubt will one day find. You are judging him on what the Crown claims happened immediately after their consensual encounter. In order to prove a case, it is incumbent on the prosecution to determine means, motive and opportunity.

'Let's take the first of these. By what means did this young woman meet her demise? The simple truth is that the Crown does not know. She suffered head injuries, that much is clear, but there is some degree of doubt as to whether or not these injuries were necessarily inflicted by a third party. You have heard from Dr Grainne that it would be possible for somebody to fall backward, perhaps landing on rocks, and do damage to the back of the skull such that it would be indistinguishable from a third party exerting force. A car accident, he said, would cause similar damage. Is it so beyond the realms of possibility that this young woman, inebriated and confused, attempted to make her way back to the vicarage where she had been staying and fell foul of a grotesque accident, one that left her concussed, wounded, desperate? The answer is no, it is not impossible.

'Secondly, what opportunity did this young man have to commit such an act? There are no witnesses to any such violence. In fact, during the course of the evening in question, nobody saw evidence of any anger or frustration. Nobody has witnessed anything other than two young people enjoying each other's company.

'Which brings me on to the third area of proof that the Crown must establish, and this is an area they've simply neglected in every way. Why? What possible reason did this young man have to attack and kill Meryam Martin? He is a man with everything to live for, a man blessed with the fortuitous combination of wealth and privilege. Why would he throw all that away? You have seen him on the stand. This young man is not of psychopathic bent; he is of an articulate and generous nature. Character testimonies have confirmed this.

'The Crown has attempted to batter Mr Drummond's character, but nothing sticks. He stopped writing a diary, like any teenage boy who scribbles away one minute and then drops it like a stone the next, and this is somehow meant to indicate his capacity for murder.

'We have heard from his best friend, his cousin, Benjamin, who attests to the defendant acting quite normally in the days, weeks and months following the night in question. Do you reasonably believe, beyond any reasonable doubt, that the young man before you carried out a savage attack, and then went on living his life as if nothing had happened, knowing full well there was the body of a woman concealed in a shallow grave on his father's estate? You have heard of his character from dozens of people – his tutors at Cambridge, his sports coach, his peers – and do they, or do they not, all attest to Mr Drummond being an amiable and generous young man who has never shown the slightest hint of violence?

'I will say to you once more, this is a grave responsibility you bear, and you must judge each piece of evidence laid before you, but the evidence you have seen is entirely circumstantial, and I'm afraid that is the weakest type of proof a prosecution can offer. I will urge you not to end this young man's life on a story concocted only with this type of evidence. It would be a gross dereliction of duty.

'Finally, let's not forget the victim here. Miss Martin was, by all accounts, a vivacious and alluring young woman who captured the hearts of those she came across. Her premature death is a tragedy, and yet the cause of that death remains a mystery. I hope, and you may cherish that hope too, that one day the true account of what happened to Miss Martin that night will emerge. Until that day, I'm afraid you have no choice but to find the accused not guilty of her murder.'

The barrister turned away from the jury with a flourish and sat back down.

The judge put on his spectacles and said, 'Ladies and gentlemen of the jury, I would first like to thank you for the impeccable attention and patience you have demonstrated throughout this trial. It is not often the son of a prominent Member of Parliament finds himself charged with such a grave offence. The interest from the media has been intense, and will continue to be so over the coming weeks and, dare I say, months. The fortitude you have demonstrated during these four weeks will no doubt be necessary to lean upon once more. I am going to ask the bailiff to take you to the jury room to consider your verdict. I will require a unanimous verdict in this case.'

Outside court number one, I sat on a bench in the corridor with Natasha, drinking a tepid cup of coffee from a plastic cup. From time to time, a member of the defence team came to update us. The jury were still deliberating, they explained. They had asked for several clarifications from the judge. No, they did not know whether that was a good or bad sign.

'It's going to be all right,' I said, but that's all I had to say, a simple banality. I didn't think things were going to be all right at all.

'Tremendous to know everything's going to be hunky-dory,' Natasha said, deadpan. 'Have you nobbled the jury?' She tapped her foot impatiently.

Eva came striding down the corridor, waving her arms. 'We're being called back in.'

Natasha dabbed her eyes with a handkerchief. 'Whatever happens, when all this is over, please come home.'

We hurried back to court number one. Tom was already standing in the dock, his head bowed, his hands clasped behind his back. Two of the female jurors, I noticed, were in tears. Reporters with their notepads poised were getting ready to run from the courtroom and phone through their copy to the news desks.

The clerk ordered the court to rise and the judge entered the courtroom. He took up his seat, removed his glasses and poured himself a glass of water from a decanter. Then he told us to sit.

'Ladies and gentlemen of the jury,' he said. 'I thank you wholeheartedly for your diligence in pursuing justice. You have gone about your task with attentive minds and open hearts. You understand the faith this great court puts in you, and now you find yourself nearing the time when you can be free citizens again.'

Tom closed his eyes and rocked back and forth on his heels.

The judge continued, 'You have given me a series of questions on which you have asked for clarity. I have tried to do my best to answer these in open court. You have asked me to define "reasonable doubt". You have questioned whether you can opt for an alternative charge; you cannot. You have asked me whether speculation and the fanfare around this case can be factored into your decision-making. They cannot.

'There is a simple decision at the heart of this case. Do you feel the prosecution has convinced you, beyond any reasonable doubt, that the defendant murdered Meryam Martin and then disposed of her body to cover up the fact? If you are not convinced beyond reasonable doubt, then you cannot deliver a guilty verdict. I have tried to give you sound direction, as permitted under the law. Presiding juror, can you confirm you have reached a unanimous verdict?'

The woman with her white hair tied in a grey bun stood up. Her shaking hand held a notepad. 'I cannot, your honour,' she said.

'Do you feel confident you can reach a verdict if I grant you more time for deliberation?'

The woman shook her head. 'We're a long way off, I'm sorry to say.'

The judge removed his spectacles and placed them on the lectern. 'If I were to accept a ten to two verdict, would that materially change things?'

'It would not, your honour.'

The judge said, 'Mr Thomas Drummond, the jury has failed to reach a verdict, and therefore this trial concludes, albeit without a verdict. You are free to leave the court. Mr Harris, it will be up to the Crown to decide whether to lodge an application for a retrial. You have a month, as you are no doubt aware.'

The courtroom exploded with noise. Natasha threw her arms round me and hugged me tight. There were gasps and cheers from the public gallery. Eva covered her face with her hands. Reporters ran for the exit doors. The judge called for order. Someone shouted, 'Rot in hell, you piece of shit.'

In the midst of the chaos stood Tom Drummond. He lifted his gaze towards the public gallery. I held Natasha close. She had buried her head in my chest and was weeping. When Tom saw me, the faintest of smiles appeared on his lips. He put his fingers to his mouth and blew a silent kiss.

Act V

Chapter 33

A month later, the family flew to Tenerife, escaping the media scrum camped outside Merryvale Manor for the gentle rhythms of life in Santa Cruz. On the terrace of the Hotel Borges Castillo, the day would begin with pastries filled with custard and whipped cream, which we dipped in sweet black coffee. After breakfast, Tom and I ventured into the mountains where the moisture-laden clouds bathed the landscape in a cool mist. We took winding paths past tangled laurel trees and agave plants that sprung up like prehistoric crocuses. If you looked closely enough, you could spot lizards basking on the black rocks. From time to time, we came across small farms where workers tended to sweet potatoes, yams and fruit trees. At the summit, we smoked cigarettes and looked down with awe at the minty blue of the ocean and the whitewashed villas that lined the craggy coastline. We always made sure we arrived back in time to join the rest of the family on the terrace for lunch. Under the shade of a white umbrella, we drank ice-cold white Rioja as we mopped up tapas dishes of salty cheese and garlicky chorizo with loaves of warm bread.

Most afternoons, Rupert and Eva retired for a two-hour siesta, while Natasha and I preferred to read du Maurier and Agatha Christie paperbacks on sun loungers by the pool. She read passages from her books out loud as she massaged suncream into my back and shoulders. She was like the Natasha of old: quick-witted, warm and sensuous. Away from Merryvale, from the baggage of her school expulsion and the catastrophe of her short-lived marriage, she recovered the lightness of being that had marked her out as special. As the strength of my feelings returned, I too felt high on the sun, serotonin and hormones.

Tom kept himself to himself, preferring to spend the afternoons walking through the city. He returned by eight to join us in the restaurant for supper, and would tell stories about the museum he had explored that traced the influence of Freemasonry on the city, or the unusual church he had found with five naves. Since the conclusion of the trial, he was sometimes withdrawn and tetchy. When mildly pressed by Eva to 'cheer up' or 'at least show us that lovely smile', he would erupt into a tantrum that could last for hours. At night, he put on his velvet smoking jacket and spit-polished shoes, and sat in front of the mirror sweeping his hair into a side parting. Then he went out without a word, only to return in the early hours, stinking of tobacco and red wine, and sometimes something more potent.

We shared a suite on the top floor of the hotel, with a balcony that overlooked the harbour. One morning, we were smoking and looking down at the yachts tied up on the waterfront. Tom, who was dressed in a vest and a pair of underpants, leaned back in his chair and rested his bare feet on the balustrade. 'Seems we've all moved on, doesn't it?' he said, flicking a trail of ash into a potted cactus at his feet. 'Keep calm and have another bloody sangria.'

'Everyone just needs a holiday,' I said, feeling the faint breeze on my arms. Every morning, the trade winds swept a cooling cloud bank in off the Atlantic.

'Let me ask you a straight question,' Tom said.

'Of course.'

He flicked the smouldering butt over the balcony. 'Why *did* you do it?'

'What?'

'I have a few theories,' he said, warming to his theme. 'Firstly, you genuinely believe I'm innocent, which is very sweet of you, but if that's the case, then, I still thought you'd probably tell the jury everything you knew and leave justice to take its course. You've inherited your mother's little Church of England morality, you see. I was certain you were going to blurt it out when you took the stand. So, I'm not certain about theory one, not certain at all. Theory two is more convincing. It goes like this. You found your exile from Merryvale to be intolerable. You suddenly felt unwelcome in the place you call home. You felt deprived of Eva's affections. So, you lied in court to win back their affections and be welcomed back to Merryvale.' He paused to drag on his cigarette. 'Theory three is an extension of theory two. Theory three says Mother went a bit further, and did something really mean to twist your arm, something financial, perhaps?' He waved his index finger in the air. 'They cut off your college fund. That's it, isn't it?'

'You don't sound very grateful,' I said, swallowing back a lump in my throat.

'I'm just curious,' he said, closing his eyes and appreciating the heat of the sun as it emerged from behind a cloud. 'I have a fourth theory, too. Do you want to know?'

'Go on,' I urged.

He opened his eyes and pointed a deliberate finger at me. 'You know who did it; therefore you know it can't be me.'

'That's ridiculous.'

Tom stretched his arms above his head and let out an exaggerated yawn. 'Shall we go up the mountain? It seems to be the only place I can think straight.'

We took our now familiar route through the streets of Santa Cruz to a run-down taverna on the periphery of the town where the trail started. A pair of stray dogs sniffed at our legs, until Tom frightened them away with a dramatic roar. We passed a young hiking couple who had made the summit for sunrise. Tom led the way, nimbly scrambling over rocks for the initial ascent, before the path evened out and became more manageable. The heat slowed my progress, and I had to stop several times for water breaks, wiping the sweat from my brow with the arm of my T-shirt. Tom became a small figure in the distance, driving himself forward. When I reached the summit, he was sitting cross-legged on a rock ledge, staring out to sea. A hundred feet below him, the ocean was a shimmering expanse of blue and green. He motioned for me to join him. 'Sit. There's something I want to tell you,' he said.

I sat beside him. The waves crashed on the rocks below. The air seemed to throb and vibrate in the heat. The crickets chirped.

Tom said, 'I'm sorry for teasing you, back at the hotel. I haven't thanked you for what you did, and partly it's because I know my parents put intolerable pressure on you, and that's not what I would have wanted. I don't want to inherit that sort of power from them. I don't want to inherit anything from them.'

I had been alarmed by his change in mood since we had arrived. He had been mean-spirited with a dollop of self-pity and a smouldering anger, but, up on the mountain, he was reflective and sad.

'Let me tell you something about Rupert,' he said, and with a wistful smile and a shake of the head, he went on, 'he brought Meryam into the household as his personal plaything. He was paying her to sleep with him. She told me all about it.' He snorted in disgust. 'Revolting, isn't it? The thing is, he's stuck in the conservatism of his era when all he ever really wanted to do was embrace the beatniks and go and get laid. Instead, he has to keep going down to Westminster and meeting his constituents and putting on dinner parties and garden tea dances, and all the time he's got Mother watching him like a hawk. I think it all just drove him quite mad, and bringing Meryam into the home was an act of gross insubordination, equivalent perhaps to Profumo. He thought, *if that old fruit can screw Keeler, then I can go one better.* I think he probably *wanted* the world to know. The headlines would redress his growing feelings of emasculation.'

'Step back from the edge a little,' I said, feeling a wave of nausea in my stomach.

Tom breathed in through his nostrils. 'There's nothing to be frightened of up here.' He got on to all fours and inched a little further to the edge. 'Imagine those last moments. Would you have time to have any thought at all?'

I reached for his hand, but he waved it away. 'We should get back for lunch.'

Tom stood up, held his arms aloft and swung them in full circles. 'Yes, lunch, of course. That's how we measure out our lives. Then there will be supper, and the day ends, and then the same day will begin again.' He turned to face me. 'Do you ever think you were better off out of it? That your banishment was a lucky escape?'

I shook my head.

'Well, I need to get away for my sanity. There are a few people I've met during my late-night excursions. There's a biker called Pascal who has a cottage in Andalusia. Right at the foot of the Costa Blanca. I'm done with all this; I'm done with Cambridge. It's disgusting, don't you think, all this wallowing in privilege, like pigs in shit?'

'Tom the radical now?'

'The world has changed, and I feel as if I'm watching from the sidelines, waiting to be swept away, but I'm not going to wait around and let that happen.' He was close to the edge again.

I stood up and made a small movement towards him. 'Move away from the edge – you're scaring me.'

Tom knelt down by his rucksack and pulled out a letter. He handed it to me. It was from his lawyer. The Crown was pursuing a retrial.

He said, 'I really can't do it all again. I think I'd rather jump off this cliff.'

'Oh Tom, if you run—'

'They'll think I'm guilty. So be it. Everyone does anyway.'

'That's not true,' I said, feebly.

'Really? I don't even think you're sure.' He puffed out his cheeks. 'Come on, let's go and have lunch,' he said, jumping off the boulder onto the mountain path. 'You know how Eva's a stickler for punctuality.'

Chapter 34

Rupert had slung a wreath of flowers over his neck and was attempting to cajole Eva and a pair of terrified German tourists into a conga around the courtyard. In one corner, three young Spanish guys with timples and castanets played a frantic Canarian folk song. Some of the locals clapped their hands and stamped their feet.

'My son,' Rupert shouted in the ear of the German woman, 'is a free man. We're celebrating the delicious taste of a future restored. Excuse my mixed metaphors, I'm thoroughly pissed.' He patted the German on the back and resumed dancing, his arms up above his waist, his big arse jutting out. Eva, bronzed and rested, shimmered in front of him in a black cocktail dress. Every now and then, she beckoned furiously for us to join them, but Natasha, Tom and I remained at the table, finishing off a large jug of tinto de verano.

Tom had waited until the right moment over dinner to inform his parents about the retrial, but the right moment had never come, and now he was forced to endure the spontaneous celebration of a false dawn. He pulled the collar of his shirt up and slumped back in his chair. In a year's time, he was due back in court number one.

Natasha rested her chin on her hand and gazed at me across the table. She had put on a little weight and her complexion, tanned and moisturised, was blemish-free for the first time in months. 'We'll just pretend they're not with us,' she said, with an open smile.

She had been filling me in on the state of her marriage. 'I realised down in Cornwall on our honeymoon that I'd made a total mess of everything. I know this sounds ridiculous, but when he came out of the bathroom with a towel round his waist, I just knew. He had a very hairless pink chest and a perfectly smooth round belly. It struck me he looked like a bar of soap. It's hard to get particularly excited about getting into bed with a piece of soap.

'I told him then and there that I was having second thoughts. You know me, I can't deny my feelings when they come calling. Just as I said that, his towel dropped to the floor. It must have been terribly humiliating for him. He didn't know whether I was being serious at first; he sort of laughed in shock, but his expression soon turned to a sneer and then full-blown contempt. He just turned and went back into the bathroom. The last I saw of him that night was his little pink bottom, which was also perfectly round. Anyway, he's filed for divorce. Someone told me he has moved into a house in Dorchester with a girl called Veronica who looks like a hamster.' She paused to knock back her drink. 'Can you believe what a mess I've made of all this?'

'It's not as if you weren't forewarned,' I said, flatly. There was something vulgar about Natasha's delivery; perhaps it was because she appeared on some level to revel in the chaos she had caused. I realised, perhaps for the first time, that I just wanted her to stop.

Rupert and Eva shepherded the sheepish-looking German couple towards the table. 'This is Gay-ord – am I saying that right?' my uncle said, having to shout over the music. 'Gay-org? That must be Kraut for George, is it, old chap? George would be simpler. This is George, he's an estate agent. And his charming wife Ursula writes for a consumer magazine, darling. I thought you might want some tips about getting into the industry.' He put a hand on Natasha's bare shoulder. 'My daughter here,' he said to

Ursula, 'has a new ambition every week, but lacks the motivation to see anything through.'

Natasha gritted her teeth and mouthed, 'Help,' in my direction.

Eva said, with a twinkle in her eye, 'Last year, she got married for all of two days.'

Rupert let out a wheezy laugh. 'Twice the adult lifespan of a mayfly.'

Georg and Ursula exchanged an uneasy glance.

Rupert recovered his composure and, to nobody in particular, said, 'It was a good bash, though. The Prime Minister was on the guest list.'

'As Daddy was saying,' Eva said to Natasha, 'Ursula writes features for a consumer magazine in Mainz.'

Natasha flashed a facetious smile. 'That's awfully kind of you to come over, Ursula, but I'm not planning on writing for a consumer magazine,' she said.

I felt a sudden sharp stab of longing for Clara. I should have visited her parents' home and marvelled at her old man's train set in the attic. Made love in the single bed in her childhood bedroom. Sat in normal pubs with normal, decent people on Swindon High Street. But it was all too late.

Eva had drawn up a chair and lit a cigarette. 'Why are you so crabby?' she said to Tom. 'You have a face like a slapped fish.'

Tom groaned, shifted forward in his seat and rapped the table with his knuckles. 'Mother, Father, there's something you need to know,' he said. 'Nat, you too. Ursula, Georg, you're more than welcome to hear my news too. Anybody else?' He gave an exaggerated look around the courtyard.

Rupert's smile vanished; he held the back of Eva's chair.

'Your little dance was premature, I'm afraid,' Tom said. 'I'm to face a retrial.'

Eva's hand shot to her mouth.

Natasha's face crumpled. 'The bastards,' she said, with a whimper. 'They can't do that. How can they do that when there's no evidence?'

'Christ,' Rupert muttered, placing a palm on his chest. He was still wearing a flowery wreath one of the musicians had placed over his head. 'Not sure my heart can take much more of this.'

'You must telephone Channing tonight,' Eva said to Rupert. 'He'll need to issue a statement in the morning, expressing our grave disappointment at the decision.' She clapped her hands together and said, 'Children, look at your glum faces. We carry on, that's what we do.'

Later that night, I emerged from the bathroom to find Tom shoving items of clothing into a rucksack. He zipped it closed and swung it over his back. 'You can keep the rest of my stuff. You don't need much here to get by, do you? I think that's why I feel so alive out here. Everything's stripped back.'

We hugged.

Tom stood there, impossibly handsome, but with tired red eyes and a weary, half-hearted smile. For a brief moment, I thought he was going to be just fine, whatever choices he made.

I went to speak, but he held his middle finger to my lips. 'It's done now. It's over,' he said softly. Then he opened the door and peered into the corridor. 'I'll get going. Tell Mother I'm sorry, but she won't be hearing from me again. I know she's done her best. Tell sis this is for the best – she'll understand – and you can tell Rupert whatever the hell you like.' Halfway down the corridor, he stopped, turned around and flashed his marvellous white smile. 'Go back inside now, Ben. Try to live a good life,' he said.

That night, I lay on the bed, unable to sleep. Sir Anthony's summing-up played over and over in my mind. *It beggars belief, does it not, that Tom Drummond was capable of concealing another character, something monstrous and dark?*

Chapter 35

Only a small party awaited us on the front porch of Merryvale Manor when we arrived home on a damp Tuesday afternoon. Mrs Kinney stood in her white apron and black uniform, hands clasped behind her back, her grey hair tied back into a neat bun. Next to her stood Cresswell in his walking boots and green dungarees. Bess, now old and half-blind, was curled up at his feet. When she saw me, she shuffled forward and made a whelp of pleasure.

Mrs Kinney was in an agitated mood as we followed her into the entrance hallway. There were many issues to sort out, she explained, not least the fact that the new cook had departed at the end of the month and the cellar was empty. A spring-clean was needed, she said. The rats from the woodshed had started to encroach into the kitchens. A layer of rust had formed on Alphonse's suit of armour, the curtains gave off a musty, stale smell, and stains peppered the carpet in the salon.

'Mrs Kinney, we will go through your considerable to-do list one item at a time,' Eva said. 'But first we really must have a pot of tea and some toast and marmalade. I'm sure we don't need a cook for that.'

'Marvellous to be back,' Rupert said, without emotion.

Natasha said, 'I would love a chocolate biscuit with my tea.'

'We've had the reporters bothering us, all over the village,' Mrs Kinney said. 'We've had nobody running the budget.'

'Yes, yes, it must have been positively awful,' Eva said. 'I promise we'll get everything shipshape soon enough. Right now, we're welcoming Benjamin back home for the first time in a long time.'

Mrs Kinney said, 'And Master Tom?'

'He's extended his holiday,' Rupert said.

Mrs Kinney rolled her eyes. 'Does his bedsheets need changing, then?'

Eva said, 'Yes, Mrs Kinney, proceed as you would. He'll be home with us soon enough.'

Natasha's fingertips touched mine. 'I'm so glad you're back with us at Merryvale,' she said in my ear. 'I missed you awfully.'

Rupert poked his head into the dining room and then reappeared. 'May I ask, dear Mrs Kinney,' he said, 'do you happen to know the whereabouts of my brother?'

'He's in the salon, sir.'

Rupert tapped my shoulder. 'Benjamin, I'd like you to come with me.'

In the salon, Channing rose from an armchair and rubbed at the heavy bags under his eyes. His silk dressing gown had fallen open, revealing a rug of dark chest hair. A cloud of body odour followed him across the room.

'You look a shambles, man,' Rupert said, wrinkling his nose.

'And you have presided over one,' Channing said. 'Hope your days in the sun were worth it.'

'The fish was good,' Rupert said, defensively. 'Gambas as large as your arm.'

'Reassuring to hear you enjoyed the fish.'

'The cheese as well,' Rupert said. 'Just how bad is it?'

'The boy has a scheduled court appearance on Thursday to set a date for the new trial. If he fails to appear, the judge is likely to issue an arrest order.' He went to the drinks cabinet and unscrewed a bottle of Scotch. 'Anyone?'

Rupert massaged his temples in a circular motion. 'Tom's been under considerable strain. He'll come to his senses.'

Channing poured generous splashes of Scotch into three tumblers, then handed a glass each to me and Rupert. We stood facing each other. The room was cold and musty and there were no logs in the fireplace.

Channing had a pinched expression. 'If you're back, you'd better make yourself useful. Firstly, we need the low-down on Tom. Do you know where he was going?'

'He didn't say,' I replied.

'You've turned lying into an art form,' Channing said, with a snort of derision. 'Did he indicate his intentions?'

'He mentioned mainland Spain, among lots of places. Cuba, for example.'

'My children,' Rupert said, shaking his head, 'are going to get me fucking deselected.'

Channing said, 'While you've been topping up your tan, I've been putting out fires everywhere. The vicar has started a petition in the village calling for a by-election. Someone has emptied a bucket of red paint over the front gates for three nights in a row. Simon Wingfield has used his newspaper column to call on you to hold a candlelit vigil by the lake in memory of Meryam. It's not going away, brother.'

Rupert knocked back his drink. 'Bad blood is certainly brewing,' he said, balefully. 'Even the *fucking vicar*. The amount of wine from my cellar he's drunk... the gall of the man. Perhaps we should host another open-house day, and bring all the villagers in for tea and cake. Show them there is a new start at Merryvale, and we're going to do things differently.'

'These people despise us,' Channing said.

'Now, I don't think that's true,' a chastened Rupert said, jutting out his chin. 'We just have some bridge-building to do.'

'We could span the Golden Gate Bridge across the Frome and they'd still hate us,' Channing said. 'That's the politics of envy, right there – it's consuming the whole country.' He went over to the drinks cabinet and brought the bottle back. 'Have another stiff one, dear boy. I'm afraid I've not told you the worst of it.'

'Worse than calamitous? Did the Greeks have a name for that?'

Channing refilled our glasses. He clinked his tumbler against mine. 'You performed well on the witness stand,' he said. 'And now you're back home we're going to have to put our backs up against the wall and take the onslaught. I'm thinking, Rupert, we let all the shit hit the fan first before we devise a comeback strategy. Just take the punches, for now.'

Rupert said, 'My son is on the run. I'm going nowhere.'

Channing landed a punch on Rupert's arm. Rupert held up his fists in a defensive position. They briefly played out a mock fight, their cheeks flush with alcohol. Everything in life was a game to be played, a match to be rigged, and the odds always seemed to fall in their favour.

In the stale air of the windowless salon, I thought of Tom, perhaps on the deck of a ship heading for Morocco or Cadiz, his blonde hair rippling in the breeze. Whatever he had done, however much he was concealing from me, at least he had made a bid for freedom. I was not so brave. A few months of cold treatment in Cambridge, and I had lied under oath in order to be embraced back into the fold. And for what? A cut-short trip to Tenerife, and the keys to get back into the madhouse.

Rupert had sunk into the velvet armchair and hooked one leg over his knee. 'What's the worst of it, then? Sock it to me.'

Channing coughed into his hand. 'The Sunday papers are sniffing around. *The Times* claim to have got hold of some material. They say they've spoken to an old boyfriend of Meryam's called David Fallowhill. Ring any bells?'

Rupert shot forward and gasped for air. He cupped his chest with his hand.

'Are you OK?' I said, rushing to his side.

'Yes, yes, yes,' he said, taking slow deep breaths. His trembling hand gripped the chair. 'It's just a name I wasn't expecting to hear.'

Channing's nostrils flared. 'It's that shitter Vince Reilly who has been digging around. He's sending over a list of questions they want addressed.'

Rupert bowed his head for a moment. When he lifted his gaze, his eyes were cold and hard. 'Damn them and their questions,' he said quietly.

Channing said, 'If he knew about the arrangement…'

Rupert drew back his arm and hurled the tumbler across the room; it shattered upon impact with the bookcase. 'Do these people think they have the right to ask me anything?'

Chapter 36

During the next few days, we gave Merryvale Manor its most efficient spring-clean in decades. Cresswell and I swept the dust and debris from the terrazzo floor in the entrance hall before scrubbing every tile with a hot sponge. We took down the chandelier in the dining room and removed and dusted each piece of detachable glass. Mrs Kinney removed the ceramic pots from the display cabinets and cleaned them with cotton wool balls dipped in vinegar. Channing bought a big ginger tomcat we called Vincent and set him to work rounding up the rats in the cellar. Eva gave the salon a makeover, adding fine satin cushions to the chaise longue and dusting the bookshelves. Rupert hired an under-gardener and, under Cresswell's tutelage, the gardens of Merryvale slowly began to regain a sense of order.

One afternoon, I helped Cresswell dig up an ugly tree stump on the lawn. We had dug a hole around the stump and hacked at the roots with an axe. Bess sat nearby, her tail gently wagging. After a few hours of graft, we stopped for a break. Cresswell pulled out a pouch of tobacco from the top pocket of his lumberjack shirt and rolled a cigarette.

'There's a dream I have,' he said, gazing back at the old house with a weak smile. 'There's a cliffside cottage, fifty miles from here. Your uncle bought it years ago as a getaway. It needed work, and they never got round to it. Lonely old place has been rotting ever since. Rupert's going to let me take on the job of doing it up. Better than mowing the lawn and drinking myself blind. I'll take the dog for company, get myself some sea air... a nice place for Bess to see out her days.'

'Well, we'll miss you terribly,' I said. 'And dear old Bess.'

Cresswell scratched a red blister above his earlobe. 'Rupert's given me a little pot of money too... enough to get by on. He's a man of many faults, but he looks after his own.'

We were disturbed by the honking of a car horn. About a hundred yards away, at the end of the driveway, a small yellow car had pulled up in front of the entrance gates. The driver wound down their window and waved in our direction.

'Not another bloody reporter,' Cresswell said.

The car horn sounded again. From the driver's side, a woman got out and shouted something inaudible. I turned away quickly, not wanting my picture in the papers.

Cresswell said, 'Best we keep away from the press.' He whistled towards Bess. 'Let's walk a little. Give the old girl some exercise.'

We crossed the lawn towards the woods, drinking whisky from a leather hip flask we passed back and forth. Bess limped by our side.

Cresswell said, 'I read the newspapers. During the trial.'

'You did?'

'Every day.'

'And what did you think?'

'You said some nice things about Tom Drummond.'

'Um... nothing I didn't believe.'

Cresswell glanced at me. 'You sure about that?'

I scoffed. 'Of course.'

There was no birdsong as we walked through the woods. Cresswell pointed at a red discolouration on the trunk of a tree near the path. 'There's blight in this forest,' he said, and he coughed and spat out the contents of his mouth into the vegetation. 'There's nothing you can do about it once the rot sets in. The forest is dying.'

We walked the rest of the way in silence. The lake was murky brown and smelt of minerals and crushed vegetation. Water lilies larger than dinner plates padded the surface. A lone duck with a red bill and purple breast glided through the reeds. We stood side by side as Bess sniffed tentatively at the shallows.

After a while, Cresswell said, 'When Tom were a boy, he used to come round to the cottage all the time. A good kid, not spoiled at that age. He followed me about the garden, asking all sorts of questions. What's this? Why you doing that? Why does Bess run in circles before she shits? He never stopped. And what he really liked was me to tell tall stories, make things up to scare him. So I would tell him about the wolves in the woods that sometimes crept up to the house to eat scraps from the kitchens, and the witch who lived in the village. And I told him all sorts of stories about the Ooser, how it was the devil, and how you should never walk past it in the hallway without saying a little prayer, else it would come looking for you in the middle of the night. The little fella would squeal with delight and go running off to tell his sister.'

'I never knew this,' I said, and I knelt down on my haunches and patted Bess's flanks. She growled at the ripples on the surface of the water.

Cresswell sipped from the hip flask. 'I also told him my war stories. That's how I met his uncle. Served with him in France.'

'Wait, you knew Channing during the war?'

'That's why I'm here, lad. He fixed me up after the war, got me a job at Merryvale. There was a favourite story Tom would ask for over and over again. About the time Channing saved my life.'

'I'd love to hear it,' I said.

'It was 1940 and we had lost our regiment trying to get to Dunkirk. We knew there was only going to be a few days before the city was captured by the Germans. We travelled by night, using the canal for navigation. On the second night, we heard German voices from the woods that lined the canal. There was a flash of torches and the sound of barking dogs crashing through the undergrowth. We slipped into the freezing waters of the canal and didn't move. We were shaking with the cold, and didn't dare to look up or move or say nothing. And then, from nowhere, this bloody great Alsatian appears on the bank, just a few feet away. Its nostrils quiver as it catches our scent, and then it looks straight at us and growls. Channing moves with the speed of a hare. He leaps out of the water, grabs the dog's head and slits its throat with his knife. The dog just keels over without making a whimper. And then Channing says we need to get the body in the canal because the other dogs will smell blood. So I haul myself out, and I've grabbed its hind legs and we're dragging it towards the canal. But Channing signals to me to wait. He flips the dog onto its back and jabs at its stomach with his knife, and he twists the knife a little, and then a little more. Then he pulled out the knife and we threw the damn dog's corpse into the water. We lay there in the cold and dark, waiting for someone to find us, but they never did, and the next morning we made our way to Dunkirk. At some point, I said to Channing that he really had it in for that dog. And he said to me, look, if you don't want a corpse to float, then drain it of air. Stab it in the guts – that was his advice.'

I cupped my hand under Bess's chin. Her lips quivered as she growled at shadows on the lake's surface. I felt a rising sense of dread. 'Why are you telling me this?' I said, unsteadily getting to my feet.

'It's a good story, lad.'

Cresswell passed me the hip flask and urged me to drink. I took a sip of whisky with a trembling hand. When Dr Peter Grainne, with his pursed smile, had speculated about the mutilation of

Meryam's corpse, the defence had painted him as a grim fantasist with a lurid imagination.

'Isn't now the time to be frank with each other?' I said.

'That's all I'm saying on the matter,' Cresswell said. 'That man saved my life, but he's got a bit of viciousness about him.'

Back at the house, the yellow car we had seen earlier was parked on the forecourt. It was a two-door hatchback with a dent in the side panel and a wing mirror fastened in place with gaffer tape. On the back seat was a box of flyers for a student protest, a dark red lipstick and half a chocolate bar.

Chapter 37

'There you are, Benjamin,' Eva said. 'We've been honoured with a surprise visit.' She motioned for me to take a seat. There was a pot of tea on the dining room table, alongside a plate of scones, some clotted cream and a large cardboard box. 'The delightful Clara has been telling me all about Squire Richard Cabell who sold his soul to the devil. Apparently, you can go and see his crypt at the church in Buckfastleigh.'

'Surprise,' said Clara, with an open smile. Her nose was pierced with a small silver stud and she had cut her hair differently; a thick fringe now skimmed her eyebrows.

Next to her, Natasha sat with a blank expression. She had not changed out of her dressing gown and was picking half-heartedly at a scone with her fingers.

'Apparently, this Cabell fellow was the inspiration behind Hugo Baskerville,' Eva said, lifting a cup of tea to her lips and blowing.

'Everyone knows that, Mother,' Natasha said.

'I didn't happen to know that, actually,' Eva said, returning her cup to her saucer. 'I happen to think Clara is very knowledgeable, and she has the most generous smile. I really don't know how you let her slip through your fingers, Benjamin.'

Clara waved her hand. 'Oh, Mrs Drummond, it wasn't meant to be. I'm far too young and curious.'

'I see,' Eva said, with a bemused expression.

'Ben didn't let anything slip through his fingers,' Natasha said. 'I think that's what you're saying, isn't it?' She tilted her chin towards Clara.

'Let's not pry into their affairs, darling,' Eva said.

I pulled up a chair and sat down. 'It's wonderful to see you,' I said, but a feeling of melancholy settled deep within my bones.

Clara smeared a large spoon of cream over her scone, and followed it up with a dollop of jam. 'Right,' she said. 'I have a little surprise. I hope it's a nice one, but suddenly I'm feeling a bit nervous.' She cleared her throat. 'You may open the box.'

'Do you want to do it, darling?' Eva said, nudging the box towards Natasha, who remained motionless. 'All right, sour puss, I'm going to have a look.' She took the box and tore at the tape that sealed it down its centre. She opened the flaps and looked inside. 'Oh my goodness,' she said, and, with a little hesitation, she lifted the Ooser free from the box by its horns.

Clara gritted her teeth. 'This is probably the last surviving Dorset Ooser,' she said, studying Eva for a reaction. 'Now, I know when I was here last you were a little lukewarm about being reunited with it, Mrs Drummond, but I was pretty sure you were just being coy. The look in your eye told me you missed the old devil.'

The Ooser's jaw fell open and a wooden tooth dropped out of its mouth.

Clara explained how she had left her phone number with John and Elizabeth Perkins. It turned out Mr Perkins had been looking for the mask in the wrong place; he found it weeks later when clearing out the garage. Mrs Perkins telephoned to say she could pick it up whenever she liked. Seeing as she was visiting a friend in Bournemouth, Clara thought she would satisfy her curiosity.

Eva said, 'When you think about it, I suppose misfortune has been heaped on this house ever since we lost our dear Ooser.

Perhaps it was keeping evil spirits at bay all this time. What do you think, darling?' She turned the mask towards Natasha.

Natasha clenched her jaw. 'I think people should listen to what people tell them the first time round.'

'Don't be so unkind,' Eva replied. She placed the mask back in the box and turned to Clara. 'It's very kind of you to bring it back to its spiritual home. We'll call it the Merryvale Ooser from now on. I'll let the museum trust know immediately, and perhaps they'd like to put it on display.'

'I just don't understand why she thinks we would ever want to see this ghastly mask again,' Natasha said.

'If you're going to be unpleasant, darling, then go and be unpleasant somewhere else,' Eva said, crossing her arms across her chest.

'I haven't finished my scone.'

'Take it to your room. Behave like a child, get treated like a child.'

Clara's face crumpled. 'I'm sorry—' she said, but Eva cut her off and said she had nothing to apologise for, and what's more, she really must stay for dinner. Mrs Kinney would prepare a guest room and she could stay the night. It would be intolerable to drive back to Cambridge so late in the afternoon.

Natasha's jaw hardened. She got up from the table and slunk out of the room without saying a word.

Eva said, 'Now, I'm going to leave you two young people to finish your tea in peace, and to reacquaint yourselves. I do apologise for the behaviour of my daughter.' She excused herself from the table and left the room.

Clara was gazing at a portrait above the fireplace – a sombre-looking fop in tight velvet breeches and nimble yellow pumps.

I said, 'That's Lachlan Drummond, from Edinburgh. He died of syphilis.'

'Quite the looker, wasn't he?' Clara said.

'Eva thinks he's the spit of Tom.'

'I can see that... just.' She gave a half-smile, and gestured towards the empty place to her right. 'Nothing changes at Merryvale Manor, then? Your cousin remains quite the drama queen. Are you still a little bit in love with her?'

'Oh, fuck off,' I said, in good spirit.

Clara chewed on a mouthful of scone. 'The irony is she's very protective of you. She dislikes me immensely.' She poured herself some tea. 'Do you remember how you never spoke about your adopted family at first? Never let on that all this was here. You only told me after we'd slept with each other for the first time. And when the dam had burst, you never stopped talking about them. You were so proud of... I don't really know... of being among them, as if some of their glow rubbed off on you, but what you never seemed to realise was that you glowed perfectly well on your own. I was always more interested in what came before.'

I thought of my mother drinking gin from a teacup while she grieved the death of her husband during the war, and of kindly Uncle Billy who put a smile on her face on Sunday afternoons and brought me gifts of fruit liquorice sticks, and I thought of old Betty, with whom I gathered around the wireless to listen to *The Goon Show*. I recalled her high-pitched laugh, which sounded like a hyena caught in a trap, and the way she looked at me whenever a punchline landed. She loved that show.

'Are you OK?' Clara said.

I felt a restriction in my throat, and then a welling up of emotion that sprang from deep in my gut.

Clara went to say something, but hesitated. She took a deep breath and then said, in a lowered voice, 'Look, I didn't just come to drop off a stupid mask. I actually came for *you*.'

'What?' I felt a flicker of hope.

Clara looked at her hands. 'I don't mean like before. I came to get you out of this house, back to Cambridge, back to your studies. George has moved in, but you're welcome to sleep on the sofa for a few months while you find your feet.'

I was confused. 'Why would you do that?'

Clara looked at her hands. 'Tom wrote to me.'

'What?'

'He asked me to come. He said if you don't leave Merryvale you'll curdle and do nothing, and you'll come to think the world is a weary place. I happen to think he's right. So this is me saying: I'm going to help you make an important decision. I'm going to accept your aunt's invitation for dinner, and I'm going to drive back to Cambridge in the morning, and I'd *really* like you to come with me.' She dabbed at her eyes with her napkin, and then, with a sharp exhalation, she stood up. 'I'm going to get my bag from the car,' she said. 'Please don't think twice about it.'

I sat motionless at the table. Instinctively, I reached for the cardboard box and lifted out the mask. The Ooser's wiry hair was matted and stained with a dark brown substance, and its eyes had the familiar look of despair. For the first time, I noticed some writing on the back of its neck. Carved into the wood was an inscription that read, *The greatest wisdom is seeing through appearances.*

Chapter 38

Later, Clara and I had dinner together – a garlicky Dover sole served with asparagus and boiled potatoes – but the rest of the family declined to join us. Clara, under the impression she had been snubbed and already thinking about the next morning when she'd be free of the Drummonds for good, said she was too full for dessert and retired to her bedroom.

Afterwards, Natasha and I were summoned to my uncle's study. Inside, Rupert paced up and down, his hands clutched behind his back. Eva sat in the armchair wearing a pair of dark glasses.

'What's going on?' said Natasha. 'Has something happened?'

Rupert grimaced. 'Tomorrow morning,' he said, 'there will be some unfortunate business published in one of the newspapers. Some tittle-tattle that's been overblown. I'm afraid there are some people who are very envious of this family.'

Eva took off her glasses and gave Rupert a withering look. 'We're going to stay with Lady Marion in Suffolk for a while,' she said.

'What?' Natasha said, her gaze darting from one to the other.

'Your father is going to resign as a Member of Parliament,' Eva said. 'I'm afraid he's been economical with the truth.'

Rupert steadied himself with a hand on the bookcase. With head bowed, he said, 'Your mother's right, I've made some mistakes.'

I already knew why he was resigning – Vince Reilly had tipped me off. In what was to be a front-page exclusive strung out over the next few days, Vince had tracked down David Fallowhill, the film critic who had been in a relationship with Meryam. He had told Vince Meryam wanted to be a London socialite, but never had enough money and was always in debt. She worked shifts at the Ken Colyer Jazz Club, where most nights she was propositioned by wealthy and powerful men seeking out the seedy pleasures of Soho. One of those men was my uncle, who became obsessed with 'fixing' Meryam, according to Fallowhill. He insisted she leave London and spend the summer at Merryvale Manor, where she could tutor Natasha in French. Lured by the promise of cash, Meryam left a shattered Fallowhill and headed for Dorset. Rupert would insist the relationship was not sexual, painting himself as a misguided philanthropist who only wanted to help a wayward woman find the right path, but the fact that he had not given full disclosure to the police during the investigation was damning.

'What have you done?' Natasha said.

'Tell her,' Eva insisted.

Rupert focussed his eyes on the floor. 'The French girl.'

'What about her?' Natasha said, looking from one parent to the other.

'Just that I had known her a little... before she came here. I wanted to give her a fresh start, you see. She had rather lost her way.'

Eva played with a strand of hair and averted her gaze.

Natasha said, 'I'm sure people will understand.'

'Well, we can only hope for some common sense,' Rupert said, with a flicker of hope.

Natasha said, 'I'll pack my suitcase, then.'

Eva said, 'Your father and I will be travelling alone. We have' – and she searched for the right words – 'some degree of work to do.'

'I believe your mother sums it up with her usual precision,' Rupert said, and he pulled a random book from the shelf and read the back cover.

'I don't want to be here on my own,' Natasha pleaded. 'What will I do with myself? Am I supposed to play cards with Mrs Kinney?'

'Ben will be here, darling,' Eva said, her bottom lip trembling. Her strained features betrayed the emotional pain she was suffering, but she was doing everything to keep it contained.

'You'll stay, won't you?' Natasha said, tugging at my sleeve.

I shook my head; I had decided to take Clara's lifeline. 'I'm going back to Cambridge,' I said.

Natasha's eyes blazed with fury. 'She ditched you, didn't she? Has she changed her mind?'

I was tired of Merryvale, tired of the lies, tired of them all. 'That's what I'm going to do,' I said.

Eva said, 'That's rather unfortunate when Nat needs your support.'

Rupert stroked his jowly chin and gazed out of the window. He appeared pallid and unwell. 'The boy's done his bit, I suppose,' he said, sadly.

'You do know she's beneath you,' Natasha said.

'Be*neath* me?'

'She's from Swindon,' Natasha said, breaking into a nervous laugh.

'I'll be leaving first thing in the morning.'

Natasha grabbed my wrist. 'You could do better, you know.' She had a pleading, frantic look. 'Stay at Merryvale with me.'

'Living your life gloriously,' I said, pulling my wrist from her grasp. 'And to think I once believed you were capable of doing that.'

Rupert emerged ashen-faced from the study just before nine. Leaning on the handrail, he made his way upstairs, his movements slow, his breathing shallow.

Channing watched him go, his jaw clenched in fury. 'Don't flake off now,' he said. 'You'll hold a press conference tomorrow. Say you should have been honest about the girl, but you were only trying to help her.'

Rupert stopped halfway up the stairs. Without turning, he shook his bowed head. 'The curtain's come down,' he said. 'Show's over.'

Chapter 39

The next morning, I was first to rise. Downstairs, Mrs Kinney had placed a pot of tea and some poached eggs on the dining room table. I asked her to join me. We talked about Cresswell's impending departure, and I asked her whether she had her own retirement plans. She told me she had a sister who had recently moved into a large property in West Cork with her husband and three cocker spaniels. The peace was regularly broken by visits from their three older children and five grandchildren. There was a cabin in the garden earmarked for Mrs Kinney, with a view of the Atlantic. She was going to take long coastal walks with the dogs, and get to know her nieces and nephews. She might even take up pottery, or watercolours.

'I wish you every happiness,' I said, smiling. 'You've been very kind to me over the years... even though I've been terrified of you half the time.'

She clasped her cup of tea with mottled hands. 'Time to go your own way too, young man. You'll only ever be a guest at Merryvale.'

'I'm going back to Cambridge with Clara after breakfast.'

Mrs Kinney sipped at her tea. 'That pleases me – she's a nice girl. Though she told me she'd have poached eggs at eight, and I can't get no rise out of her.'

'She doesn't usually sleep late,' I said.

Mrs Kinney handed me an envelope from the breakfast tray. It had a Spanish stamp. 'Seems like his hand,' she said.

Thanking Mrs Kinney, I decided to go on a final walk to Arcady with Bess. I thought about knocking on Clara's door first, but decided to let her sleep; I wanted to be alone to read Tom's letter. By the front door, I pulled on my mud-encrusted walking boots and raincoat. I called Bess, and a moment later she appeared, her eyes crusted with sleep, her hair thinning with patches of grey, but her tail still wagging. I patted her flanks. 'One for old times, girl,' I said, my eyes wet with tears. 'It's time I moved on.'

We crossed the freshly cut lawn towards the woods. For some reason, I felt self-conscious opening the letter under the gaze of Merryvale Manor. I waited until we were out of sight before tearing open the envelope.

In Tom's childlike handwriting, the letter read:

Brother, when we were in Tenerife, I was disgusted with myself, unable to look in the mirror for fear of seeing the emptiness in my eyes. The world was full of grubby, grimy, worthless little human beings sliding around in dirt. And you, Ben, in your gentleness and ignorance, came up into the mountains with me every morning, and for that, I wanted to hug you, and pray for your help, and throttle you, and diminish you. All those things at once. What each of us knows about God is a piece of the truth. We don't have to do it alone. Have you heard of the Unitarian Universalist Church? Probably not. But wait, I need to say what I need to say before I go on.

I am writing this on a beach near Huelva. The sun is going down, and the Gulf of Cadiz seems restless tonight. There is a radiant pink glow in the sky and some dark low-hanging clouds out over the horizon. Have you read Waldo Emerson? There is a phrase he uses to summarise his philosophy – the 'infinitude of the private man'. Do you like that? I like to think you do. For me, it encapsulates how I have moved from small to big, from insignificant to proud, from worthless to everything. Please don't get me wrong – it's not that I believe I'm everything; it's that everyone is everything. There is nothing that divides us, even that black cloud over there and the old man dragging his tiny fishing boat up the beach, and you in Merryvale reading this, and the crushed black beans I ate for dinner. When you realise that, nothing matters, and yet everything is possible. That's a contradiction, I hear your logical brain telling me. But life exists in the gap between contradictions. You just have to go there without any preconceptions, with open eyes and a loving heart. I can't do it justice, Ben, I really can't. I have never been good with words. This is Emerson again: 'We see the world piece by piece, as the sun, the moon, the animal, the tree; but the whole, of which these are the shining parts, is the soul.'

I am going to travel this coast, and then I will go somewhere else, probably South America, or Africa, but I will not be coming home. In fact, even the word sounds fuzzy and ill-defined to me now. That is not to say that I don't sometimes think of you, but I've realised the past needs to be shed like an old skin. I wasn't even going to write, but I wanted to say goodbye, and I realised you deserve that, and you deserve the truth.

Do you remember the scene in the driveway? Of course you do. I was reversing the car. Natasha ran across the driveway and somehow stumbled onto her knees. Mother was appalled at the spectacle that was unfolding. And Meryam, well, she was as cool as a cucumber, wasn't she? She was clutching her suitcase with those shades on and a white sun hat struggling to contain that mass of red hair. The expression on her face *was hard to read, but there was definitely a suppressed smile. I think she liked creating a little bit of chaos. She was the antithesis of Mother. She just let it all out, and had no shame. Indeed, she would probably say that shame was a bourgeois construct embraced by uptight women in country houses just like ours. When she got in the car with me, she said, 'Oh my God, is this really how you all live?'*

Do you know we have two selves – the experiencing self and the narrative self? Well, I see her now at that moment, and I think she's glorious, puffing smoke out of the window as we whizzed out of the driveway. But that is not how I experienced that moment. I was angry. She was laughing at us, at the way we lived, at everything we stood for. How fucking dare she?

We drove largely in silence for twenty minutes until we reached Dorchester. All the way the resentment in me grew and grew. We stopped at a pub because she said she wanted to buy some cigarettes, but it was closed. We drove on a little towards the station, but just before we got there, she asked if I could drive her back into town because she didn't want to catch the train so late. I told her I wasn't her chauffeur, and she laughed and said I would make a good chauffeur because I did as I was told. She said something like, 'You have a suffocating family,' or words to that effect. She said if Natasha didn't have space to breathe, she would become sick.

That's when we drove to the pub. And yes, we got steaming drunk. Pints, whisky, the lot. We were making quite a spectacle of ourselves, but it was fun, you know. She talked and talked, and it was nice to listen to her. She had a raucous laugh and a wicked sense of humour, and I had that feeling that the chase was on, that she was flirting with me.

She told me why she was really staying in our sleepy part of the world. I didn't believe her at first, but she brought in so many details I was soon convinced. Do you know what clinched it? She said Rupert had wasted his money, because the one time they tried, he went as limp as a jellyfish. I thought that sounded about right. All talk, Father, no action.

I knew we were going to end up in bed. And the worst thing was that we both seemed to revel in the idea because *of Father, not despite him. It seemed the apt thing to do, just to stick it to him in the only fashion we could. It was a hate-fuck, but not for each other, for Rupert.*

God, it's beautiful here, Ben. You can hear the cicadas, the crashing of the waves, and nothing else.

Afterwards, we left the pub and drove aimlessly through town. We stopped at a few places for food but nobody was serving, so we bought some liquor instead and drove to the coast. She said she wanted to see the sea, so I headed for the cove we used to go to as kids, near Lulworth. We got out the car and walked to the cliff edge. A hundred feet below, the waves crashed onto the limestone rocks. I told her there was a path down there, and in daylight you could roam the little sandy beach when the tide was out. We sat down on the grass. The chalky hills to the west glowed in the moonlight. Sitting here now, I have a sudden pang of homesickness, though I know in my heart that is my old self reverting to instinct. The subject and the object are one. Know that in your heart, Ben, and it all gets so much easier.

I woke up with my face on damp grass. It was still dark. I was shivering and had a sharp ache in my temples. Meryam was nowhere to be seen. I was terrified she might have wandered off the edge of the cliff. Fragments of the night before came back in flashes. We had got so drunk that we had taken off our clothes and run into the forest. We had laughed and danced and fallen over. She had crouched down on the path and let out a torrent of piss. I did the same. I had vague memories of us laughing, kissing; maybe we'd screwed again.

I ran back to the car. To my relief, she was already there. She was very angry, asking me to take her back to Merryvale. God knows why I agreed, but we drove off. Ten minutes into the journey, I realised I was going to crash the car unless I stopped. My eyes were drooping. I pulled into a lay-by and told her I needed to shut my eyes for ten minutes, then I would drive her back to the house. It was still dark. When I woke up, she was gone.

I found her a few hundred yards down the road, thumbing for lifts. I pulled over, and she got back in. 'Crazy night,' she said.

I hadn't even considered how much trouble I was in. I just wanted to be somewhere warm, get into a hot bath, change my wet clothes. Do you know what? I thought I could at least have another drink and blank it all out for a few hours.

When we got back to Merryvale, Mother's car wasn't on the forecourt, which was unusual. I told Meryam to wait in the car. I went inside. The house was very quiet – the magical moment before dawn. Everything that happened next seemed to happen very quickly. I'll write down the exchange that followed as I recall it. I've replayed it so many times in my mind that I feel as though I know word for word what everyone said, but of course some of it may not be quite accurate.

First, Natasha came down the stairs in her nightgown. 'Where have you been?' She kept repeating it over and over.

'Meryam's in the car,' I said to her. 'I've screwed up.'

Natasha pushed past me. 'What did you do?'

'Nothing,' I insisted.

'Did she come back for me?'

Then Meryam came through the vestibule and into the entrance hall. She was calling Rupert's name.

Natasha said, 'I hoped with all my heart you'd come back.'

'Where's Rupert?' Meryam said.

'He's out looking for Tom,' Natasha said.

Meryam said, 'He owes me six pounds.'

Nat mumbled something about getting some petty cash from Mrs Kinney. 'It'll all get sorted,' she said. 'Just give me two minutes to pack a bag and we can go.'

Meryam laughed and said, 'You are such a naive little girl.'

Nat's face crumpled. 'What are you talking about?'

'Nat, go to your room,' I said.

'What's going on?' Nat said. 'Don't you want to go to that Cézanne exhibition at the National Gallery?'

Meryam shook her head. 'Not with you, child,' she said.

Natasha stepped backward and slumped against the wall. The Ooser hung there next to her.

Channing came down the stairs in his blue and white striped pyjamas. He said, 'What the hell is going on down here?'

Meryam put her hands to her face and said, 'Take me home, please. Somebody just take me home. I can't bear these people.'

Natasha unhooked the mask from the wall, raised it high in the air and swung it towards Meryam's head.

It made a sickening crack.

Meryam crumpled to the floor. She landed on her front, with her left arm twisted underneath her.

Nat sprang forward and brought the mask down again, striking Meryam just above the ear. She tried a third time, but Channing grabbed her from behind and held her tight. She fought like a cat at first, but then went limp and shut her eyes, and he was able to drag her off to the salon and lock her inside.

I knelt on the floor next to Meryam. Her right eye socket had fractured, and blood pumped from a gash on her head.

There was so much of it I could hardly get hold of her. Then her arms and legs started twitching. She made a gargling sound, her whole body convulsed, and blood trickled out of the side of her mouth.

Channing came back from the salon and told me to go to my room. That's when I came to you. I don't know what I wanted from you, but when it came to it, I knew my lips were sealed.

From what I pieced together later, Channing woke Cresswell, and together they got rid of the body and cleared up the mess. By the time my parents returned an hour later, it was as if nothing had happened. As far as they knew, Meryam was on a train back to London, and I was back in my room, nursing the mother of all hangovers. I was grounded for a month, do you remember? My parents have many faults, but their complicity in this crime isn't one of them.

Listen, brother, you won't hear from me again. I need to find out who Tom Drummond is, and whether he's worth saving. Do with this missive whatever you want. Be wary of Nat. She has a terrible temper. Do you remember that old tomcat, Willy, she used to speak of so fondly? He wasn't killed by a fox. She dropped him in the lake after he scratched her face. She only admitted it to me years later. And do you remember when she was expelled from school for burning that girl's pillow? It wasn't trivial; the girl suffered third-degree burns. The rumour was that Rupert paid the family a handsome sum to keep quiet.

Why did I risk a trial to protect my sister? I could say because we're twins, and that bond runs deep, but I could also say, with greater conviction, that it was because I knew a jury wouldn't find me guilty. There was no forensic evidence linking me to the crime, no witnesses, and no motive. It just needed you to do your bit, and you duly did. The odds are stacked that way for people like me. Isn't it unfair?

I love you.

Tom

I had reached the far corner of the garden where the lawn meets the edge of the wood. I thought of Natasha's wedding night, when I had followed her down this path, towards Meryam's final resting place.

I felt numb.

I turned back towards the house. It retained a degree of grandeur, but some of the roof tiling had come loose, the windows needed a new lick of paint and the brickwork was stained and discoloured.

My mother's advice came back to me again. *We are not who we think we are, but we are condemned to be who we think we are.*

I walked back across the lawn. Cresswell stood by the wood-shed, smoking a cigarette. Clara's yellow hatchback was still parked on the forecourt.

I entered the house through the front door. As I crossed the hallway, Mrs Kinney came out of the dining room with an empty carafe of coffee. As we passed, she touched her wristwatch and said, 'There's still no raising your lady friend. I've knocked three times and she's dead to the world.'

In the dining room, Natasha was standing by the open sash window, smoking a cigarette. A silk nightgown hung loosely over her shoulders.

'Where is she?' I said.

'She's upstairs,' she said, without turning from the window. There was a bloodstain on her sleeve. She blew smoke out of the side of her mouth and said, 'Would you help me wash Bess later? She slept upstairs last night, and the house stinks. I think she'll need soaping.'

'Natasha, what have you done?' I said, feeling my legs weaken. I gripped the edge of the table for support.

'"The Merryvale Ooser" doesn't quite work for me,' Natasha said, closing the sash window with a thud and turning to face me. Her lips were smeared with dark red lipstick. 'What do you say to "the Mask of Merryvale Manor?"'

I took a few steps backward.

She came towards me and said, 'Oh please, Ben, take a seat. You really do make the most awful fuss. Where do you think we should hang it? Back in the hallway, or somewhere new? Perhaps the salon?' She cupped my cheek with a cold palm. 'I presume now you'll be staying, darling.'

Acknowledgements

Firstly, I would like to thank the brilliant team at Fairlight Books, who have gifted me their expertise with kindness, patience and warmth. My editors, Sarah Shaw and Laura Shanahan, gave invaluable advice that shaped this story into the best version it could be. Their gift for storytelling, and their commitment to creating beautiful books, are inspirational. I am also indebted to the rest of the publishing team that helped bring this book to fruition: Greer Claybrook and Swetal Agrawal in marketing; Beccy Fish in design and production; copyeditor Jacqui Lewis; Deborah Blake for her proofread; and Anna Abola for the cover design. But the writing journey started long before Fairlight. I owe a huge thanks to my friends at Writers' Tears, the supportive writing group every author needs. My wonderful Mum and Dad ignited my passion for books, and gave me a loving home to explore my imagination. I love them dearly. Finally, and foremost, there's my wife Anna, my first editor. She makes dreams become possible and is the greatest gift.

About the Author

Pete Sherlock is an investigative journalist at the BBC, based in Birmingham. He started his journalism career working for several local newspapers across London, and has won a Wincott Award for data journalism and an award for editorial innovation at the Drum Online Media Awards. He is also a volunteer mentor for students wanting to break into journalism. Pete inherited his love of literature from his mum, and he studied English Literature at the University of Birmingham. He has been writing short stories and poems ever since. *The Mask of Merryvale Manor* is his debut novel.